# UNNATURAL WASTAGE

*Recent Titles by Betty Rowlands from Severn House*

# UNNATURAL WASTAGE

## Betty Rowlands

This first world edition published 2012
in Great Britain and in the USA by
SEVERN HOUSE PUBLISHERS LTD of
9–15 High Street, Sutton, Surrey, England, SM1 1DF.
Trade paperback edition first published
in Great Britain and the USA 2013 by
SEVERN HOUSE PUBLISHERS LTD

British Library Cataloguing in Publication Data

Rowlands, Betty.
  Unnatural wastage.
  1. Reynolds, Sukey (Fictitious character)–Fiction.
  2. Policewomen–Great Britain–Fiction. 3. Detective and
  mystery stories.
  I. Title
  823.9'14-dc23

ISBN-13:  978-0-7278-8214-1  (cased)
ISBN-13:  978-1-84751-454-7  (trade paper)

*To my dear son Michael,*
*in ever-loving memory.*

*All Severn House titles are printed on acid-free paper.*

Severn House Publishers support The Forest Stewardship Council [FSC],
the leading international forest certification organisation. All our titles that
are printed on Greenpeace-approved FSC-certified paper carry the FSC logo.

Typeset by Palimpsest Book Production Ltd.,
Falkirk, Stirlingshire, Scotland.
Printed and bound in Great Britain by
MPG Books Ltd., Bodmin, Cornwall.

# PROLOGUE

The hand that held a half-slice of toast and marmalade paused briefly in mid-air as the attention of its owner was drawn to a headline reading, 'Further Shake-up at Maxworth's' in the business section of the local paper. As the toast was slowly masticated, the reader studied with growing interest the report that followed.

Following the death of Gareth Maxworth, managing director and great-grandson of the founder of the old and established biscuit and confectionery manufacturer, Maxworth Foods, the new chief executive, Anton Maxworth – Gareth's nephew – lost no time in calling in a firm of consultants to conduct a review of the entire organization. 'My uncle was a great man and a very good man, but he resisted change,' Anton said during a recent interview. 'The problem was that he was still living in the early twentieth century. I think if he'd had his way we'd still be using the double-entry method of bookkeeping. After I qualified he put me in charge of the Accounts Department. It took forever before I could get him to allow a computer into the place. And as for the machinery, some of it's so old it's a miracle Ben Webb, our production manager, has managed to keep it up and running. It's only the quality of our products and the support of so many of our established customers that has kept our heads above water this past couple of years, but it couldn't have gone on much longer. That's why we're opening this new factory; the present one is totally unsuitable for the new machinery we've ordered.'

The words 'new factory' caused the reader to pause for a moment to butter another slice of toast and spread it thickly with marmalade before continuing to read. Anton Maxworth had issued a statement to the effect that a proportion of the existing employees would be offered jobs at a new plant being built in Birmingham.

> 'Our existing premises are unable to accommodate the new machinery we need to improve production. Regrettably, but inevitably, jobs in several departments will have to go, but we hope that this will largely be achieved through natural wastage.'

Had there been another person in the room, he or she would have been intrigued at the various expressions that flitted across the reader's features: first surprise and a hint of regret, possibly at the loss of a local employer at a time when jobs were increasingly hard to find; next a narrowing of eyes and knitting of brows; and finally, after several minutes of deliberation while the toast and a second cup of coffee were consumed, a hard, calculating and totally mirthless smile.

# ONE

The sharp click of the cat flap acted as an alarm clock and Patsy Godwin, already on the verge of waking, smiled as she opened her eyes and noted with satisfaction the morning sun piercing the curtains. Once again, the weather forecast had been accurate. She yawned, stretched her limbs with a little sigh of contentment and rolled over under the duvet to await Henry's regular morning visit. He snaked round the half-open bedroom door, leapt on to the bed and settled into the space she had made for him, purring with satisfaction.

'It's going to be a lovely day, Henry,' Patsy informed him. His purring increased in volume as she caressed his thick, soft fur. 'Ideal weather for my first visit to my cousin Kate in her new flat,' she went on. 'She's moved, you know . . . remember I told you? She's quite a bit older than I am and the garden got too much for her so she sold Elmfield – that's her house up in the Cotswolds, we used to love going there, didn't we? – and bought a flat near Bristol. Well, it's *in* Bristol actually, although she's pretending it's in a village. "A couple of miles from the city centre, but very handy for shops and buses," she says. She's been there for nearly six months, but every time I mentioned coming to see her she kept putting me off because she wanted to get everything straight first. She's always been very house-proud, you know. So that's why I haven't been before. But I'm afraid, Henry,' Patsy added after a moment's pause and with a note of regret in her voice, 'you'll have to stay at home and mind the house today. Pets aren't allowed in Sycamore Park.'

Abruptly, Henry ceased to purr. 'I don't pretend he understands every word,' she would say to friends who remarked on the way her pet appeared to respond when she spoke to him. 'It's my tone of voice that he recognizes. He really is very intelligent, you know.' And the friend would smile and agree that Henry was indeed a very remarkable cat.

\* \* \*

'You've really landed on your feet here, Katy,' said Patsy, as she accepted a glass of orange juice and helped herself to a handful of nuts from the dish on the low table in front of them. They were seated in two comfortable chairs on the balcony of the second-floor flat, which overlooked a well-tended garden bordered by sycamore trees with a distant view of the Welsh hills in the background. 'Lovely flat in a quiet cul-de-sac with a fantastic view and the village shops in walking distance – it seems ideal.'

'Yes, I do feel I've been very fortunate,' Kate Springfield agreed. 'I had a buyer for Elmfield and found this flat all in the course of just two weeks. I got it at a very favourable price,' she added, discreetly lowering her voice. 'Mr Branksome had just been offered a job overseas – in South Africa I think – and was anxious for a quick sale, so when I said I'd sold my house and there was no chain, he jumped at my offer.'

'How many flats are there here?'

'Forty; twenty in this block and twenty in that one.' Kate pointed to a second building of identical design on their left. 'Being at right angles to ours and facing north-west they don't have quite such a nice view or get so much sun as we do.' Her smile as she sipped her orange juice held a hint of complacency.

Patsy gestured with her glass at a low brick-built structure tucked discreetly among the trees in one corner of the garden. 'They get a nice view of the potting shed, though. It's a fair size,' she added. 'I suppose the gardener needs some quite large machinery to do the lawns and keep all the shrubs under control.'

'What?' Kate leaned forward to see where Patsy was pointing. 'Oh you are a goose, Patsy – that's not a potting shed; it's our own mini recycling centre. It's all very well organized; there are separate bins for bottles and papers and several big skips for household waste. We put that in black plastic bags and Wilkins, the caretaker, puts them all in the skips and the council collects everything once a week.'

'Who looks after the gardens, then?'

'Two young men – they work very hard and, as you see, they do a very good job. They come in a van with "Green Fingers" painted on it, which is rather appropriate, don't you think?'

'The management company seems to have thought of every-thing,' said Patsy. 'So where's the catch?' she added mischievously. 'You've been here almost half a year – you must have sniffed out something wrong by now. Any wife-swapping parties? Or mysterious foreigners suspected of being illegal immigrants or drug dealers?'

'Don't be ridiculous, dear,' said Kate, administering a gentle slap on her cousin's wrist. 'This is a very respectable neighbour-hood. The only foreigners I know of are the two American gentlemen in the flat opposite mine – Jared is some sort of businessman who travels a lot, and Larry owns an art gallery in the city. They're both very nice – they invited me in for supper a week after I moved in. Larry is a superb cook; I told him he's good enough to be a chef.'

'You're no mean cook yourself,' said Patsy warmly. 'There's a delicious smell coming from your kitchen.'

'Oh well, there are a few things I do reasonably well,' said Kate modestly. 'About Jared and Larry,' she continued reflectively, 'it seems a bit odd to me, two gentlemen living together, but as they're both bachelors and best friends – and Jared's away a lot – I suppose it suits them.'

Patsy hid a smile at her cousin's unworldliness and said, 'I'm sure it does. You're very lucky to have such friendly neighbours.'

'Oh, I am,' Kate agreed, 'and there are plenty of other nice people here. I met some of them a week or two ago. We have what's called a residents' association and I thought it would be a good idea to join so I went along to one of their meetings. It seemed a good opportunity to get to know a few more people.'

'I'm sure it was.' Patsy nodded approval. 'Was it an interesting meeting?'

'To be honest,' said Kate, 'I didn't understand a lot of what went on. It was their annual meeting so there was some formal business – election of a new chairman, or chairperson I suppose I should say – and a discussion of last year's accounts and so on, which of course I didn't know much about. Although two of the residents – a man and a woman – were having quite a fierce argument about something in the accounts. And –' at this point Kate leaned towards Patsy and once again lowered her voice – 'it seemed to me that it was getting a bit personal. One or two people sitting near me were shaking their heads and making tutting noises, which made me think those two people weren't exactly good friends.'

'That sounds intriguing,' said Patsy. 'Have you found out anything more about them?'

'Well, yes, I have actually.' Kate gave a slightly embarrassed cough. She drained her glass and stood up. 'Help yourself to a refill if you want one.' She indicated the jug of chilled juice that stood on the table. 'I have to go and check on the food. Come in with me if you like while I tell you. It's just possible we can be overheard out there and I don't want anyone to think I spread gossip.'

'Thanks, I'll bring this.' Patsy picked up the jug and they went back into the flat. In the small but well-equipped kitchen Kate opened the oven and inspected the contents of a covered roasting dish before sliding an apple pie on to the bottom shelf and closing the door. 'We'll be eating in about fifteen minutes. The vegetables are all ready to be cooked.' She pressed buttons on the microwave and the turntable began to move.

'You were going to tell me about these people who were having a spat over the accounts,' Patsy reminded her.

'Ah yes, so I was. Their names are Fenella Tremaine and Marcus Ellerman. They're about the same age – mid to late forties at a guess although it's hard to tell nowadays – but from the way they speak it's obvious they come from rather different back-grounds. He's very well spoken and she's . . . well—' Kate spread her hands and made a vague gesture with the oven cloth. 'I don't want to sound snobbish and I'm sure she's very clever – she certainly seemed to know what she was talking about and so did he. I'm told they work for the same company although whether that's got anything to do with the way they disagree with one another I've no idea.'

'Who told you this?'

'A gentleman who lives in the other block. People were handing out glasses of wine after the meeting and we got chatting. As you know I don't drink alcohol,' she added hastily, seeing Patsy's eyebrows lift, 'but there were soft drinks as well. His name's John Yardley and he's very charming,' Kate went on, with a slightly self-conscious smile. 'He's a widower; he retired a few years ago and after his wife died he moved here. He's very handsome, too; he looks a bit like that film director with the Italian sounding name.'

'You mean Martin Scorsese?'

Kate nodded. 'Yes, I think that's who I'm thinking of.'

'Wow, he sounds dishy!' said Patsy. 'Just the right age for you, by the sound of it! Perhaps you've made a conquest?'

'Oh, I assure you, it was nothing like that!' said Kate earnestly. The microwave gave a beep and she opened the door. 'You go and sit down at the table, dear, while I dish up.' Knowing from experience that it would be pointless to offer help, Patsy obeyed.

It was a warm day in late July, and when they had finished their lunch the two women returned to the balcony. Kate brought a cafetière, encased in a padded cosy bearing a picture of a beaming, mustachioed gentleman of South American appearance, and filled two cups with coffee. 'He is rather fun, isn't he?' she said, seeing Patsy's smile. 'I brought him back from my trip to Brazil last year.'

'He looks very jolly,' Patsy agreed. 'This certainly seems a very peaceful spot,' she remarked between sips of coffee. 'Apart from the odd passing car, all you can hear is birdsong and the wind rustling the trees.'

'Yes, it's usually pretty quiet,' Kate agreed. 'It gets a bit noisier at weekends and during the school holidays, of course, but nothing to complain about. Most of the people here are very considerate.'

At that moment they heard the wail of a siren. 'Perhaps we spoke too soon,' Patsy remarked.

The sound grew louder by the second. 'They're coming this way,' said Kate uneasily. 'Perhaps it's an ambulance – maybe someone's had an accident or been taken ill.'

'I think you're right.' Patsy was on her feet and leaning over the balcony. 'It is an ambulance and it's stopped outside your rubbish shed. Perhaps a resident got drunk and fell into one of the skips!'

'You shouldn't make jokes like that . . . it might be something serious,' said Kate as she got up to look. 'In fact, I think it is. Look, one of the paramedics is using his phone.' By this time several other people were craning over their balconies; a few had actually emerged from the building to see at close quarters what was going on, but a second paramedic waved them away.

The arrival of several police cars confirmed the impression that the situation was indeed serious, but it was not until some time later that they learned that the body of Fenella Tremaine had been found in one of the rubbish skips.

# TWO

'You know something,' said Detective Constable Vicky Armstrong to her colleague, Detective Constable Sukey Reynolds, 'I reckon the villains must have gone on holiday . . . we haven't had a serious new case for a couple of weeks.'

'Which is why we've all been asked to have another go at cases that have run into the sand,' said Sukey. 'As it's our turn to cover the weekend shift, at least it gives us something to do.'

'I reckon we got the short straw,' Vicky grumbled. 'It's obvious there was nothing suspicious about this residential home death.' She leaned back in her chair and flexed her shoulders. 'I have a feeling it's only because the woman's son is some local bigwig and is threatening to sue the police for negligence that DCI Leach has agreed to take another look at it.'

'He's probably after some massive amount of compensation,' said Sukey.

'They say he's a millionaire several times over,' Vicky pointed out.

Sukey grinned. 'Maybe he's keeping an expensive mistress.' She pushed back her chair and stood up. 'Let's nip to the canteen for a cuppa.'

'Good idea.'

At that moment, Detective Sergeant Greg Rathbone strode through the door of the CID office and bore down on them. 'Forget the cuppa; put whatever you're doing on hold and be in DCI Leach's office in ten minutes. That includes you three as well,' he added to the other members of his team, DCs Mike Haskins, Tim Pringle and Penny Osborne, who were seated at their desks working on similar assignments. There was a note of anticipation in the chorus of 'Right, Sarge!' that greeted the instruction.

'Something interesting happened, Sarge?' asked Vicky.

'Something big by the looks of things,' Mike remarked as he closed his case file and slid it into a drawer.

'You'll soon find out,' Rathbone snapped and marched out of the room without another word.

'He didn't look very happy,' said Penny. 'I wonder if there's been some sort of cock-up and someone's pointed the finger at us.'

'Not necessarily,' said Sukey. 'He may have personal problems – he's been on edge for the past few days.'

'Well, you seem to know him better than we do,' Vicky remarked, not without a hint of resentment.

'He has confided in me once or twice,' Sukey admitted. 'But I don't ask questions – I just leave it to him if he wants to get something off his chest.'

Vicky shrugged. 'If you say so.'

When the team entered his office, DCI Leach was seated at his desk with a mug of coffee in one hand and a sheet of paper in the other.

'Any of you know Sycamore Park?' he asked.

'Yes sir, it's a rather posh block of flats just north of the Downs,' said Penny. 'They have a Neighbourhood Watch arrangement with PC Dandridge from the local nick. It's pretty quiet, so he tells me – just an occasional case of theft from an unlocked car or attempt to break into one of the garages.'

'You know Dandridge then?' said Leach. Behind his steel-framed glasses his keen blue eyes held a sympathetic twinkle.

Penny blushed. 'Yes, sir, we've been out once or twice.'

'Good. He should have some useful first hand information from their Neighbourhood Watch rep. You and he can liaise in the enquiry into something a bit more serious than the odd theft from a car.' The team waited expectantly as he paused before saying, 'Murder, in fact. The caretaker at Sycamore Park, a chap called Wilkins, found one of the residents – a woman – lying on a heap of plastic bags of rubbish in a skip. He thought at first she'd been taken ill while dumping some rubbish in the skip and just toppled in. He called an ambulance, but when the paramedics arrived they found the woman was dead and called the police. Uniformed are already in attendance, securing the scene.'

'Do we have any idea of the cause of death, sir?' asked Sukey.

'According to initial reports, the body was partially covered by a bag of rubbish that the caretaker heaved into the skip before he noticed it. When they moved it to one side to check her pulse they noticed a knife between her shoulder blades.'

'Well, that saves us the trouble of hunting for the weapon,' Rathbone commented. 'What's the betting it's a standard kitchen knife anyone could buy from a high street store anywhere?' he added gloomily.

'We may be lucky there, Greg,' said Leach. 'The initial report mentions that the handle is quite distinctive – it could be oriental.'

Rathbone shrugged. 'Well, there are quite a few of those around as well. Some people bring them home as souvenirs. How many flats are there in Sycamore Park, by the way?'

'Forty, in two separate blocks; that means a lot of house-to-house visits. I've had a word with the Super and he's given me the OK to draft in extra uniformed to get statements from all the residents and pass them to you. You will weed out anything that looks remotely useful and farm them out among your team.'

'Right, sir. Has Doc Handley been informed?'

'Yes, he's on his way to the scene, so you get down there ASAP with one of your DCs.'

'As they say, there's not much doubt about the cause of death, Sarge,' said Sukey as she surveyed the body. The woman was lying half on her side across a heap of black plastic bags full of household waste that were piled almost to the top of a large green skip, one of three standing against the brick wall of the shed. A knife with an elaborately carved handle protruded from her back. 'A pretty distinctive weapon, too – there can't be that many of that particular design around.'

Rathbone grunted. 'Let's hope you're right. With luck someone will recognize it and come forward.' He swung round on his heel and spoke to the nearest member of the team of uniformed officers who were enclosing with plastic tape an area that included a wide space round the shed as well as the tarmac path leading to it. 'Tell that lot to get out of the way!' he shouted at the nearest police officer, indicating with a wave of his hand the curious crowd of onlookers who were trying to see what was going on. 'This is a crime scene and we don't want people trampling around destroying evidence.'

'Right, Sarge.' The officer raised his voice a fraction and said, 'Please, ladies and gentlemen, keep well out of the way. If any of you saw anything, or has any information that you think will help us, please wait to speak to a detective. Otherwise, give us your names and addresses and then go home. There's nothing for you to see. A statement will be issued later.' He made shooing gestures with his hands and the crowd, which by this time numbered fifteen or so, reluctantly withdrew a short distance, stopped beside a line of parked cars, and waited.

'Here's Doc Hanley,' said Sukey, nodding in the direction of a white Ford Focus backing into an empty parking space. The pathologist got out and strode towards them, bag in hand.

'That was quick,' Rathbone commented. 'I don't recall anyone saying it was urgent.'

A faint smile flickered across Hanley's thin features. 'I was on my way to the morgue when I got the message and it only meant a short detour so I thought I'd come straight here. Where's the body?'

'In here.' Rathbone indicated the skip. Its hinged lid had been left open by the paramedics and had not, so far as he had been able to ascertain, been touched since they left.

Hanley studied the body in silence for a few moments. Then he glanced upwards and said, 'I take it you want the lid of the skip left open?'

'That's how it was when the paramedics found it. We haven't questioned the caretaker – the man who found the body – so we don't know if that's how the killer left it.'

Hanley grunted. 'Better get a tent up in case it rains. That roof doesn't look very waterproof.'

'I've already ordered one.'

'Good.'

For the next few minutes the two detectives stood and watched as the pathologist, with long, delicate fingers, gently probed the area round the neck and eyes. After a few moments he straightened up. 'It's more than likely the cause of death was the knife wound,' he said, 'but I can't be sure until I get her on the slab.'

'What about the time of death?' asked Rathbone.

'There's dried blood on the clothing round the wound, but not enough of it to give an accurate estimate at this stage.'

'Any idea if she was killed here, or brought here after death?'

Hanley's grin included both Rathbone and Sukey, who had been taking careful notes. 'You're the detectives. Send her along once the CSIs have done their stuff and I'll do my best.'

Rathbone nodded. 'Thanks Doc, will do.' The containment of the scene had been completed and the team were awaiting further instructions. He went over to the sergeant in charge and said, 'What about the man who found the body?'

'That was the caretaker.' The sergeant referred to his notebook. 'His name's Frederick Wilkins and he has a flat on the ground floor of the other block. According to the paramedics he seemed calm enough when they arrived – he didn't see the knife as it was concealed by the bag of rubbish he'd just lobbed into the skip – but when he heard the woman was dead he had a bit of wobbly so they told him to go and sit down over there.' The sergeant pointed to a wooden seat, one of several placed at intervals round the lawn.

'Well, he's not there now,' said Rathbone.

'One of the residents –' at this point the sergeant referred again to his notebook – 'a gentleman called Marcus Ellerman, went over and spoke to him. He asked me if it would be OK to take him into his flat and give him a drop of something to calm him down as the poor chap was really shaken up. I agreed as long as they both waited in Mr Ellerman's flat – that's number sixteen on the fourth floor of this block – until someone from CID called to take a statement. As a matter of fact,' the sergeant added, 'I was quite glad to get Ellerman out of the way. He's an officious type; he kept demanding to know what had happened. Once he left the scene the rest of the ghouls became a bit more amenable.'

'Right, we'd better have a word with both of them. Flat sixteen, I think you said?'

*      *      *

The door was opened by a well-built man with a tanned complexion and thick, iron-grey hair. He was wearing fawn trousers and an open-necked shirt with the sleeves rolled up to the elbow, revealing tanned and muscular forearms. Sukey guessed his age at somewhere in the mid or late forties.

'Mr Marcus Ellerman?'

'It's Doctor Ellerman. Who wants to know?'

'Detective Sergeant Rathbone and Detective Constable Sukey Reynolds.' The two held up their IDs, which Ellerman scrutinized carefully. He looked for a second time at Sukey's and remarked with evident approval, 'Your mugshot doesn't do you justice!' before standing aside to admit them.

'As you have already heard, sir,' Rathbone began, 'the caretaker, Frederick Wilkins, discovered a woman's body two or three hours ago.'

'That's right. According to Wilkins it's that of Fenella Tremaine, a resident here. She lives – lived – in flat number thirty.'

'The victim has not yet been officially identified, sir, but we shall be very grateful for any information you can give us. Now, I understand that as Wilkins appeared to be in some distress you obtained permission from Sergeant Drury to allow him to wait in your flat until our arrival.'

'That's right. He's in here.' Ellerman led them into a spacious sitting room with windows overlooking the gardens. 'Wilkins, the police are here. They want to talk to you.'

A man of about his own age, somewhat leaner and dressed in jeans and a sweatshirt, hastily got to his feet. 'I don't know anything about it,' he said in a tremulous voice. 'I hardly knew the lady, so why would I murder her?'

'What makes you think she was murdered?' said Rathbone.

'I heard one of the paramedics say something about a knife.' He glanced at Ellerman. 'You heard it too, didn't you, sir?'

'I did. And these two –' he gestured at the two detectives beside him – 'wouldn't be here if it wasn't murder.' He swung round and said, 'That's right, isn't it?'

'Not necessarily, sir.' Sukey sensed that it gave Rathbone a certain satisfaction at being able to contradict him. 'The CID are called in to investigate any unexplained or suspicious death, but it doesn't always turn out to be murder.'

'Let's not split hairs. Just get on with your questions so that Wilkins can go home.'

'An excellent suggestion, sir,' said Rathbone. 'We'll escort him there.' He went over to Wilkins, who was still on his feet and fiddling nervously with the handkerchief with which he had been wiping sweat from his hands. 'All we need at this stage is for you to tell us exactly what happened, but I dare say you'll feel more comfortable in your own place. Am I right?'

Wilkins nodded. His relief was evident and Sukey guessed that he found Ellerman intimidating. 'Yes, Sergeant.'

'We shall, of course, need a statement from you as well, sir,' Rathbone told Ellerman as he showed them out.

'Naturally.' The tone was curt and the manner unfriendly. Sukey sensed that he had been hoping to be present while Wilkins was being questioned. 'I'll be in for the rest of the evening.'

In the modest living room of the caretaker's flat an armchair was positioned facing the window. Beside it was a low table on which stood a plate and a mug, both empty, suggesting that the caretaker had been eating a meal while enjoying the view across the garden.

Wilkins picked up the used crockery and cutlery with a mumbled apology. 'Excuse me while I put these in the kitchen. Please sit down.'

The detectives sat on a couch and waited. Wilkins returned a moment later and turned his chair round to face them.

'Right, Mr Wilkins,' said Rathbone. 'I understand that when you saw Ms Tremaine lying in the skip, your first thought was that she'd been taken ill?'

'That's right. That's why I called the ambulance.'

'How did you suppose she got in there?'

Wilkins passed a hand over his forehead. 'I . . . I don't know . . . I didn't think,' he said hesitantly. 'My first thought was that she needed help. It never entered my head that she was dead, let alone murdered. Then I heard that talk about a knife in her back – is that really true?'

'I can confirm that we are investigating a murder,' said Rathbone, 'and the murder weapon was a knife – one of a somewhat unusual design, possibly oriental. Full details will be issued to the media and naturally the public will be asked if they recognize it.' He leaned forward and fixed Wilkins with a direct stare. 'Do you happen to own a knife that might answer that description?'

The caretaker met the gaze without flinching. 'No, Sergeant,' he said firmly.

'Or have you seen anything like it? In one of the residents' flats, for example?'

This time Sukey noticed a momentary hesitation before Wilkins replied, 'I hardly ever go into any of the flats.'

Rathbone nodded. 'I see. Now, according to what you told the police, you thought she must have been taken ill while throwing a bag of rubbish into the skip, overbalanced and fallen in.' He paused for a moment before saying, 'That's a bit unlikely, don't you think? The skip must be at least four feet high – anyone of normal height would have to be standing on something to lean over the edge and just topple in.'

Wilkins' brow puckered and he shook his head. 'I suppose so, but I didn't stop to think . . . I mean, I just opened the skip, threw in the bag of rubbish and went to close the lid . . . and then I saw her lying there and called nine nine nine on my mobile.'

'What time was this?' asked Rathbone.

'Some time after two – I don't remember exactly.'

'Is that your normal time for taking rubbish to the skip?'

'No, and it isn't even my usual day. The residents leave their bags of rubbish outside their front doors and I pick them up every morning from Monday to Friday, put them on my barrow and wheel it to the skip.'

'And today's Saturday, so why were you there this afternoon?' asked Sukey.

'I had some rubbish of my own to get rid of and I wanted to get it out of the way.'

'What kind of rubbish?'

'I'm redecorating my spare room and I spent this morning stripping off the wallpaper. After I'd had my lunch I put it all with some other stuff into one of the black plastic bags we use and carried it to the tip.'

'Now, Mr Wilkins,' said Rathbone, 'I want you to think very

carefully and tell me exactly what you did when you entered the shed where the skips and rubbish bins are kept. I counted four skips, by the way, and the body was found in the one farthest from the entrance. Why did you go to that particular one?'

'I knew it was the only one that still had some room in it, although it was very nearly full. I reckon if it'd been half empty I mightn't even have seen the poor lady.'

'Presumably the lid was closed when you got there?'

'Yes. I raised it and threw the bag in, and I was about to let the lid fall when I happened to look down and . . . there she was.' Wilkins momentarily closed his eyes at the recollection. 'I called the ambulance and it came very quickly and . . . that's all I can tell you. Honestly!' He looked from one to the other, his expression apprehensive, as if expecting his story to be challenged.

'It must have been quite a shock,' said Sukey sympathetically. Wilkins responded with a nod and a faint smile.

'I presume you collected the rubbish and took it to the skips yesterday morning as usual. Did you go there again that day?'

'No.'

'Or this morning?'

'No.'

'Have you ever noticed anyone else going there?'

'Oh yes, Sergeant. Some of the residents take their own bottles and paper and so on to the recycling bins. Sometimes I see them, but of course I'm not always around.'

'Presumably Ms Tremaine used to take her own stuff to the bins?'

Wilkins nodded. 'That's right.'

'Can you remember the last time you saw her there?'

Wilkins pondered for a moment. 'I can't remember exactly, but I've a feeling it was quite late one evening not long ago, when I was coming home from a visit to The Swan. That's the pub in Hope Lane.'

'And you've seen her alive since?'

'Oh yes, I'm sure I have.'

'Has she lived here long?'

'All I can say is she was here when I came, about eighteen months ago.'

'So you've known her for some time. Have you noticed anything different about her behaviour recently?'

Wilkins compressed his lips and appeared to be thinking. 'I wouldn't say as I know her exactly,' he said after a moment. 'To be honest, Sergeant, I've never had much to do with her. She doesn't stop to chat like some of the other folk who live here.'

'Have you ever seen her in conversation with any of the other residents?'

For the second time Wilkins hesitated for a few moments before saying, 'No one in particular that I can think of.'

'Well, thank you Mr Wilkins, you've been very helpful,' said Rathbone. Once outside the front door, he said, 'I don't think he had a very high opinion of Ms Tremaine, although he was careful not to say anything critical about her. On the face of it his story sounds reasonable, but I'm not ruling him out at the moment. Make a note to check his bag of rubbish, by the way. Now, let's see what Doctor Ellerman has to say for himself.'

'Did you notice those cushions in Ellerman's flat, Sarge?' asked Sukey as they made their way to the other block.

'You mean the ones with elephants embroidered on them? Yes, I did. And the handle of the knife has an oriental looking design as well, hasn't it? That could be interesting.' He pressed Ellerman's bell and waited. 'I see the CSIs have arrived,' he added, glancing over his shoulder at the white vans parked alongside the police vehicles. The lock on the front door was released and they went in.

# THREE

'You took your time!' Ellerman snapped. He glanced at his wristwatch as he closed the door behind Rathbone and Sukey. 'There's something I want to watch on the television in fifteen minutes so that's all the time I can give you.'

'That's no problem, Doctor Ellerman,' said Rathbone. 'We can always speak to you again if necessary.'

Ellerman gave a non-committal shrug and led them into his sitting room, sat down in an armchair and took a mouthful from a drink on a table at his elbow. He made a peremptory gesture with the glass towards a sofa and said, 'I suppose you'd better sit down.'

The two sat down and Sukey took out her notebook. 'Perhaps you could begin by telling us exactly what you saw this afternoon,' said Rathbone.

Ellerman took a further swig from his drink before replying. 'I was doing some work in my study after lunch when I heard the sirens. I didn't take much notice at first – I often hear emergency vehicles haring along the main road – but when they got closer and then stopped I went to the front window and looked out. There was an ambulance by the shed where the rubbish containers are kept and Wilkins was talking to the paramedics and gesturing. They all went in and a couple of minutes later Wilkins came out – tottered out would be a better word; he looked as if he'd seen a ghost. One of the paramedics was using his mobile and it looked as if something serious was up so I went down and investigated. Wilkins was practically gibbering and kept saying Fenella Tremaine – or *Mizz* Tremaine as he called her – was in one of the skips and he thought she was ill but they said she was dead and someone had stuck a knife in her back. Then the police arrived and started swarming all over the place. I spoke to the sergeant and tried to find out exactly what had happened but he was pretty officious and wouldn't tell me anything. He spoke to Wilkins, but the man was in such a state he couldn't get any sense out of him so I offered to bring him up here and give him a stiffener. The sergeant agreed and the rest you know.' Ellerman finished his drink, stood up to replenish his glass, sat down again and crossed his legs. 'Next question?'

'We understand Ms Tremaine was a resident here,' said Rathbone. 'How well did you know her?'

'We happen to work for the same company.'

'Which is?'

'Maxworth Foods.'

'There was an article about them in the *Echo* recently,' said Sukey. 'I understand there's a big reorganization in progress under the new chairman involving a move to new premises and some loss of jobs.'

Ellerman turned to look at her. There was surprise in his expression, and a hint of admiration in his tone as he said, 'You're not just a pretty face are you?'

Sukey ignored the comment and said, 'So you were colleagues?'

'I didn't say that.' He hesitated for a moment before saying, 'Look, there's no sense in trying to hide it because you're sure to find out one way or another. Fenella and I didn't hit it off. We had diametrically opposed views on a number of things, including how our department should be run. In fact, there are a number of people who find her difficult to deal with, but so far as I know no one disliked her enough to kill her. And I can assure you I didn't.'

'So you work in the same department as Ms Tremaine,' Sukey commented.

'Haven't I just said so?'

'Which is?'

'Administration and Accounts. Should really be two separate departments but they were lumped together under the late chairman. There used to be an overall supremo – pompous know-it-all, thought he was God Almighty – but he retired and so far no one's been appointed to take his place.'

'Presumably the decision will depend on the result of the shake-up DS Reynolds referred to a moment ago?' said Rathbone.

'I suppose so.'

'I imagine it's quite a well-paid, responsible position for which there would be considerable competition?' Ellerman made no reply, but took a further pull at his drink. 'Do you consider yourself eligible, sir?'

'I certainly have the qualifications and experience.'

'Which are?'

'I have a law degree and an MBA – that's a master's degree in business administration.'

'Thank you sir, I'm aware of what an MBA is.' Sukey could tell from the edge to Rathbone's voice that he was becoming irritated with Ellerman's condescending attitude, but he merely said, 'And your doctorate, sir?'

'Human Relations in the Workplace.'

'What about Ms Tremaine?'

'I believe she has – had – a degree in some arts subject, but she was taken on at Maxworth's as an accountant.'

'Presumably she is qualified?'

'Yes, either chartered or certified – I'm not sure which.' Ellerman looked at his watch, reached for a remote control and waved it towards a large television. 'Your time's up. I'll see you out. You can get me in my office if you want to ask any more questions.'

'We shall certainly want to speak to you again, sir,' said Rathbone as he and Sukey followed him to his front door, 'so perhaps you'll let us know if your business commitments require you to leave the area.'

'You can contact us on this number.' Sukey handed Ellerman one of her business cards.

He took the card and looked her directly in the eye. 'It would be a pleasure talking to *you* at any time, Constable Reynolds,' he said in a voice that made Sukey think of oiled silk before closing the door behind them.

Once outside the building, Rathbone exploded. 'If there was a prize for being the most ill-mannered, condescending, self-opinionated oaf in the city, Ellerman would be a front runner!' he exclaimed.

'He also fancies himself as a bit of a sexpot,' Sukey commented drily.

Rathbone, his pent-up irritation relieved by his outburst, gave a chuckle. 'Yes, I noticed him giving you the eye. I have to admit he's a good-looking bastard. It would be interesting to know what the overall supremo who retired thought of Doctor Ellerman! I wonder,' he said in a sudden change of tone, 'if his dislike of the late Fenella Tremaine had something to do with the fact that he tried it on with her and got the elbow. She must have been an attractive woman.'

'He gave us to understand that she rubbed quite a few people up the wrong way,' Sukey pointed out.

'I suspect he's inclined to exaggerate when it suits him. Wilkins might have been a bit shaken by his discovery, but "practically gibbering" sounds a bit OTT.' Rathbone knitted his brows and thought for a moment. 'I wonder why he was so keen to get Wilkins into his flat.'

'Perhaps he thought Wilkins might have noticed him and Fenella crossing swords about something and wanted to persuade him not to mention it to us,' Sukey suggested.

'Maybe. It'll be interesting to hear how far other people, among both the neighbours and their colleagues at Maxworth Foods, share his opinion of Ms Tremaine. By the way, how come you know so much about the company?'

'Harry Matthews has been following the story for the *Echo* and we were talking about it the other day.'

'Ah yes, your young news-hound,' said Rathbone. 'So you two are still an item?'

'In a manner of speaking, Sarge,' Sukey admitted with a smile.

'Good luck to you. OK, let's see how the CSIs are getting on.'

By the time they left Ellerman's flat the ambulance and police cars had left and been replaced by a mobile police station. They went inside and found Sergeant Drury and a uniformed constable drinking tea.

'We could do with a cuppa if there's one going,' said Rathbone. 'We've just been interviewing a witness who sat swilling scotch without offering us so much as a sniff at the bottle, and informed us he could only spare fifteen minutes before his favourite telly programme started.'

Drury gave a sympathetic grin. 'That wouldn't be Mr Ellerman, by any chance?'

'Got it in one, but it's *Doctor* Ellerman, he'd have us know.' Rathbone's tone was sardonic. 'He admitted he didn't like the victim "before we heard it from anyone else" he was at pains to tell us. He went on to add that she wasn't flavour of the month with a lot of people, either here or at work, but that he didn't know of anyone who'd want to murder her. That included himself, of course. He's employed by the same company as she was, by the way – Maxworth Foods.'

'We didn't know that,' Drury handed mugs of tea to Rathbone and Sukey, which they accepted gratefully, 'but we do know that he and the deceased weren't exactly best friends. One of the statements we have here –' he took a sheet from a folder and handed it to Rathbone – 'is from a Mr John Yardley. He lives at number thirty on the third floor in the second block and he mentioned a rather acrimonious argument between the two of them at a recent residents' meeting – not the first, he told us.'

Rathbone was scanning the statement. 'He says he used to be her line manager before he retired, but knows nothing of her private life,' he commented. 'We'll see him tomorrow.'

'There's another statement here – a joint statement by two ladies. One of them – a Miss Kate Springfield – has lived at number eight for the past six months. The other is her cousin, Miss Patricia Godwin, who was spending the day with her. They're both what my father would have described as "maiden ladies of a certain age". Miss Springfield claims she's hardly spoken to Tremaine and knows nothing about her except that she was at the residents' meeting I just mentioned and witnessed the "difference of opinion" as she called it with Doctor Ellerman. She was rather upset and wanted her cousin to stay with her overnight, but Miss Godwin insisted she had to go home to feed Henry.'

'Her dog?' said Sukey.

Drury grinned. 'No, her cat. Quite a remarkable animal, I understand.'

'Well, if Kate has only lived here for six months she's unlikely to know much about any bad relationships between neighbours,' commented Rathbone, 'but as she witnessed the spat between Tremaine and Ellerman we'd better pay her a visit. Needless to say, we'll be having another talk to him as well.' He drained his mug and stood up. 'That's all for now. See you tomorrow.'

'It's turned out to be quite an interesting weekend after all,' said Vicky drily as she and Sukey headed for their respective cars.

First thing the following morning DCI Leach summoned Rathbone and his team to his office. 'Right, troops,' he began, 'I'll bring you up to date and then I'll have your reports. The victim has been formally identified as Fenella Tremaine, aged forty-five, by her daughter, Nancy Brotherton, who lives in Bath. She hadn't seen her mother for some time and it appears they weren't on the best of terms – they fell out over Nancy's choice of partner. She appeared shocked, but not particularly grieved by her mother's death and we'll certainly need to talk to her again. Any questions?'

Penny Osborne put up her hand. 'Did Nancy recognize the murder weapon, sir?

'She said she'd never seen it before, and so far as she knows her mother never had any interest in oriental gizmos. Not that we've any reason to think she was stabbed with her own knife. We've called a press conference for eleven o'clock tomorrow and I'd like to give them something to prove we haven't been taking it easy just because it's the weekend. I've gone through your initial reports and there are obviously a lot of questions we'll want answers to. The first is, did the killer stab Tremaine as she was dumping a bag of rubbish and heave her body into Sycamore Park, or was she killed somewhere else and brought to the skip by car and her body thrown into the skip? Any thoughts on that, Greg?'

'Well sir, as the caretaker picks up the black bags of rubbish and takes them to the skips daily Monday to Friday, there doesn't seem to be any reason why she should be taking stuff there. However, he told us that she was one of a number of people who sometimes take their own empty bottles, food cans, newspapers and so on to the recycling bins. CSIs will be checking the contents for fingerprints and also sifting through the contents of the bags she was lying on . . . after they've done all the necessary checks for blood and so on.'

'So she could have been there to dump her empties, the killer happened to be there at the same time, complete with knife, stuck it into her back, heaved her up into the skip and scarpered. That sounds a bit unlikely, don't you think?'

'If the killer was a resident he might have seen her heading for the shed with a bag of stuff, seen his opportunity and followed her.'

'So we're talking about a premeditated killing?'

'Things do seem to point in that direction, sir.'

'Has Doc Hanley given us an approximate time of death?'

'He thinks she'd been dead for eight to ten hours, so somewhere between ten and midnight on Friday.'

'What about lighting?'

'Sunset was just before nine, but the sky was clear so there'd have been some natural light for another hour or so. There are security lights, but all except a few at the entry and exit points to the estate are switched off at midnight. According to Sergeant Drury, there had been some arguments about this in the past. Some people wanted to keep them on all night while others were keen to see their electricity charges kept to a minimum.'

'I wonder if that was behind the spat between Tremaine and Ellerman that Miss Springfield mentioned,' said Leach. 'It seems you've got plenty there to be going on with, Greg. Has anyone anything else to add?'

Vicky Armstrong put up her hand. 'Excuse me, sir, but something's occurred to me that could be relevant.'

'Yes Vicky, what is it?'

'I've been doing some work on the Holmwood Care Home case. The son of one of the former residents is trying to sue them for causing the death of his mother by negligence, even though the verdict was death from natural causes with no suspicious circumstances.'

Leach nodded. 'I remember. What about it?'

'Well, sir, it may be a coincidence, but one of the people he wants to call as a witness is Fenella Tremaine.'

# FOUR

Back in the CID office, Rathbone said, 'Let's get our priorities right,' and marched over to the vending machine. When they were all settled with their mugs of coffee he sat down at his computer and opened a file. 'Up till now,' he went on, 'we've been working on the assumption that the motive for Fenella Tremaine's murder lies somewhere in Sycamore Park and that the killer is most likely a resident. Now, however, it seems that Vicky's hit on an unexpected new lead which might point us in a different direction. So here's the programme for today.' His fingers moved over the keyboard as he spoke. 'Vicky and Sukey, you are to locate the person who's planning to sue the Holmwood Care Home and get him to tell you the circumstances of his mother's death, who he blames for it and in particular why he was hoping to cite Fenella as a witness. You'll need to visit the home and talk to the staff, of course, but I suggest you first have a word with the director of the company that runs it. And be tactful – they're probably feeling pretty sensitive at the moment on account of all the media interest.'

'Right, Sarge,' said Vicky.

Rathbone moved the mouse, clicked and then waved his coffee mug towards DC Haskins, 'You, Mike, will have another go at Wilkins. I thought he was a bit evasive when I asked him about Fenella and her relationship with the other tenants; I had a feeling he didn't like her very much, so dig a little deeper. He also indicated that he's had friendly chats with other residents and it's possible he's picked up the odd comment along the way that may have given him an idea of how they feel about her. I notice from some of the witness statements,' he was scrolling down the screen as he spoke, 'that some mixed opinions were expressed. One lady claimed not to know her very well but said, "She was often heard criticizing the caretaker or cleaners or the gardeners for not doing their jobs properly. I'm sure she did it with the best of intentions, but . . ." Another witness was more forthright and described her as a busybody. One woman said, "I don't wish to speak ill of the dead, but she did tend to throw her weight around and that upset some people." See what Wilkins has to say about that.'

'Will do, Sarge.'

'You, Tim –' Rathbone pointed at DC Pringle – 'will call on Mr Yardley. He witnessed the spat between Fenella and Ellerman but all he said about it in his statement –' here Rathbone scrolled back until he found the quote he was looking for – 'was that it had "something to do with how the sinking fund was apportioned between the two buildings" and that "the pair of them always seemed to find something to argue about". He knew Fenella as an employee in his department, but it might be as well to get an idea of what he personally thought of her – and of Ellerman, for that matter. Meanwhile, of course, uniformed are collecting more statements for you to go through. I'm particularly interested in any remarks or opinions about Fenella that have been overheard recently, or any instances of arguments with neighbours other than the spat at the meeting.'

'It's pretty evident that she wasn't the most popular resident on the estate, Sarge,' said DC Penny Osborne, 'but most of the criticism seems to have come from women. Maybe they were jealous. You did say she was quite good looking, so perhaps—' She broke off in some confusion; despite having worked in the department for some time as part of his team, she had not yet completely overcome her initial awe of him, or of his sometimes unpredictable moods.

Rathbone nodded. 'Could be. Anyway, Penny, I want you to go and see Miss Springfield and find out a bit more about the spat at the residents' meeting. And tomorrow I want to see Ellerman again and also have a talk to Anton Maxworth, so first thing in the morning set up interviews with them. I have to attend the press conference at eleven so make it as soon as possible after that. You can sit in and take notes, and then you can come with me to Maxworth's.' He printed off the list of assignments and handed them out. 'Right, you lot, you've got work to do, so get on with it. Being Sunday not everyone will be available, but there are still some outstanding witness statements to follow up,' he added as an afterthought.

'Why d'you suppose the Sarge is taking Penny instead of you to see Ellerman?' asked Vicky as she and Sukey sat down to plan their approach to Mr Bradley Donaldson. 'I thought you and he were sort of partners.'

Sukey shrugged. 'It's true we've worked quite closely on a number of cases, but I think he probably wants to build up Penny's confidence by giving her more experience in dealing with difficult witnesses. And from what I've seen of Ellerman so far he seems to go out of his way to be difficult.'

'You're probably right. I've thought once or twice that Penny needs toughening up a bit.' Vicky hesitated for a moment before saying, 'I wondered for a moment . . . don't get me wrong . . . whether he might be a tad jealous of your relationship with Harry Matthews?'

Sukey stared at her. 'Jealous of Harry? There's nothing between me and the Sarge apart from the job. To be honest, I found him rather patronizing at first and I had to work hard to earn his respect, but I think it's fair to say he takes me seriously now – most of the time anyway! It's true he has confided in me once or twice about his family problems,' she added after a moment's thought. 'He had some worries a while back – he was afraid his ex was going to move north to be near her sick father, which would have meant he'd no longer be able to have his son for alternate weekends, but that problem solved itself when the old man died.'

Vicky nodded. 'I see. Right, let's see if this guy Donaldson is at home and find out if he can add anything to what he's already said about his mother's death at the Holmwood Care Home. He'll be hopping mad when he finds someone's topped his star witness!' She reached for the phone, but it rang before she had time to pick it up. 'Armstrong. Yes . . . put him through.' She mouthed, 'It's him!' at Sukey and then said: 'Good morning sir. I was about to call you . . . yes . . . yes . . . of course . . .'

The caller's voice was so penetrating that Sukey could hear most of what he was saying, which seemed to amount to a demand for the entire Avon and Somerset Police Force to drop work on its other cases and focus all its energies on unmasking the killer of Fenella Tremaine. When at last Vicky managed to get a word in edgeways she said, 'May I suggest, sir, that my colleague and I come to see you to take a detailed statement? . . . I'm sorry . . . no, I'm afraid that isn't possible without evidence . . . there are procedures that we have to follow, including interviewing certain other people, but we have to have a word with you first . . . yes, I understand how you feel and I assure you the case is being given the highest priority . . . yes, we can come now. If I may have the address . . . thank you, sir. We'll be with you in half an hour.' Vicky gave a grimace as she put down the phone and wiped imaginary sweat from her brow.

'I gather he's a mite concerned about Fenella's demise?' said Sukey.

Vicky gave a hollow laugh. 'In spades. He's quite convinced that her killer is the member of staff at the Holmwood Care Home that he blames for his mother's death and that the motive was to stop her giving evidence to support his claim against the home for negligence. He only wanted us to go there straight away and arrest the woman.'

'He makes Ellerman sound like a pussycat,' said Sukey wryly. 'You've been doing a bit of work on the case; what have you found out so far?'

'Like I said earlier, he refuses to accept the official verdict of accidental death and of course he sees Fenella's murder as proof that he was right all along.'

'What's his background?'

'He owns a company with a factory in Avonmouth that makes garden tools. He must be filthy rich; he lives in a very exclusive area just west of the M5 on the way to Weston-super-Mare, in a house called, would you believe, Excalibur, which is his company's brand name.'

'I've got a pair of secateurs with that name,' Sukey commented. 'I use them to prune the roses on my patio.' She put on her jacket and picked up her bag. 'I can't wait! Let's get rolling!'

An ornate pair of wrought-iron gates in a design incorporating a pair of scimitar-like shapes swung silently open as Vicky and Sukey approached. They were admitted to the house named Excalibur by a man of indeterminate age with an impassive expression, who meticulously scrutinized their IDs before escorting them through the house to a conservatory with a spectacular view over the Bristol Channel.

'Detective Constables Armstrong and Reynolds, sir,' he announced, in a voice as colourless as his appearance.

The man who rose to his feet and approached them with a hand outstretched in welcome was about sixty, of medium height, on the portly side, with a high colour and a shining bald pate. 'Bradley Donaldson,' he boomed, vigorously pumping their hands. 'Glad to meet you! Sit down, sit down!' His voice echoed round the confined space, making Sukey think of an army sergeant-major bellowing orders on the parade ground. He indicated a pair of basket chairs that matched the couch where he had been sitting. On a table in front of them was a tray with a Thermos jug and three cups and saucers. 'Pour us some coffee, Evans, there's a good chap!' The manservant obeyed, handed round the cups, offered milk and sugar and then retreated into the house, closing the door behind him.

'Now, sir,' Vicky began, 'it so happens that shortly before we learned of the discovery of Ms Tremaine's body I had been asked to review the case of your mother's death.'

Donaldson grunted. 'It was about time someone took me seriously, and now I've been proved right, haven't I? Maybe if your lot had got their fingers out earlier, poor Fenella would still be alive and those so-called nurses who were supposed to be caring for my mother would be behind bars before they could cause any more distress.' His voice suddenly faded; he pulled a handkerchief and dabbed his eyes. 'Sorry about this,' he said gruffly. 'My mother was very dear to me – and to my children. She was getting on in years, of course, and increasingly frail, but she still had all her marbles and she looked forward to my visits. I can still see her face, the way it used to light up every time I went to see her—' Once again, he was cut short by emotion.

'Please be assured of our sincere sympathy,' said Sukey quietly.

He nodded, put away the handkerchief, took a deep swig of coffee and continued in his normal voice. 'All right, let's get on with it. What do you want to know?'

'You referred to Ms Tremaine as "Fenella",' Vicky began. 'How well did you know her?'

'She used to visit an elderly woman who usually sat beside Mother in the lounge in Holmwood and we got chatting.'

'A relative?' asked Sukey.

'No. I think she was a woman who used to look after her when she was a child. She called her "Auntie Peg" and said she was the only person who ever really loved her.'

'Why do you suppose that was?' asked Vicky.

'I gather her father walked out soon after she was born and her mother took it out on the child, as if she was in some way responsible for the breakdown of the marriage.'

'That must have had a pretty damaging effect,' Sukey remarked.

'I'm sure it did. She – Fenella – was in some ways an odd mixture. With Auntie Peg she was gentle and loving, but in her dealings with the staff she was a bit of a battleaxe. If she wasn't satisfied with the treatment the old lady was getting she'd lay into the staff in no uncertain terms.'

'Has Auntie Peg been told about her death?'

He gave a sad smile and shook his head. 'It wouldn't mean a thing to her. She calls all the female staff "Fenella" – one woman is the same as another to her.' He made an impatient gesture. 'Shall we stick to the point? I don't see what this has got to do with the death of my mother or Fenella's murder.'

'It's important that we find out as much as possible about Fenella's background,' Sukey explained. 'We know she had a daughter, Nancy, who identified her body. Did she ever mention her?'

Donaldson appeared surprised. 'No, never. Were they close?'

'We understand they had their differences,' said Sukey, 'but there is nothing to indicate that the relationship has any bearing on the case.'

'Now, according to the medical report submitted at the inquest,' said Vicky, 'your mother suffered what was in effect a comparatively mild stroke which in a younger, fitter person would not have been fatal, but in her case—'

'I know what was said at the inquest,' Donaldson broke in angrily, 'and I made the point then that had the staff been doing their job they'd have noticed there was something wrong and called the doctor, in which case she might still be alive. I couldn't prove it, of course – not at the time. It was only when Fenella told me what she overheard that it became clear that not only was it due to negligence, but there was a deliberate cover-up.'

'What did she overhear?'

'She had occasion to go to the office one day some time after Mother's death and as she approached she distinctly heard two members of staff talking. One said, "Her time was up anyway," to which the other one replied, "That's why I didn't say anything."'

'And you assumed they were speaking about your mother?'

'Well, it was obvious wasn't it?'

'Why didn't this come up at the inquest?'

'This was after the inquest – in fact, it was the day after Mother's funeral, which was reported in the local paper. Mother was a local councillor for many years so a lot of people turned up and Fenella was sure that was what they were talking about. She got in touch with me straight away and I immediately said, "I knew those so-called carers weren't doing their job properly," and asked her if she'd be willing to give evidence in court and she said she would. And there's your motive for murder, ladies. What more do you want?'

'Mr Donaldson, as you are no doubt aware, Fenella Tremaine's body was discovered in a rubbish skip on the Sycamore Park estate, which is several miles from here,' Sukey pointed out. 'Have you any theory as to why that should be the case?'

'That's for you to find out; there could be half a dozen reasons. They almost certainly know where she lived – not being a relative, she wouldn't have been allowed to visit Auntie Peg without producing satisfactory credentials so her address would be on file in the office.'

'We'll need their names, of course.'

'Got them here.' Donaldson handed over one of his business cards with two names written on the back.

Vicky slid the card into her pocket. 'Thank you, sir, we'll be in touch. And thank you for the coffee.'

As the two detectives prepared to leave, Donaldson rose to his feet and said, 'Anything else I can do . . . anything at all . . . just let me know.'

'Thank you, sir,' Sukey repeated and then added as an afterthought, 'In case you're asked, I'd advise you not to say anything to the press about this interview.'

'Don't worry. I'll keep shtum until you've made the arrests.' He picked up a small brass bell and rang it vigorously. 'Evans will see you out.'

'It looks as if we have to take this seriously,' said Sukey as they returned to the car. 'I guess our next step is to go to the home and interview these two women. The Sarge said we should contact whoever's in charge beforehand. You've been doing the research – I take it you've got the details.'

'Yes, but I vote we go and get something to eat first,' said Vicky. 'I'm starving; that mean old so-and-so didn't even offer us a biscuit with our coffee.'

'OK,' Sukey agreed. 'We may as well go back to HQ and call the home from there.'

# FIVE

'So, Penny, how do you feel after your first press conference?' asked Rathbone while the media representatives were being escorted from the building shortly before midday on Monday.

'It was fascinating, Sarge,' said Penny enthusiastically. 'I thought the way DCI Leach handled some of the questions was quite masterly. That journalist from the *Bristol Evening Echo* had obviously done his homework – he knew about Fenella Tremaine being called as a witness in the case that Mr Bradley Donaldson is bringing against the nursing home and he did his best to get more information.'

'Ah yes, young Harry Matthews,' said Rathbone. 'As a matter of fact he's been helpful to us more than once by turning up bits of evidence. He also nearly got himself and Sukey killed in a tattoo parlour a while back,' he added with a grin. 'We've laughed about it since, but it wasn't funny at the time.'

'I heard about that, of course, but I didn't recognize him.' Penny thought for a moment and then began hesitantly, 'You don't suppose—' and then broke off in evident embarrassment.

'Suppose what?' said Rathbone impatiently.

'It's just that I believe he and Sukey have been seeing each other quite a lot lately.'

'It wouldn't surprise me. They're neighbours. What of it?'

'Well, Sarge, there's been a lot of stuff in the papers lately about journalists finding out personal details of people involved in criminal cases by hacking into their mobile phones and listening to their voice mail. Could that be how Harry Matthews got his information about Fenella?'

Rathbone frowned. 'I've always thought him pretty high principled in spite of being a journalist. I wouldn't like to think of him turning out to be that sort of low life, especially as he's a friend of Sukey's.' He thought for a moment. 'I'm pretty sure, from what Matthews said just now, that everything he knew was already public knowledge. Donaldson isn't exactly a shrinking violet – he'll talk to anyone who'll listen.'

'So what happens next, Sarge?'

'As far as you and I are concerned, a quick snack in the canteen before our appointment with Doctor Ellerman. A word of warning,' he added drily. 'Mind you don't fall under the spell of his fatal charm!'

'You can see why they need new premises,' Rathbone remarked as they approached the three-storey red-brick building. 'That pile was put up at the beginning of the last century; it was probably the last word in high-tech disguised as architecture in those days.'

'It looks more like a country house from here,' Penny remarked as, after they had been admitted by a uniformed guard, they drove through the gates and followed the drive that ran through well-tended lawns bordered by flower beds on either side. 'You'd never associate it with an industrial company.'

'Wait till you get round the back,' said Rathbone.

Following the signs, Penny found a space in the car park and switched off the ignition. 'Yes, I see what you mean, Sarge,' she said, glancing at the heaps of metalwork and various unidentifiable pieces of machinery which were being loaded on to heavy trucks. 'It looks like a scrap-metal yard.'

'Which is more or less what it is,' commented Rathbone. 'Most of that stuff is well past its sell-by date. That's why the company's moving to a new purpose-built factory. I wonder if our friend Ellerman will be one of the unfortunate victims of "natural wastage",' he added as they made their way to the front of the building and entered by the main door. 'It could be that his arrogant manner is a cover-up and that he's as scared of losing his job as the rest of the staff.'

The receptionist smiled and nodded as she inspected their IDs and said, 'Doctor Ellerman is expecting you so please go up. His office is on the second floor.'

'I hope this lift doesn't break down,' said Penny as the old-fashioned metal cage creaked its way upwards.

'It's in keeping with the terminal state of the premises,' commented Rathbone.

Ellerman's office was at the front of the building overlooking the garden. On this bright summer afternoon the room had a cheerful aspect, despite the dark panelling on the walls, the dull red carpet and curtains and the narrow sash windows. On a sunless day in winter it would, Penny thought, be thoroughly depressing.

When they entered, Ellerman was seated behind a huge mahogany desk. Two chairs had been placed in readiness facing him, and with a gesture and a brief, 'Good afternoon,' he indicated that they should sit down. 'I see you've brought another attractive member of your harem, Sergeant,' he said, with an approving glance at Penny.

'DC Osborne is a valued and highly professional member of the team that is currently investigating the murder of Fenella Tremaine,' said Rathbone.

'I'm sure she is,' said Ellerman, showing no sign of being abashed by the detective's curt tone. 'Let's have your first question, Sergeant.'

'First of all,' Rathbone took from his briefcase a photograph of the murder weapon, 'Do you by any chance recognize this knife – or can you recall seeing one like it?'

'I take it this is the murder weapon?' Ellerman studied the picture briefly and handed it back. 'I've seen plenty of knives with this sort of handle in India – they're in all the tourist shops.'

'Do you own one?'

'Do I look like someone who brings back kitsch from oriental bazaars?'

'When I was in your flat yesterday I happened to notice two cushions on which elephants were embroidered with silver threads. They looked to me as if they might come from India.'

'Oh, those.' Ellerman appeared for the moment nonplussed, but quickly recovered. 'Frankly I think they're hideous but my wife – my late wife, that is – persuaded me to buy them. I keep meaning to throw them out, but somehow I've hung on to them for sentimental reasons.'

'That's understandable, sir. Now, with regard to the knife, do you happen to know anyone who owns one of a similar design to this?'

Ellerman hesitated for a fraction of a second before shaking his head and saying a firm, 'No. Next question?'

'All right.' Rathbone put the photograph away. 'Now, Doctor Ellerman, you have already admitted that you and Fenella Tremaine had your differences. Were they confined to your business relationship?'

Ellerman sat up straight and gripped the arms of his chair. 'What are you suggesting?' he demanded.

'I'm not suggesting anything, sir. I'm merely asking a simple question. Let me put it another way. Apart from your professional disagreements, what was your personal relationship with Ms Tremaine?'

'There was nothing whatsoever about our relationship that you could describe as personal, except that I didn't like her.'

'She appears to have been a very attractive woman and I've noticed you have, shall we say, an eye for the ladies.'

Ellerman gave a dismissive snort. 'I can still admire a pretty woman, Sergeant, but Fenella Tremaine was definitely not my type. For one thing, she had a very aggressive manner that made me – and quite a few other people – want to disagree with her even when she was in the right.'

'For example?'

'There was a bit of a problem recently with people lighting a barbecue on their balcony. It happens now and again and it isn't usually a problem, but on this occasion they were having a bit of trouble which meant there was rather a lot of smoke and some people couldn't sit on their balconies. Fenella went storming round and told them they were causing a nuisance and threatened to report them to the management. They're a very nice young couple who've only been here a short time and they were really upset and embarrassed, especially as she was delivering this tirade in front of their guests.'

'Not exactly the most tactful way of dealing with the situation,' commented Rathbone.

'Tact wasn't her strong point, Sergeant.'

'What would you say were her good points?'

'Well . . .' Ellerman frowned and thought for a moment. 'I'm sure she had very high principles and she took pride in her surroundings and often made sensible suggestions for the way the estate is run, but –' he spread his hands in what seemed to Penny an uncharacteristically helpless gesture – 'I suppose the kindest thing I can personally say about her is that on the whole she meant well.'

'Thank you for your frankness, sir,' said Rathbone. 'Now, I understand you have a residents' association here – was she on the committee or did she have any official standing?'

'She used to be on the committee; she got someone to nominate her as treasurer a year or two ago but she didn't get enough support so she resigned in a huff.'

'So who is treasurer?'

'I am.'

'I understand that at a recent meeting of the residents' association you had a disagreement with her that more than one witness described as "rather heated".'

'Oh, you heard about that did you?' said Ellerman through his teeth. 'She was questioning the way the sinking fund is handled in the accounts. It was just nit-picking really; the stupid bitch always had to find something to complain about.'

'Could that be said about your differences here?'

Ellerman was silent for several seconds. 'Not really. I have to admit that she does know her stuff when it comes to accountancy; our differences were more about admin, how the department should be run and so on.'

'How well are you getting on with the new managing director – Mr Anton Maxworth?'

Again Ellerman hesitated. 'All right so far.'

'And Ms Tremaine?'

'Let's say she was careful to keep on the right side of him.'

'Doctor Ellerman, I want your honest opinion on what could be a very significant factor in this case,' said Rathbone. 'Under the proposed reorganization of the company, it seems likely there will be changes in your department – changes which may mean some of the staff losing their jobs.' He paused; Ellerman waited impassively for him to continue. 'If one single person within the company were to be appointed to run the entire department, it appears that you and Ms Tremaine would be the most likely candidates. That's right, isn't it?'

Ellerman nodded. 'I suppose so.'

'And the loser might be without a job?'

Suddenly Ellerman leaned forward and banged his fist on the

desk. 'It's obvious isn't it?' he shouted, 'All right, I did see her as a rival, but if you think I killed her just to clear the field for myself you can think again. I'm not saying another word without my solicitor.'

'What did you make of that, Penny?' asked Rathbone as they made their way back to reception, using the stairs this time as the lift was engaged.

'Well, Sarge, the statements from the paramedics described the knife in Fenella's back as looking "sort of oriental" and he quite likely overheard them talking about it.'

'So?'

'So he was obviously prepared to be shown a picture of it and asked if he recognized it, and his reply came out so pat it was almost as if he'd decided how to answer in advance.'

Rathbone gave an approving nod. 'Go on.'

'When you started questioning him about the cushions and went on to ask him if he or anyone he knew owned a knife similar to the murder weapon, he seemed to tighten up. Suppose he was lying and that he does own such a knife? He's never attempted to hide the animosity between him and Fenella – in fact he made a point of telling us about it before anyone else did – but it was when you as good as suggested that with her out of the way the job was as good as his that he started to lose it. Even if he didn't kill her, it must have hit him that he's a prime suspect, which won't do his chances of promotion much good.'

'Very well put, Penny,' said Rathbone as they reached the bottom of the stairs and returned to reception. 'I can see you weren't deceived by the spot of flattery he threw in your direction!'

'I thought it was a bit pathetic, Sarge.'

'No threat to PC Dandridge of Neighbourhood Watch?'

She gave a shy smile. 'Definitely not.'

'Good. Now for Mr Anton Maxworth.'

'Mr Wilkins?' The man stopped and switched off the machine with which he was vacuuming up odd leaves and scraps of rubbish from the paths round Sycamore Park. 'Yes?'

'Detective Constable Haskins.' Mike held up his ID. 'Could

I have a word? I was hoping to catch you yesterday, but you weren't at home.'

'It was my day off and I spent it with my mother.' Wilkins stared fixedly, first at the card and then at Mike, before saying uneasily, 'I've told your people everything I know.'

'That was on Saturday, shortly after you discovered Ms Tremaine's body,' Haskins reminded him. 'At the time you were – understandably – in a state of shock. We're hoping that now you've had time to recover you may be able to recall something that slipped your mind at the time . . . something that could help us find the lady's killer.'

'I've been over it in my mind enough times and nothing new has come up.'

'Just the same, I'd like to run through it with you once more,' Haskins insisted.

Wilkins gave a resigned shrug. 'All right. What do you want to know?'

'It's a bit public here,' Haskins objected. During their brief exchange two people had walked by on their way to the car park; each had raised a hand and greeted Wilkins while casting unmistakably curious glances at the detective as they passed. 'Why don't we go to your place?'

Wilkins shrugged, pushed the machine into an open garage that housed among other items the trolley he used for transporting bags of waste, and closed the door. He remained silent as he led the way to his flat, but the minute they were inside with the door closed behind them, and before Haskins had time to utter a word, he said in a hoarse, unsteady voice, 'I swear to God that I didn't do it!' He rubbed sweating hands on his jeans and gazed at Haskins in obvious terror. 'I can guess what some of them have been saying among themselves and it's true she gave me a hard time once or twice, but I never laid a finger on her. You must believe me!'

'Take it easy, Mr Wilkins,' said Haskins. 'No one's accusing you of anything, but the fact that you discovered the body makes you a key witness. We need all the help we can get in tracking down Ms Tremaine's killer. Now, why don't we go and sit down and talk calmly?'

'If you say so.' Wilkins led the way into his sitting room and slumped into a chair. 'OK, let's get it over with.'

'We have reason to believe,' Haskins began, 'that she had, shall we say, differences of opinion with a number of people at Sycamore Park and inevitably there has been a certain amount of gossip. Several witnesses have referred to occasions when she has been heard criticizing various members of the maintenance staff, including you, for the way they carry out their duties. You said just now that she "gave you a hard time once or twice". Would you like to be a little more specific?'

'She was always picking on me.' Wilkins stared at his feet. 'I'd only been here five minutes and she started telling everyone I wasn't up to the job and the estate didn't look half as good as when the previous chap was here.'

'Did you get any other complaints?'

'In the early days, one or two people pointed out things that Jeff – the previous caretaker – used to do that I wasn't doing.'

'For example?'

'Things like sweeping up the area round the skips after the council men had emptied them. I said I thought that was the council men's job but the people just laughed and said things like "you're joking", so I've done it ever since.'

'Did you mind being told off for things like that?'

'It wasn't telling off; not in that case. I was new to the job and they were just being helpful.'

'Did you feel Ms Tremaine was just being helpful?'

Wilkins raised his eyes. 'Not at the time,' he said slowly, 'and now I come to think of it, she might have been trying to prove something to herself. She'd been here longer than most of the other residents and she acted like she knew more than everyone how things should be done and she upset quite a few people. Just the same,' he added with a hint of regret in his voice, 'she didn't deserve to die in a rubbish skip with a knife in her back.'

'Let's talk about the knife for a moment,' said Haskins. 'Had you seen one like it before?'

Wilkins shook his head. 'I never saw the knife. It was one of the paramedics that spotted it. I said that in my statement.'

'All right; I just wanted to be sure. Now, I'd like you to look carefully at this.' Haskins took a photograph from his bag. 'This is a picture of the murder weapon, which was shown to the media at this morning's press conference. Do you by any chance recognize it?'

Wilkins stared at the picture; his eyes widened in mingled astonishment and alarm and for a moment he appeared unable to speak.

'I can see you do,' said Haskins. 'Where did you last see it?'

Wilkins swallowed before replying, 'In Doctor Ellerman's flat.'

# SIX

'**G**ood afternoon, Sergeant Rathbone, Constable Osborne! My name's Anton Maxworth.' A man whom Penny judged to be in his early fifties stood up and held out a hand across a desk which, in contrast to the one in Ellerman's office, was of a simple, modern design that looked slightly out of place against the sombre, old-fashioned decor. He was clean-shaven, with a fresh complexion and neatly trimmed dark hair. 'Sit down,' he went on, indicating a group of comfortable chairs placed round a low table by the window. 'Would you like tea or coffee?'

'That's very kind of you, sir,' said Rathbone. 'Coffee would be very acceptable, thank you.'

Maxworth pressed a button; a woman's voice answered and he said, 'Coffee for three, please.' He took a seat opposite them and said, 'This is a terrible business. I knew there was some tension between Fenella and Marcus, of course, although they were both careful not to let it get out of hand in front of me – or the other members of the department for that matter.' He broke off as there was a light knock on the door and a young woman entered with a tray. 'Thank you Anne; just leave it on the table and I'll pour.' She went out and closed the door; Maxworth filled three cups from a cafetière and offered milk and sugar. 'Now, how can I help you?'

'We understand that certain organizational changes are taking place within your company, pending the removal to new premises,' Rathbone began. 'Doctor Ellerman hinted that the department in which both he and Ms Tremaine have been working for some considerable time is likely to be scaled down, but that they were both hoping to be considered for a new appointment as head of department. Is that correct?'

Maxworth gave a brief smile. 'Partly,' he said, 'that is, I've already appointed a couple of people with IT skills to set up a new computerized system to handle the accounts and administration. I've also advertised a new post of company secretary who will, of course, have overall charge of the department, and there have been a number of very promising applicants.'

'Has the position been advertised internally, sir?' asked Penny.

'Naturally. And both Tremaine and Ellerman have applied.' He paused for a moment to take a mouthful of coffee before adding wryly, 'Neither of them has been shortlisted. So if he's the one who stuck a knife in her to make sure he got the job, he was wasting his time.'

'Are you saying you suspect Doctor Ellerman of murdering Ms Tremaine?' asked Rathbone.

'I didn't say that.' A troubled look flitted across Maxworth's expressive features. 'It was just a bit of "gallows" humour – and in rather poor taste in the present circumstances I suppose. I assure you, Sergeant, that I have no reason whatsoever to suspect Doctor Ellerman.'

'Could I ask your reasons for not considering either him or Ms Tremaine for the new post?'

'It's very simple really. Fenella Tremaine did a first-class job in the department but she simply isn't . . . wasn't . . . management material. Marcus Ellerman is highly qualified and knows his job backwards, but human relations aren't his strong point. Ironic, isn't it? "Human Relations in the Workplace" was the subject of his PhD thesis, but he's not very good at putting his theories into practice and he's inclined to rub people up the wrong way.'

'Didn't someone say that about Ms Tremaine, Sarge?' said Penny.

Maxworth's eyebrows lifted. 'Someone in this company?'

'No, sir, one of their neighbours in Sycamore Park,' Penny explained.

'That's right,' said Rathbone, 'and Doctor Ellerman, who also lives there, gave us to understand that she had upset several of them recently.'

Maxworth raised his eyebrows. 'I hadn't realized they were neighbours.' He got up, went to his desk, called up a file on his computer and began jabbing at his keyboard. 'So they are.' He frowned. 'Sycamore Park,' he said, almost to himself. 'I've got a feeling I know of someone else who lives there.' He returned to the table and sat down. 'No,' he said after a moment, 'no one comes to mind. It's probably irrelevant anyway.'

'Probably,' Rathbone agreed, 'but if you should happen to remember, perhaps you'd let us know.'

'Of course. Have you any more questions?'

Before Rathbone could answer, his mobile rang. He got to his feet saying, 'Excuse me, please,' and headed for the door. When he returned, Penny could tell immediately from his expression that the call had been significant. 'I apologize for the interruption Mr Maxworth,' he said. 'I must ask you to excuse us for the moment. We may need to see you again later.'

'What's up, Sarge?' asked Penny as the door to Maxworth's office closed behind them.

'You'll find out in a couple of minutes.' Without waiting to summon the lift, Rathbone charged up the stairs to the second floor, banged on Ellerman's door and flung it open without waiting for a response.

Ellerman sprang to his feet. 'What the devil do you mean by barging in like this?' he demanded.

'Sit down, Doctor Ellerman,' Rathbone snapped. He opened his briefcase, took out the photograph of the murder weapon and threw it on the desk. 'I showed you that less than an hour ago and asked you if you recognized it – remember?'

Ellerman nodded. 'I remember. What about it?'

'DC Osborne, please read Doctor Ellerman's reply.'

Penny hastily consulted her notebook. 'His reply was, "I've seen plenty of knives with this sort of handle in India. They're in all the tourist shops."'

'And what further question did I ask, and how did he reply?'

'You asked Doctor Ellerman if he owned one, Sarge, and he replied, "Do I look like someone who brings back kitsch from oriental bazaars?"'

'Right, Doctor Ellerman,' said Rathbone. There was a hint of steel in his voice that Penny could not recall having heard before.

'You have already admitted bringing back from India those embroidered cushions we saw in your flat.'

'I've already told you; I bought them to please my wife.'

'Would you describe those items as "kitsch"?'

'To be honest, yes, but Julie liked them.'

'What about knives with decorative handles?'

'They're hardly the sort of thing to appeal to a woman.'

'No, but some men have an interest in weapons. Doctor Ellerman, I'm asking you for the second time, do you recognize this knife?'

'And I'm telling you, for the second time,' said Ellerman defiantly, 'that I shall answer no further questions without my solicitor being present.'

'Supposing I were to tell you that we have a witness who claims to have seen a knife identical to this one in your flat?'

Ellerman's jaw dropped and his normally healthy colour faded. 'What witness?' he asked in a hoarse voice.

'Do you deny owning such a knife?'

Ellerman shook his head, but it appeared to be in disbelief rather than a denial. When he made no reply, Rathbone said, 'In the circumstances, Doctor Ellerman, I suggest we continue this interview at headquarters. If you wish to contact your solicitor before we leave and ask him to meet us there, you are free to do so.'

'Am I being arrested?'

'Not at the moment. Let's say that we believe you have information concerning the murder of Fenella Tremaine and that you are helping us with our enquiries.'

Ellerman stood up. Every vestige of self-confidence seemed to have deserted him; he even appeared to Penny to have shrunk in stature. 'I prefer to call my solicitor from police headquarters,' he said. 'If you don't mind, I'll have a word with my PA before we leave.' He pressed a button on his desk and said, 'I have to go out unexpectedly. Any messages can wait till I come back.'

At police headquarters Ellerman made a call to his solicitor and was then shown into an interview room and offered a cup of tea, which he declined. Within fifteen minutes a tall, spare, white-haired man wearing heavy horn-rimmed glasses and carrying a briefcase arrived and introduced himself as Jason Pollard. 'I am Doctor Ellerman's legal adviser and I wish to confer with my client in private,' he said.

'It's the normal procedure, sir,' said Rathbone. Penny judged from his curt response that he was irritated by the man's officious manner. He held open the door of the interview room. 'Your client's in here. I don't know about you,' he said to Penny as he closed the door behind Pollard, 'but I could do with a snack and a coffee.'

'Have we got time, Sarge?' asked Penny.

'If they're ready before we are they'll just have to wait, won't they?' He went over to a vending machine and fed it with coins.

Fifteen minutes later, Pollard emerged, beckoned and said, 'We're ready for you now, Sergeant.'

'With you in a moment, sir.' Without any show of haste, Rathbone swallowed the rest of his coffee and threw the plastic cup into a bin along with an empty crisp packet. Penny did the same and they followed Pollard back into the interview room.

When all four were seated Rathbone switched on the tape recorder. For a moment Penny thought Pollard was about to object, but all he said was, 'I'm sure this matter can be cleared up very quickly, Sergeant. My client has assured me that he knows nothing about the death of Fenella Tremaine and that he is perfectly willing to answer any questions you may wish to put to him.'

'All right, let's start with the murder weapon, shall we?' Once again, Rathbone produced the photograph. 'Doctor Ellerman, you have twice avoided giving me an answer when I asked if you recognize this knife. I am now asking you that question for the third time, and I want a straight answer.'

Ellerman nodded. 'Yes, I recognize it.'

'Do you possess such a knife?'

'Yes.'

'Where is it?'

'It's in my flat.'

'Exactly where in your flat?'

'In a glass fronted display case in the living room. It's with various other knick-knacks I . . . that is to say, my late wife and I . . . brought back from our travels.'

'You mean "kitsch"?' said Rathbone with a touch of sarcasm.

'I told you, Sergeant; Julie liked to have a memento from every trip.'

In response to a glance from Rathbone, Penny asked, 'How long have you been a widower, sir?'

Ellerman frowned. 'Is that relevant?'

'It might be,' said Rathbone.

Ellerman glanced at Pollard, who gave a slight shrug as if he too considered the question unimportant. 'Just over six years,' he said.

'Were you living in Sycamore Park at the time?'

'No. We had a house in North Bristol.'

'Was it your wife's idea to buy the knife?'

'No, as it happens it was mine. I was intrigued by the workmanship. It was quite expensive, in fact, not the usual mass-produced junk.'

'And it has been in your display cabinet ever since your return from your trip to India?'

'Yes.'

'So why, when I showed you the photograph, did you deny recognizing it?'

'I . . . I didn't want to risk the press finding out that I owned such a knife . . . I didn't want the publicity.'

'Because you thought it might damage your chance of promotion?'

'Yes.'

'Didn't it occur to you that the simplest way to prove it wasn't your knife was to invite us to see it for ourselves?'

'You might have thought I had more than one – people do sometimes buy these things in pairs.' Ellerman clasped his hands together and thumped them against his chest in a sudden burst of emotion. 'All right, I admit I lied . . . I suppose I panicked, but I swear to you I didn't touch her. I only bought the one knife and it's in my flat. Why don't we go there now and I'll show it to you?'

'Just what I was about to suggest.' Rathbone switched off the tape recorder and stood up.

\*   \*   \*

'It's in here.' Ellerman slid aside one of the glass doors of the wall-mounted display cabinet. He reached towards the back of the lower shelf and then withdrew his hand with a muttered expletive.

'What's the problem, sir?' asked Rathbone.

'It's not here . . . the bloody thing's gone! Some thieving bastard must have nicked it and used it to kill Fenella!'

'When did you last see it?' asked Rathbone.

'How should I know? I walk past that cabinet every day without looking inside.'

'You haven't shown it to anyone recently?'

'No. No one.'

'Who has been in your flat recently?'

'I don't do much in the way of entertaining but . . . I suppose the last time was when I invited the committee for drinks the day after the residents' association meeting. It gave the new members a chance to get to know each other, but the main reason was to settle the query about the accounts that was still outstanding.'

'That was when you had a rather public disagreement with Ms Tremaine?'

'That's right. Needless to say, she wasn't among the guests.'

'So it wasn't purely a social gathering, sir?'

'Not entirely. As I've just said, there were a few points arising from the meeting that needed clearing up. Because of the disagreement the chairman ruled the matter be adjourned for further discussion and this was agreed on condition that residents would be advised of the decision as an appendix to the minutes of the meeting.'

'Can you remember everyone who came to your flat?'

'Of course.' Ellerman opened a bureau and took out a note book. He scribbled some names, tore out a sheet and handed it to Rathbone.

'Thank you, sir.' Rathbone handed the note to Penny. 'Anyone else you can think of? Workmen for example? Do you have a cleaning lady?'

Suddenly Ellerman snapped his fingers. 'Wilkins!' he exclaimed. 'He must have taken it. He does odd jobs for the residents now and again . . . he was in here a few days ago adjusting one of the windows. He hated Fenella because he believed she tried to get him sacked . . . he must have seen the knife and taken it. He knew her habits . . . he must have been lying in wait for her and . . .' His voice rose in triumph. 'He's your killer, Sergeant!'

# SEVEN

'**M**r John Yardley?'
'Yes.'
'DC Pringle.' Tim held up his ID.
'Ah yes, you want to talk about Fenella Tremaine.' Yardley held the door open and stood aside for Tim to enter. 'Do come in.'

'Thank you, sir.'

'Please sit down.' Yardley indicated one of a pair of armchairs placed on either side of the window and sat down on the other. 'This is a terrible business,' he said gravely. 'Poor Fenella . . . murdered and dumped in a skip like a bag of rubbish. Terrible!' he repeated with a sad shake of his head.

'I see from the statement you made to one of our uniformed officers –' Tim referred to his notebook – 'that as chairman of the residents' association you were present at a recent meeting when she had a rather acrimonious disagreement with Doctor Ellerman. Would you care to enlarge on that, sir?'

Yardley gave a slightly rueful smile. 'Oh dear, that was rather unfortunate, and in a way I felt partly responsible. You see,' he went on, in response to Tim's surprised expression, 'before I retired I was on the board of directors of Maxworth Foods.'

'Who are also the employers of both Doctor Ellerman and Ms Tremaine?' Yardley gave a nod of agreement. 'Yes, I understand you held a senior position there, but that doesn't explain—'

'I was the head of the Accounts and Administration depart-ment,' he explained, 'and shortly before I retired there was a sudden, unexpected vacancy when a senior member of the staff died very suddenly of a heart attack. It couldn't have happened at a worse time from the company's point of view; the auditors were working on the annual accounts and the deadline for filing them was fast approaching. Fenella Tremaine had been employed in the department, on the accounts side, for two or three years and was very competent. The chap who died had always spoken very highly of her and in the circumstances, having sought the then chairman's approval, I took the decision to offer her the job. Only one person objected, and that was Doctor Ellerman.'

'What were the grounds for his objection?'

'It was obvious it was personal as they'd had a few disagreements in the past. To be frank, Constable Pringle, Ellerman can be some-what overbearing at times and I have a feeling he was a bit of a misogynist in matters of business into the bargain. I wouldn't have described Fenella as a feminist, but she had proved herself capable of standing up to him and I decided to take the risk.'

'And it was shortly after her appointment was confirmed that you retired?'

'That's right, at the next Annual General Meeting.'

'Were you aware that under the proposed reorganization of the company, she and Ellerman were potential rivals for an important position in the department?'

'Oh yes, I'm a shareholder as well as drawing a pension, so I naturally continue to take an interest in the company's fortunes. I recently met the new chairman, Anton Maxworth. A very capable man; the company will do well under his leadership. I must say,' he added after a moment's reflection, 'it never entered my head that either of them would resort to murder to get the job.'

'So you think Ellerman killed Ms Tremaine?'

'I didn't say that.' Yardley's response was swift and emphatic. 'But of course, I seem to have read somewhere that anyone's capable of murder if the stakes are high enough.'

Tim nodded. 'It's true we can't take anything for granted. Now, sir, at the time of your retirement were you living in Sycamore Park?'

'No. My wife and I had a house in Clevedon. She died five years ago; I was already finding the garden too much for me to manage – in fact, before she became ill we had been considering downsizing – and so I bought this flat and moved in just over three years go.'

'Before you moved in, were you aware that both Doctor Ellerman and Ms Tremaine were living here?'

'No.'

'Had you known, would it have affected your decision to take this flat?'

'Of course not – why should it? The place suits me as it's got all the features I was looking for. I admit it was quite a surprise when I bumped into Fenella a couple of days after I moved in; we'd both been out shopping and came back at the same time. She looked rather taken aback when she saw me.' Yardley gave a smile, as if amused at the recollection. 'We haven't had much to do with each other since, at least on a personal level. As a matter of fact I think she still thinks . . . thought of me as the boss. And she lives . . . lived in the other block. It was some time later that I realized Ellerman lived here as well.'

'Have you had much contact with him?'

Yardley gave an emphatic shake of the head. 'As little as possible. Almost up to the time I retired he never lost an opportunity to make some derogatory remark about Fenella. Soon after I moved in here I joined the residents' association and after a while I became chairman of the committee. Ellerman became treasurer and Fenella secretary and it wasn't unusual for the two of them to have a spat over something or other – in fact it was almost par for the course. Someone once said a scriptwriter could turn it into a sitcom called the "Fenella and Marcus Show".' He gave a wry grin. 'Ellerman tried at first to get me on his side, but mostly I told him they had to sort it out between them.'

'And presumably you said the same thing to Ms Tremaine?'

'Oh, Fenella never appealed to me for support – as I said earlier, she could stand up for herself. She didn't really enjoy being the secretary though; admin wasn't really in her line. She'd rather have been treasurer and eventually she resigned from the committee altogether. I can't say I blamed her.' He frowned and passed a hand over his forehead. 'Such a pity she was the one who had to die,' he said, almost to himself.

Tim cleared his throat. 'Now, sir, about the run-in they had at this meeting – as chairman, you were presumably involved in some way?'

'I intervened to rule that the matter of the accounts be referred back to the committee for further discussion. There were other matters on the agenda and at the rate we were going we'd have been there all night.'

'Was the matter eventually settled?'

'Oh yes. A new committee was elected and we had a meeting a week or so later and came to an agreement very quickly. As I said, Fenella had already resigned and we agreed to adopt Ellerman's suggestions. I have to admit that in this instance I was in agreement with him.'

'Where did this meeting take place?'

'In Ellerman's flat.'

'May I have the names of the other people present, sir?'

'Of course. Apart from myself and Ellerman there was the new secretary, Jennifer Freeman, who lives at number twenty-five in this block, and two American chaps called Whittington and Worsley who live in the other block – not sure which number. They're both very amiable types; they turned up once at a previous residents' meeting when we were short of committee members and agreed to join. They help out with admin jobs like printing off and distributing notices, shoving copies of minutes through letter-boxes, that sort of thing.'

'That's very helpful background information, sir,' said Tim. 'Now I want to turn to a rather different matter. Our enquiries so far have indicated that from time to time Ms Tremaine aroused some ill-feeling among the other residents because of her habit of complaining; for example, about the way they park their cars or allow their children to ride their bicycles along the paths or kick balls around. We understand she also complained to the management company on these and other matters. Would you care to comment on that?'

'To be honest, I think in most cases she had a point,' Yardley replied without hesitation. 'Not everyone is as considerate of other people as they could be, and I've had occasion myself to chase up the estate manager on matters of maintenance. It wasn't so much what she said to people, more the way she said it. She had this rather assertive manner, you see, but she was basically a well meaning and kind person. For example, I know for a fact that she used to pick up shopping for one or two of our residents who are housebound. And I recall hearing some of her colleagues at Maxworth's speak highly of her, particularly the juniors in the department, who used to say how helpful and supportive she could be, especially when Ellerman picked on them if they made a mistake.'

Tim put away his notebook and stood up. 'Well, thank you very much, Mr Yardley, for being so frank.'

'I've recalled you at short notice because there have been some significant developments,' said DCI Leach as his team assembled in his office late on Monday afternoon. 'I've considered your brief verbal reports and it's pretty clear that at least four people may have had a motive for killing Fenella Tremaine. The first to consider is Doctor Marcus Ellerman; apart from his personal dislike of her he's admitted seeing her as a rival for a new position shortly to be created in the department where they both worked. Having at first denied ever having seen the murder weapon, he was eventually forced to admit that he owned it. When he was unable to produce it he accused the caretaker at Sycamore Park of having stolen it and used it to kill Fenella. Anyone care to comment?'

'There is one point I forgot to mention, sir,' said Rathbone.

'Yes, Greg?'

'At our first interview with Ellerman we – that is, Penny and I – had a strong impression he was prepared to be questioned about oriental knives and had decided on the line he was going to take. He was self-assured to the point of arrogance until faced with evidence that he possessed the actual murder weapon, when all the bluster went out of him. It may be that his solicitor primed him how to react if he was unable to produce the knife. His display of shock-horror when it wasn't where he claimed he kept it was pretty convincing and then he immediately went on to accuse Wilkins.'

'We'll certainly detain him for further questioning,' said Leach. 'I'll leave that with you for the time being, Greg. Now, our second suspect is the caretaker Frederick Wilkins. When interviewed the day Fenella's body was discovered he admitted not being exactly a fan of hers but emphatically denied murdering her. Mike, you told me that when you saw him this morning he appeared uneasy throughout the interview. Then you showed him the photo of the murder weapon; are you quite sure his astonishment when he recognized it was genuine? Or could he, like Ellerman, have expected the question and prepared himself for it?'

Haskins thought for a moment. 'All I can say, sir, is that it struck me at the time as being absolutely genuine.'

'It'll be interesting to see how he reacts when he learns that he's suspected of having stolen the knife,' Leach remarked. 'You'd better go and see him again, Mike. I'm not inclined to eliminate him at the moment.'

'Will do, sir.'

'That brings me to Sukey and Vicky's report of their interview with Bradley Donaldson, who is currently suing the Holmwood Care Home for negligence. Fenella had agreed to give evidence against two nurses, who presumably stood to lose their jobs and possibly be struck off if found guilty.' He glanced at Sukey and Vicky. 'I take it you haven't yet had a chance to pursue that line of enquiry?'

'No, sir,' said Sukey. 'A Mr and Mrs Brian Seaton are joint owners of Holmwood and I spoke to Mrs Seaton. She didn't exactly bend over backwards to be helpful – she's probably worried about the home's reputation if and when the press find out we're interviewing any of her staff – but she soon grasped the fact that we were making our approach through her out of courtesy and that we'd talk to the women concerned whether she agreed or not. She's promised to make a private room available for the interviews.'

'So when are you seeing them?'

'Ten o'clock tomorrow, sir,' said Vicky.

'Good,' said Leach. 'There are a couple of other things we have to consider. Sukey, both you and Penny commented on Ellerman's roving eye, so it's fair to assume he's a womanizer. He's already dismissed a suggestion that he found Fenella attractive, and it may be true, but I think we need to dig a little deeper into his past. The same goes for Fenella herself – she may have a secret life that she's managed to conceal from her neighbours. So far a search of her flat hasn't revealed anything of much help to us and hardly anything in the way of correspondence apart from letters from charities to thank her for donations. We think she probably did most of her business affairs such as banking on her PC. We've taken it away for examination but it'll be a while before we get any results there. It's interesting to note –' at this point he referred to the file on his desk – 'that further house-to-house visits have revealed several neighbours who made more positive comments about her, saying things like "she was a really good person under that no-nonsense exterior" and "we could do with a few more people with her high standards".'

'Which suggests that the ones who rushed forward to give their opinions were people who'd had a brush with her and possibly come off worst,' Rathbone remarked.

'That wouldn't surprise me.' Sukey detected a note of world-weariness in Leach's voice before he added, with an unexpected spark of humour, 'I note that one person described her as "a bit of a lush who used to sneak down to the recycling centre after dark to dispose of her empties".' Leach turned to DC Pringle. 'You, Tim, mentioned that John Yardley's comments were on the whole positive, didn't you?'

'That's right, sir,' said Tim, 'but on reflection there is one thing he said that I thought rather strange. He said, "It's a pity she was the one who had to die" – as though he had some kind of gut feeling that one of them was for the chop.'

'Do you think he suspects Ellerman then?'

'He was careful not to say so but yes, I think he probably does.'

'If Ellerman was aware of Fenella's habits of sneaking down after dark with her empties, sir, he could easily have watched out for a suitable opportunity,' suggested Vicky.

'It's only hearsay of course,' said Leach, 'and we certainly didn't find a large amount of booze in her flat, but of course she may have disposed of a lot of empties just before she was killed. Forensics are checking the contents of the bin for prints, but it was pretty full so it's a mammoth task.' He turned to Rathbone. 'Right, Greg, it's over to you. I'd like all the written reports on today's interviews by the end of this afternoon. Make sure everyone knows exactly what they've got to do tomorrow.'

# EIGHT

'I'm afraid, Henry,' Patsy Godwin informed the cat that was purring contentedly on her lap, 'that I'm going to have to abandon you again – for a couple of days this time. Awfully sorry!' she added as the purring abruptly ceased. 'But don't worry, you aren't going to starve. I've asked Mrs Puffitt to come in twice a day and give you your food and milk. You know how fond she is of you,' Patsy coaxed, giving him an encouraging tickle behind the ears. 'She always brings you titbits on cleaning days.' After some hesitation the purring began again, although the volume was noticeably lower.

'You see, Henry,' Patsy continued between sips from a cup of tea, 'Cousin Kate is in a tizzy because she can't make up her mind whether or not to tell the police who she saw, or thought she saw, the night before that awful murder was discovered. She keeps saying she doesn't want to throw suspicion on an innocent person, and she can't be absolutely sure and so on and so forth, but if she says nothing and the person she isn't sure she saw goes on to kill someone else she'll feel absolutely dreadful. We've spent ages on the phone and I've told her till I'm blue in the face that she really should tell the police and in the end she said she would if I'd go with her and stay overnight in case they want to talk to her again. You do see my problem, don't you? Oh, all right, suit yourself if you want to sulk,' she added crossly as the cat jumped off her lap and stalked out of the room, his tail held erect as a symbol of disapproval. Patsy finished her tea, washed up her cup, saucer and plate, and went to pack an overnight bag.

'Good morning. Please come in.' The speaker, a slim, apple-cheeked woman of about fifty, escorted DCs Vicky Armstrong and Sukey Reynolds into a pleasantly furnished sitting room where a woman who appeared a few years older was already seated on a couch in front of the window. She sat down beside her and waved a hand at two chairs facing them. 'Please sit down,' she said. 'My name's Patricia Godwin and this is my cousin, Kate Springfield, who has some information she thinks may be helpful to your enquiries. She has asked me to sit with her while she talks to you. I hope you have no objection?'

'None whatsoever,' Sukey assured her. 'We appreciate your response to our appeal for further information, Ms Springfield. Just in case you're worried about publicity,' she went on, noticing the agitated movement of Kate's hands, 'any information you give us at this stage is confidential and we won't release your name to the press.'

'That isn't what I'm worried about,' Kate said hurriedly, 'although of course I wouldn't want my name to be in the papers so thank you for saying that, but what worries me is not being sure about whether I'm doing the right thing you see, and . . . well, I did think of saying something to that nice young officer who came to see me yesterday morning, DC Osborne, but all she asked about was that disagreement and in the end I didn't—'

'Ms Springfield, it's not unusual for people to feel hesitant about speaking to the police,' Sukey interposed, sensing that the witness had a tendency to ramble on and anxious not to be late for their appointment at the Holmwood Care Home, 'so just relax and tell us what's on your mind. We're talking about the evening of last Friday, the twenty-sixth of July, aren't we – the evening before Ms Tremaine's body was discovered? What exactly happened that you think might be important?'

Kate glanced at her cousin, who gave an encouraging nod. 'It was a little before ten,' she began. 'I'm sure of that because it was nearly time for the news. It was getting dark so I went to close the curtains.'

'And while you were doing that, did you look out of the window?' Sukey prompted.

'Yes . . . that is, no. I mean, I'd left the balcony door open and before I closed it I stepped out on to the balcony to get a breath of air. It was rather a warm evening, you see.'

'And did you look around?'

'Yes, I suppose I must have done,' said Kate. 'And then I saw,' she went on, speaking slowly at first but then in hurried, staccato bursts, 'or I thought I saw . . . I didn't think anything of it at the time . . . after all, he lives here and there was no reason why he shouldn't be there . . . although of course it was rather late . . . it was only after we heard the dreadful news of the murder, that I remembered it . . . and I kept thinking about what happened at the meeting.' Kate broke off and put her hands to her eyes. 'Oh dear!' she wailed. 'I can't be sure it was him and it might not have anything to do with this dreadful business.'

'Suppose you let us be the judge of that,' said Vicky. 'Just tell us what you saw. You said "he" – you're certain it was a man?'

'Oh yes, I'm pretty sure of that.' Kate began to sound more confident. 'A well-built man, quite tall.'

'How was he dressed?'

Kate closed her eyes as she tried to recall the image. 'Let's see. I'm sure he wore trousers, not shorts, quite light coloured, and a shirt with long sleeves. No jacket; as I said, it was a warm evening.'

'Very good,' said Vicky. 'What was he doing?'

'He wasn't *doing* anything.' Kate began to hesitate again. 'He was just there, and I only saw him for a few moments. He seemed to be looking this way and that, almost as if he'd heard something.'

'Did you recognize him?'

'Oh dear, that's what I can't be sure of . . . I don't want to accuse an innocent person.' Kate became visibly distressed and her cousin put an arm round her shoulders and pushed a tissue into her hand.

'Just saying you thought you saw a certain person in a certain place at a certain time doesn't amount to an accusation,' Sukey began, doing her best to conceal her impatience. 'Even if it is the person you thought you saw, he may have had a perfectly innocent reason for being there. So just tell us who you thought this man was.'

There was a long silence while Kate blew her nose, dried her eyes on the soggy tissue, swallowed hard and whispered. 'I thought it was Doctor Ellerman.'

'Can you say why you thought it was him and not some other person of similar build?'

Kate frowned and thought for a moment before saying. 'I've

only lived here a short time so I don't know many people. I particularly noticed Doctor Ellerman at the meeting because he had a lot to say and there was that disagreement so I paid a lot of attention to him.'

'Yes, we know about the meeting,' said Sukey. That was some weeks ago, we understand. Let's go back to Friday evening. How clearly did you see him? Is there a light in that area?'

'It wasn't quite dark, you see . . . and when I first saw him he was in shadow and then he stood still for a moment like I said, looking around, and then he walked away and I just came indoors.'

'Do you mean he was in shadow at first and then moved into the light?' asked Vicky.

'It wasn't exactly light where he was standing; just less dark.'

'The security lights by the waste centre are comparatively dim,' Patsy Godwin interposed. 'I don't imagine they expect people to go there after dark.'

'That's what struck me as strange; I mean, that anyone should be there as late as that,' said Kate, with a surge of confidence as if her cousin's comment strengthened her justification for speaking out.

'You said he moved away – do you mean back into the shadows?'

'No, in the other direction.'

'Towards the front door to the flats?'

'No, past the side of the building and out of sight.'

'Did you hear anything? Voices, perhaps, or a car starting up a few moments later?'

Kate shook her head. 'No, I came in and shut the door. As I said, I thought nothing of it until—' Her momentary flash of confidence seemed to evaporate and she began pounding closed fists on her lap. 'Oh, dear, I do hope I haven't been wasting your time!' she exclaimed.

'On the contrary, Ms Springfield,' said Sukey, 'it's possible you have given us extremely valuable information. I have just one more question about the meeting where Doctor Ellerman and Ms Tremaine had what we understand was a rather strong difference of opinion. What makes you think it has anything to do with this murder?'

'They had been arguing for several minutes . . . they really became quite cross with one another, and then . . . just as the chairman intervened . . . I'll never forget the way he . . . Doctor Ellerman looked at Mrs Tremaine as he sat down . . . almost as if he'd like to . . .'

'Like to what?' said Vicky.

The response came in a barely audible whisper. 'Kill her.'

'I thought we'd never get away!' said Vicky with some feeling as she and Sukey returned to their car after thanking Kate for her help and giving repeated assurances that she had done exactly the right thing in talking to them. 'The old bat did go on a bit – we'll have to get a move on if we're going to be at Holmwood by ten.'

'We'd better report back to the Sarge,' said Sukey. 'You drive; I'll call him on the way.'

By the time they reached the entrance to Holmwood, Sukey had given DS Rathbone a brief outline of Kate Springfield's observations, which he pounced on with a rare show of enthusiasm. 'Let's see what the cocky bugger has to say about that!' he almost gloated. 'Well done the pair of you!'

'It seems we've collected some Brownie points.' Sukey grinned as Vicky turned in through the gates of Holmwood Care Home.

'Great. Let's see if we can rack up a few more.'

They pressed the bell beside the front door of the modern, brick-built building and were admitted by a young olive-skinned woman wearing a spotless white overall and a blue headscarf. 'Mr Seaton is in the office,' she said in a soft, lilting voice as they showed her their IDs. 'Please come this way.'

Brian Seaton was tall, fair-haired and unexpectedly youthful in appearance. He rose to meet the detectives with a smile of welcome, revealing immaculate teeth. 'My wife told me to expect you and she apologizes for not meeting you herself,' he began as he reached across the desk to shake their hands and invited them with a wave at a couple of chairs to sit down. 'She's having a discussion with the doctor – we're rather concerned about one of our residents. I do assure you,' he went on earnestly, 'that the well-being of all our residents is of paramount importance to us and we have been greatly distressed by Mr Donaldson's allegations. The coroner's verdict at the inquest indicated quite clearly that no blame attached to any of our staff, so we completely refute his charge of negligence.'

'As I explained to your wife on the telephone,' Vicky began, 'we are currently investigating the murder of Ms Fenella Tremaine. As part of our investigations we are trying to build up a picture of her background and private life. We understand that she was a frequent visitor to one of your residents; we don't know the lady's name but we understand Ms Tremaine used to call her Auntie Peg.'

'Ah yes, Peggy Thompson,' said Seaton. 'Yes, we've heard about what happened to poor Ms Tremaine of course – terrible business!' He assumed a suitably serious expression to match his tone, and quickly added, 'but I hardly think you expect to find her murderer here?'

'We have to follow up every lead, no matter how apparently irrelevant,' Sukey explained. 'Perhaps you didn't know that Ms Tremaine and Mr Donaldson became acquainted during their visits here?'

Seaton nodded. 'Oh yes, we were aware of that.'

'After his mother's funeral, Ms Tremaine got in touch with Mr Donaldson. She had read the report of the inquest into his mother's death, during which he claimed that had the nursing staff been more attentive she might not have died. During their conversation she mentioned an exchange she had overheard between two members of your nursing staff – an exchange that on reflection she thought might be significant.'

Seaton frowned and raised his eyebrows. 'What conversation was that, and how did she come to overhear it?'

'She mentioned two names – Sally Carter and Barbara Melrose,' said Vicky. 'Were they on duty at the time Mrs Donaldson died?'

'I'll check.' Seaton spent two or three minutes consulting his computer before saying, 'Yes. They were both on duty that day. They are two very experienced and conscientious nurses and they have both worked here for several years.'

'We're not here to examine their credentials,' Sukey assured him. 'We just want to ask them a few questions, so if you would kindly—'

'Yes, yes, all right.' Seaton stood up, walked round the desk and opened the door. He led them along a short corridor and showed them into a small, windowless room lit by a skylight. 'If you'll wait here I'll go and find them,' he said and went out, leaving the door open. A few moments later he returned escorting two young women in neat blue uniforms. 'Here they are,' he said, with an air of an uncle presenting two favourite nieces. 'These ladies are detectives,' he informed them after introducing each of them by name, 'But don't worry – they don't bite!' He gave each an encouraging pat on the arm and withdrew, saying over his shoulder to Sukey and Vicky, 'Do pop into the office before you leave – my wife would like to meet you.'

The moment the door closed behind him, Sally Carter said, 'This is about Fenella Tremaine's murder, isn't it?'

'Suppose you let us ask the questions,' said Sukey. For some reason she had found Brian Seaton's manner intensely irritating and she spoke in a sharper tone than usual. 'We want you both to cast your minds back a couple of months to the death of Mrs Donaldson, a former resident here. We understand that you were both on duty the day she died.'

'That's right,' said Barbara Melrose. 'We had to attend the inquest; the coroner was very kind and he seemed satisfied that we did everything we could for her.'

'It appears that the old lady's son doesn't think so, and we are informed that you were overheard later saying something that suggested otherwise. To be precise –' she referred to her notes – 'our information is that one of you said, "Her time was up anyway," to which the other replied, "That's why I didn't say anything." Would either of you care to comment on those remarks?'

Two pairs of eyes widened, two jaws dropped and hands were clapped to two mouths. For a few seconds the nurses struggled to control themselves, failed, and exploded into giggles. 'Perhaps you'd like to share the joke?' Vicky suggested.

'Oh dear, do we have to? It's really very embarrassing – and we might lose our jobs if it gets back to him,' said Sally.

'Of course, he might give us a bonus if we promise not to tell Carla,' Barbara tittered.

'If it turns out that you're withholding vital information you stand to lose more than your jobs,' Sukey snapped, at which the women hastily straightened their faces. 'What you have just said appears, on the face of it, to go some way to refute Mr Donaldson's claim to have found evidence of negligence. However, it is possible it opens a rather different can of worms. And you are right; we are also looking into the murder of Fenella Tremaine. So it might be in your interests to come clean. When you said you might lose your jobs if it gets back to him, do we take it you were talking about your employer, Mr Seaton?' The two women exchanged glances and then nodded.

'You reckon he plays away?' asked Vicky. Again they nodded. 'And the one whose time was up anyway – would that by any chance be Fenella Tremaine?'

'We reckon so,' said Barbara. 'We could see they fancied each other. He used to make a point of coming into the lounge when she was visiting Peggy Thompson and you could tell by the looks they gave each other and the way they exchanged whispers. They would have realized none of the old dears would notice anything and it probably didn't occur to either of them that we might be keeping an eye on them.'

'You've both been here a considerable time – had he had other affairs?'

Sally shrugged. 'Who can say?'

'Has he tried it on with either of you?'

'No, we reckon he's too smart for that.'

'Do you think his wife knows – or suspects?'

'It's none of our business,' said Barbara. 'Look, is that all you want to ask us? It's nearly time to make the mid-morning rounds.'

'Yes, that's all for now, and we can assure Mr Donaldson that you have given a completely satisfactory explanation of the conversation that Ms Tremaine overheard,' said Vicky.

'And you won't say anything about . . . you know?'

'There's no need for us to take formal statements from you at the moment,' said Sukey.

# NINE

DS Rathbone had barely completed the formalities prior to resuming the previous day's interview with Marcus Ellerman when he was called away to take the call from Sukey, reporting on the visit she and Vicky had paid to Kate Springfield. When he returned to the interview room Penny could see immediately that he had learned something significant. He resumed his seat and reset the tape recorder. He leaned forward with his chin jutting out and his eyes narrowed in a manner plainly calculated to intimidate.

'All right, Doctor Ellerman, let's recap shall we?' he began. 'First, although you were aware, from an overheard conversation, that the knife in Fenella Tremaine's back had a distinctively carved handle, you were evasive when questioned about some souvenir items that you and your wife brought back from your overseas travels, even when knives with decorative handles were specifically mentioned. Second, when shown a photograph of the actual knife used to kill Fenella, you stated – having given the picture only a cursory glance – that you had never seen one like it. And third –' with each new point Rathbone jabbed the table with a forefinger – 'when pressed to look more closely at the photograph and answer the question again you refused to do so without first consulting your solicitor. Are we agreed so far?' Ellerman nodded. 'Please answer aloud for the tape.'

'Yes.'

'Fine. So now, having consulted your solicitor, you decide to admit not only to recognizing the knife but actually owning one of identical design, which you immediately offer to produce. Would you care to explain why, if you were so confident of being able to show us your own knife, you didn't say so in the first place?'

Ellerman cast a pleading glance at Jason Pollard, who gave an encouraging nod. 'I admit it was stupid of me,' he said lamely, 'but . . . I suppose I panicked. I'd already lied about it or, as you say, been evasive, and like I said, I thought you might suspect I had a second knife, but I swear I bought only one and I had no idea it had gone. Surely, it's obvious it was stolen by the killer. Wilkins is the only person other than personal friends who've been in my flat recently, so surely he's the one you should be questioning, not me. For God's sake, Sergeant!' He raised his hands, palms upwards, as if in supplication. 'If I was planning to murder Fenella, which I emphatically deny, do you think I'd have been stupid enough to stab her virtually on my doorstep and with my own knife?'

'You'd be surprised at the stupid things even people with a lot of letters after their names do in the heat of the moment,' said Rathbone. He leaned back in his chair and said in a casual tone, 'By the way, Doctor Ellerman, where were you between nine thirty and midnight last Friday?'

Ellerman appeared taken aback at the sudden change of direction. He glanced at Pollard, who indicated with a nod that he should answer. 'Let's see, what was I doing last Friday?' He thought for a moment before saying, 'Ah yes, I was at home, catching up with some work. We'd had rather a busy day at the office and I brought some accounts back with me to check.'

'What time did you arrive home?'

'I don't remember the exact time . . . probably shortly after seven o'clock.'

'So from then on you were at home on your own all the evening?'

'That's right.'

'You didn't go out at all? To get something to eat or drink, for example?'

'I took something from the freezer, heated it in the microwave and ate it sitting at my desk.'

'Did you have any visitors?'

'No.'

'Did you receive any phone calls?'

'Not that I remember.'

'Or make any calls?'

'No.'

'What time did you go to bed?'

'About midnight, I suppose.' Ellerman appeared both bewildered and uneasy as Rathbone pressed on with his questions. 'Look, what is this all about?'

'So we have only your word for it that you were indoors, in your own flat, from approximately seven o'clock until midnight? In other words, you are unable to produce a single witness who can confirm what you have just told us.' Ellerman drew a sharp breath and opened his mouth, but no sound came out. 'Supposing I were to tell you,' Rathbone continued, 'that we have a witness who saw you in the recycling area at Sycamore Park at about the time when, according to the forensic pathologist, Fenella Tremaine was murdered with your knife. What do you have to say to that?'

'I'd say they were lying!' Ellerman's colour flared. He cast a despairing glance at Pollard, who appeared momentarily trans-fixed, and then half rose with his hands raised. To Penny's alarm he appeared to be about to attack Rathbone, and the uniformed officer keeping guard grabbed his shoulders and pulled him back into his seat. 'Sergeant,' he said in a hoarse voice, 'I give you my word that I did not move from my flat on the evening in question. Who is this witness anyway? I demand to know!'

'Please Doctor Ellerman, calm down!' said Pollard. He turned to Rathbone. 'I understand that according to medical reports this murder took place some time between nine thirty and midnight. My client has stated quite definitely that he did not leave his flat all evening, so it is obvious that it was some other person your witness saw.'

'Of course, that's it!' said Ellerman, his earlier anger giving place to relief at what he evidently saw as a reprieve. 'It must have been Wilkins. I said it was Wilkins, didn't I? He's the man you should be questioning, Sergeant, not me.'

'How would you describe Frederick Wilkins, Doctor Ellerman?'

Ellerman's frown was almost a scowl. 'I don't know . . . I've never taken much notice of his appearance, except he always looks scruffy, even when he's off duty.'

'Would you say he was well built?'

'Not particularly. On the scrawny side if anything.'

'About how tall? Medium height? Six feet or over?

'Oh, for God's sake, how am I supposed to know? Not particu-larly tall – about average height I suppose.'

'Not particularly tall, scruffy and on the scrawny side,' Rathbone repeated. 'That hardly fits in with our witness's description, which was of "a well-built man, quite tall, dressed in light-coloured trousers and a shirt with long sleeves" – not exactly scruffy.'

'All right, so it might not have been Wilkins your witness saw,' Ellerman conceded with some reluctance. 'All I'm saying is that it wasn't me. It must have been someone else who fits that description, not necessarily the killer. It still doesn't put Wilkins in the clear, does it?'

'All right, we'll leave that for the moment. Now let's go back to the knife. There are fingerprints on the handle but it would appear that an attempt – a rather clumsy attempt – was made to wipe them off. When this interview is over an officer will take your prints for comparison.'

'Of course my prints will be on it – it's my knife! Whoever killed Fenella left them on to incriminate me!'

'So why would he attempt to wipe them off?'

Ellerman, who by this time appeared thoroughly rattled, passed a shaking hand over his forehead. 'How should I know? People do stupid things . . . as you yourself reminded me a little while ago,' he added in what seemed to Penny a desperate attempt to regain some kind of initiative.

At this point Pollard intervened. 'I assure you, Sergeant, that my client will have absolutely no objection to having his fingerprints taken,' he said. 'However, I must point out that although he admits having been less than frank with you during your earlier enquiries, it is clear that you have nothing but hearsay and circumstantial evidence to connect him with the murder of Fenella Tremaine. Unless you can produce some hard evidence on which to base a charge, I must insist that you release him without further delay.'

'Wait here while I arrange for an officer to take your prints,' said Rathbone curtly. He left the room briefly. Once outside he called DCI Leach and gave him a report on the interview. On his return he found Ellerman wiping ink from his fingers.

'All right, you can now prove that I have at some time handled my own knife,' he remarked with a hint of a sneer. 'I take it I'm free to leave without a stain on my character?'

'You are being released on police bail,' Rathbone informed
him curtly. 'Your solicitor will explain what that involves.'

Barbara and Sally resumed their duties and Sukey and Vicky
went back to the office. Sukey tapped on the door, which was
slightly ajar. A woman's voice called 'Come' and they entered
to find Brian Seaton and a thin-faced woman in a dark-blue
nurse's uniform standing side by side at an open filing cabinet,
apparently studying the contents of a folder. They looked up as
the detectives entered and Sukey was immediately struck by the
contrast between Seaton's smile of recognition and the woman's
wary, almost hostile expression.

'Ah, you're back!' he said. 'Carla dear, these are the—'

'Two meddlesome detectives, who are calling the standard of
our care for our residents and the integrity of our staff into question,' she interrupted. 'I trust you are satisfied that there is no
justification for the allegations made by Mr Donaldson and we
shall expect a full apology.' She glared at them both from behind
round and unflattering spectacles

'Mrs Seaton,' said Sukey, 'there has never been an intention
on our part to make any kind of judgement on your standards of
care. We are investigating the murder of Fenella Tremaine, who
has been a frequent visitor here and who is reported to have
made certain statements which we are obliged to investigate. And
I'm pleased to inform you,' she added quickly, anticipating an
acid response, 'that after speaking to the two nurses in question,
Barbara Melrose and Sally Carter, concerning a snatch of conversation said to have been overheard by Ms Tremaine, we have
found nothing to support Mr Bradley Donaldson's allegations.
We shall inform him accordingly, and we appreciate your and
your husband's cooperation.'

'These allegations,' said Carla Seaton, 'exactly what were they
and what was the conversation about? Surely we have a right to
know.'

'It was a purely private conversation,' said Vicky, 'and we are
satisfied that it had been totally misunderstood and bore no
relevance whatsoever to the death of Mrs Donaldson.'

'So what exactly did Carter and Melrose say to one another
to cause all this misunderstanding, as you call it?'

'As my colleague has just informed you, it was a private conversation.' Sukey could hear her tone becoming sharp in response to the other's aggressive manner. 'All we can say is that everything has been explained to our satisfaction, so we won't waste any more of your time.'

'Thank you so much.' Seaton hurried to the door and opened it. 'I'll show you out.' He led them back to the entrance, pausing on the way to greet an elderly man, leaning heavily on a stick, who was heading with faltering steps towards the lounge. 'Hurry up Alec, you'll be late for elevenses!' he said and the old man's wrinkled face lit up in a smile. 'They do love a word of encouragement,' he said as he opened the front door. As they parted he shook them both by the hand and said, 'I really think you two young ladies are much too pretty to be chasing murderers!' They acknowledged the remark with polite smiles and returned to their car.

'What do you make of that set-up?' said Vicky.

'I wonder if she suspected her husband was having it off with Fenella Tremaine?' said Sukey. 'From the look of her, I'd say she was capable of murder.'

'Well, you can hardly blame him for having a bit on the side,' Vicky replied. 'I'll bet she's not much fun in bed. You certainly gave her the rough edge of your tongue, by the way. I've noticed several times recently you've sounded a bit snappy. It's not like you – is there something wrong?'

Sukey gave a deep sigh as she settled into her seat and clipped on her seat belt. 'Oh, it's nothing really. Harry's been busy all week and we haven't seen each other so we were hoping to spend time together over the weekend, but it didn't happen. And then, oh hell, I've got a birthday coming up and it's the big four zero. That's enough to depress anyone.'

Vicky burst out laughing. 'Don't be so daft! Remember the old Sophie Tucker song – "Life begins at Forty"? And –' she turned to scrutinize Sukey's face – 'you don't look a day over thirty so stop worrying. First opportunity you get, give Harry a night to remember!'

Sukey peered in the vanity mirror. 'Not too many lines, I guess. Thanks for the advice Vicky; you're a pal.'

'No probs.' Vicky turned on the ignition and drove slowly

back to the gate. 'For the record, I'm only a few months behind you!'

Back at headquarters, Rathbone listened to the team's verbal reports before saying, 'Just to bring you up to date this end, we had to let Ellerman go for the time being, but he's by no means out of the frame. I've spoken to DCI Leach and as he's already shown signs of aggressive behaviour we're agreed we need to find out a bit more about his past. He may even have form. We now know a bit more about Fenella. It's interesting that she had an affair with the joint owner of the care home she used to visit; she's probably had other lovers, so that's another line of enquiry that needs following up. There may be other vengeful wives lurking in the background, although they're hardly likely to possess oriental daggers with carved handles.'

'Excuse me, Sarge.' Penny put up a tentative hand. 'Sukey and Vicky said they thought Mrs Seaton looked as if she was capable of murder. Supposing she found out about her husband's affair? She probably knew where Fenella lived; being a regular visitor to the home she would have had to give an ID for security reasons. Supposing Mrs Seaton had a knife identical to Ellerman's and—'

'Sneaked over to Sycamore Park one dark night on the off-chance of finding Fenella presenting a sitting target in the recycling area?' Rathbone's tone was faintly patronizing and Penny looked suitably abashed. 'Ingenious, but stretching coincidence a bit too far, don't you think? Still,' he conceded, 'until we've checked the murder weapon for fingerprints we have to keep open minds. Now –' he was scrolling down his computer screen as he spoke – 'there are several names here of people who were visited during the initial house-to-house enquiries but don't appear to have been spoken to since. They're all residents of Sycamore Park: Jennifer Freeman, Jared Whittington and Larry Worsley; more significantly, they're also members of the residents' association committee and were present at the meeting in Ellerman's flat to discuss the contentious matter of the accounts that was carried over from the general meeting. In the light of the latest developments we'll have to talk to them again. We need to know exactly what happened at that meeting – how was the matter settled, was it a brief business meeting or did it turn into more of a social occasion with refreshments and if so what particular topics came up in conversation, did they notice anything of particular interest in the flat, that sort of thing. Show them the picture of the murder weapon, but be careful not to imply that Ellerman is a suspect at this stage – we don't want misleading reports in the press. The last thing we need is the media hounding him and leaving us liable to a claim for damages if he's proved innocent.'

'Sarge.' Tim Pringle raised a hand. 'Do you think I should have another word with Mr Yardley? He mentioned the meeting in Ellerman's flat and gave me the names of the other people there, but I didn't actually ask him those particular questions.'

Rathbone nodded. 'Good point, Tim. Yes, by all means have another word with him. Sukey, you go and see Ms Freeman. Vicky, see what you can find out about Fenella's past. I suggest you begin by asking her daughter how they became estranged. Penny and Mike go and see Messrs Whittington and Worsley. Meanwhile, I'll have a look into Ellerman's past history. OK.' He shut down his computer. 'Do your written reports and then go home. See you all tomorrow.'

# TEN

B efore leaving headquarters, Sukey sent a text to Harry reading simply, 'Free this evening. Are you?' Within seconds the reply came back: 'Me too. Will bring food.'

The traffic was heavy but her heart was light as she drove home. As she pulled up on the parking space outside her flat and clipped on the steering-wheel lock she heard a tap on the window and he was there, smiling a welcome, opening the car door, drawing her to her feet and into his arms. After a few seconds he took her keys, locked the car and opened her front door.

'As soon as I got your text I nipped out to get some supplies.' He indicated the supermarket bag he was carrying.' He followed her up the stairs, put the bag on the kitchen table and helped her off with her jacket. 'It's seemed an eternity since I saw you,' he said when they were both free to speak.

'Two eternities,' she agreed. 'Harry, I've missed you so much.'

'That's good.' He began unpacking his purchases and putting them away. 'I've bought steaks, oven chips and frozen peas. Not very original but I didn't think you'd want to waste too much time cooking.' His meaning was clear and Sukey felt the familiar thrill of anticipation. 'Let's start with a drink, shall we?' he went on. 'Dad and I tried this the other day –' he held up a bottle of Shiraz – 'and we thought it was OK.' He opened the bottle and filled two glasses.

They sat outside on Sukey's rooftop patio, savouring their wine and enjoying the panorama of the city basking in the early evening sunlight. 'It's been a good couple of weeks weather-wise,' Harry remarked, 'but this is the first time I've had a chance to appreciate it.'

'Me too,' she agreed. 'It's been boringly quiet lately and time seemed to drag because you've been away so much. Things started to happen at the weekend, of course.'

'Ah yes, the Fenella Tremaine murder,' he said knowingly. 'I want to talk to you about that later on.'

'Harry, you know I can't—' she began, but he cut her short.

'I'm not asking you to break the rules.'

'Then what—?'

'Tell you later.' He finished his wine and held out a hand for her empty glass. 'Want a refill?'

'Not just now, thanks.'

'Hungry?'

'Not just now . . . at least, not for food.'

Holding hands, they went back indoors together. Later, as they lay in bed and watched the light fading, Harry remarked, 'So you've arrested Marcus Ellerman for the Fenella Tremaine murder. That was some smart detective work!'

Sukey leaned up on one elbow and stared down at him accusingly. 'How did you know that?' she demanded. 'We haven't released a name; all the media have been told is that a man has been helping with enquiries.'

'Oh come on, love, get real,' he said, pulling her face towards his and sliding his free hand down her back. 'I'm a news hound,' he reminded her after an interval. 'You don't really think I'm just going to sit and wait for your lot to hand out crumbs of information, do you? It wasn't difficult; all I had to do was hang around the mobile police station at Sycamore Park and watch the action.'

'Harry, please say you're not going to run the story. He's not been charged or even detained for further questioning. It could mess things up for us if it gets into the papers.'

'I promise I won't run it until I have the official say so, although I can't vouch for any of my rivals. There is a price for my silence, though.'

'Which is . . .?' She made a suggestive movement and he gave her a gentle slap on the bottom.

'Not that, you insatiable woman!'

'Then what?'

'You let me in on the action. I've been doing a little ferreting around on my own and I have reason to believe Fenella may have a secret or two tucked away in her past.'

'What makes you think that?'

'One of Dad's old army buddies is a resident in the Holmwood Care Home and he goes to visit him now and then. When the story of Fenella's murder broke he told me he'd made her acquaintance while she was visiting a friend there. He said he thought she looked "a bit of all right" and hinted that she might be "available". I told him not to say that in front of Freddie!' Lady Frederica Sinclair, a retired lawyer, was Major George Matthews' 'lady friend', as he gallantly referred to her in company. 'Dad admits he has an eye for a pretty woman,' Harry went on, 'although he always hastens to add that there's no harm in looking.'

'I'm sorry, I can't do that kind of deal,' said Sukey, smiling in spite of herself. 'You're right, though; we already know that there's another side to Fenella and one of our team has already been assigned to finding out more. Please, Harry, stay out of it; Sergeant Rathbone – and no doubt DCI Leach as well – know you and I are pretty close and I'd be in all sorts of trouble if they found out I'd been giving you information about witnesses. But there is something you could do,' she added as a thought came into her head. 'Vicky and I had to go and check on Bradley Donaldson's insistence that there was a cover-up at Holmwood over the death of his mother. It all hinged on a misunderstanding and as far as the police are concerned there's no further interest in the place, but we did turn up some interesting background information.' She threw back the duvet and got out of bed. 'I'm hungry – and this time it is for food. I'll tell you more while we cook.'

'I have to admit I'm puzzled,' said Harry as they sat down to their steak and chips. 'You've just warned me off poking into Fenella's past because your lot are already on the case. Just out of interest, what do they expect to find? A lover with a jealous wife who found out about the affair and stuck the knife in her back?' He paused to put the last forkful of steak in his mouth. 'On second thoughts,' he added thoughtfully, 'it would help if you could prove that she'd been having it off with Ellerman. That would give him a double motive for killing her – get her off his back and leave the way clear for him to get promotion at work.'

Sukey sighed. 'It's obvious you've been chatting to some people at Maxworth's,' she said. 'I've got to hand it to you, you don't miss much.'

'That's what the *Echo* pays me for,' he said smugly. 'So what's this assignment you have for me then?'

Sukey laid down her knife and fork and drank a mouthful of wine. 'They say there's many a true word spoken in jest,' she remarked. 'As it happens, while Vicky and I were at Holmwood we discovered that the owner, Brian Seaton, plays away and one of his lovers – whom incidentally he'd recently dumped – was Fenella Tremaine.'

Harry's jaw dropped and then he burst out laughing. 'No kidding!' he guffawed. 'So Dad was right about her!' He grew serious again and said, 'You aren't suggesting his wife might be the killer, are you?'

'None of us seriously considered that as a possibility, mainly because we know the origin of the murder weapon and there seems no possible way in which Carla Seaton could have got hold of it, let alone found the opportunity to kill Fenella. Actually, Penny Osborne did tentatively raise it as a possibility and was pretty smartly put down by DS Rathbone. But thinking it over,' she went on, 'our impression of Carla, who struck us as a bit of a battleaxe and not exactly overburdened with sex appeal, was that she could be violent if provoked.'

'This needs thinking about over the dessert.' Harry brought fresh fruit salad and ice cream from the fridge and spooned it into dishes. They ate in silence for a few moments. 'It would help,' he said, 'if I had more information about the murder weapon.'

Sukey shook her head. 'Harry, I really can't give you any more details, but it would be very interesting if there happened to be some kind of link between Holmwood and Sycamore Park. I'm wondering if you could find a way of chatting up a few people at Holmwood to see what – if anything – of that sort you can uncover.'

Harry thought for a moment. 'I suppose I could drop in and see old Major Howes again,' he said. 'He's a nice old boy and like quite a few of the residents at Holmwood there's nothing wrong with his marbles, he's just wheelchair bound and couldn't bear living alone. I've been once before with Dad and he was very interested in my job – and he had a few amusing observations about some of his fellow residents. OK, I'll see what I can do.'

'That's brilliant!'

He leaned across the table until his face touched hers. 'You can express your appreciation later,' he whispered.

'Who were you calling insatiable?' she whispered back.

The following morning the team settled down to prepare for the day's assignments. Sukey searched through the file of witness statements taken during the house-to-house enquiries until she found one given by Jennifer Freeman, who lived in Block B at Sycamore Park. It was brief and read: 'I knew Fenella Tremaine only slightly. I first met her when I took over as secretary to the residents' association from her. She called on me at my flat to hand over the files and records. I offered her a drink and she stayed for an hour or so, but I haven't seen her since except just to pass the time of day when we happened to meet. I know people say she could be difficult, but I found her very pleasant and helpful. She warned me to be on my guard against Doctor Ellerman because according to her he's a bit of a bully and I'd already noticed they didn't exactly hit it off.'

'Not a lot of help, but it's a start,' Sukey remarked as Vicky returned from the vending machine with a hot drink and settled down at her own work station.

'It's always as well to be optimistic,' Vicky remarked cheerfully. 'By the way, you're looking chipper this morning. Did you see Harry at long last?'

'I did, and I took your advice.'

Vicky grinned. 'It obviously worked. So what isn't a lot of help?'

'The statement Jennifer Freeman made during the house-to-house interviews indicates only a slight acquaintance with Fenella, but I'm hoping she may have heard or seen something significant during or since the meeting in Ellerman's flat that didn't seem worth telling us about.'

'What's her background?' asked Vicky.

'She's an interior designer. She calls herself Décor for You. She gave her card to the woodie who interviewed her and I've made an appointment to see her at her showroom in Stoke Bishop. What are you doing today?'

'I'm off to Bath to have a chat with Nancy Brotherton – Fenella's daughter. She sounded pretty upset when I rang to make the appointment. I think it's only just hit her that she's lost the mother she hadn't spoken to for a long time.'

Sukey nodded. 'I can imagine. She's probably regretting not having made an effort at reconciliation and now it's too late.' She put on her jacket and picked up her bag. 'Have a good day.'

'You too.'

Décor for You sat, a little incongruously Sukey thought, between a fish and chip shop and a greengrocery in a parade which also included a hairdresser, a pharmacy and a small supermarket. The window display was simple: an armchair upholstered in dull aubergine fabric with a matching footstool, a low glass-topped table on which stood a pale green porcelain coffee pot with matching cup and saucer; a tall reading lamp behind the chair, apparently focused on a newspaper lying on the arm; a multicoloured rug in varying shades of soft green and purple that complemented the upholstery.

Sukey's entry was announced by the first few tinkling notes of 'Home Sweet Home'. A door opened at the back of the shop and a woman of about her own age emerged and said, 'Good morning,' in a vibrant contralto voice. Her appearance was striking; she had chiselled features, lustrous dark eyes and long, glossy black hair that hung in curtains on either side of her face. She wore a loose, brightly coloured dress with long sleeves, there were silver bracelets on both wrists and her long tapering fingers were heavily bejewelled.

'Jennifer Freeman?'

The woman nodded and smiled, revealing strikingly white, even teeth.

'Detective Constable Reynolds.' Sukey held up her ID.

'Do come into my office.' She led Sukey into a room with a window looking out on a small backyard. Another woman, considerably older and more soberly dressed, was standing by a desk in one corner. As they entered she picked up a bag bearing the name 'Décor for You' in gilded lettering on an ivory background. 'I'll be off now to take this swatch to the Mayhews,' she said, with a brief nod in Sukey's direction. 'Are you sure you don't want me to take the one for the Seatons at the same time? Holmwood's only a couple of miles further on.'

'Thank you, Hazel, but I have to go there again myself,' said Jennifer. 'Mr Seaton rang me yesterday to say that his wife isn't altogether happy with the colour scheme I'd suggested so we need to have another talk about it.'

'If you say so.' A meaningful twitch of one eyebrow accompanied the words. 'I won't be long.'

'Right. I'll just put this on the door.' As Jennifer followed her from the room she waved a notice reading, 'Back shortly'. When she returned she closed the inner door and invited Sukey to sit down. 'I understand you've already made an arrest, so I really don't see how I can help you,' she began. 'As I said to the officer who came to my door last Saturday after they discovered poor Fenella's body, I didn't really know her all that well.'

'Yes, I've read your statement,' Sukey said, 'but we have since learned that shortly after the meeting of the residents' association, at which there was a rather heated exchange between Fenella and Doctor Ellerman, there was a committee meeting at which you were present.'

'I'm not sure I'd describe it as heated. Bad-tempered, perhaps. Anyway, you're right. It was John Yardley who called the meeting. He's chairman of the committee but he had the decorators in so Marcus – Doctor Ellerman – said we could use his flat.'

'How long did the meeting last?'

'The formalities were over very quickly, but Marcus offered us drinks and nibbles so we stayed for a little while.'

'Were you sitting down or standing up?'

'It's funny you should ask that. We were sitting down for the meeting and when Marcus brought the drinks, but then Larry Worsley, whom I'd noticed looking round as if he was taking an interest in some things in the room, commented on one of the pictures and got up to have a closer look. He owns an art gallery so naturally we were all curious to hear what he had to say. There were one or two others that he seemed to like so we followed him around.'

'So there was a time when everyone was moving around looking at pictures?'

'That's right. Excuse me, but I don't see—'

'Just a moment,' Sukey interrupted, 'I take it you were in Doctor Ellerman's sitting room?'

'That's right, but—'

'Did you happen to notice a glass-fronted display cabinet?'

Jennifer thought for a moment. 'Yes. One of the pictures Larry was interested in was on the wall next to it.'

'Did he look at or comment on any of the things inside the cabinet?'

'He might have noticed them, but as far as I remember he was only interested in pictures. Why do you ask?'

'I'm sure you've seen this?' Sukey took the photograph of the murder weapon from her bag.

Jennifer shuddered. 'That's what Fenella was killed with, isn't it?' she said in a husky whisper. 'Yes, of course I've seen it. It's been in all the papers.'

'This knife has a very distinctive handle. When not in use it was probably kept in a sheath. Did you happen to notice such a knife in Doctor Ellerman's display cabinet?'

Jennifer started and put a hand to her mouth. 'Are you saying

Doctor Ellerman might have killed Fenella? Oh, surely not. He might have got cross with her but I can't imagine he—'

'Please answer the question,' said Sukey.

Jennifer exhaled. 'I'm sorry, I didn't really look at what was in the cabinet.' She glanced at a diamond-studded wristwatch nestling among the silver bracelets. 'Is that all? I have to go out as soon as Hazel gets back.'

'To call on Mr and Mrs Seaton, the proprietors of Holmwood Care Home?' said Sukey.'

'That's right. Do you know them?'

'It so happens our enquiries have revealed that Fenella Tremaine was a frequent visitor there.'

Jennifer's eyes flew open and Sukey detected a hint of concern in her expression. 'I had no idea,' she said, and to Sukey's experienced ear it was plain the news was disturbing. 'Perhaps she was helping them with their accounts,' she said after a moment. 'I understand that was her job.'

'She used to visit an old lady she'd known from childhood,' said Sukey, 'and we have reason to believe that those visits led to a relationship developing between her and Brian Seaton.'

'Oh, really? You just never know, do you?' Jennifer made a desperate but unsuccessful attempt to sound as if the information was of only passing interest. She stood up. 'Well, if that's really all – I'm afraid I haven't been much help.'

'As you've just remarked, you never know,' said Sukey. 'Thank you for your time,' she added as, to the accompaniment of 'Home Sweet Home', she took her leave.

# ELEVEN

Small, neatly trimmed evergreen shrubs grew on either side of the short path leading to the front door. Vicky's approach had obviously been observed, as she had barely touched the bell when the door was opened by a young woman in her mid to late twenties. She was wearing jeans and a loose blouse;

in the crook of one arm she held a rosy-cheeked baby that was contentedly sucking a thumb.

'Nancy Brotherton?' Vicky held up her ID. 'DC Armstrong.'

'Yes, that's right. I was expecting you. Do come in.' The woman led the way into a cosy sitting room with a window looking out over a small, well-tended garden. 'Do sit down,' she said, pointing to an armchair. 'I've just finished feeding Emily and I'll keep her on my lap until she's ready to go to sleep, if that's all right.'

'Of course it is,' said Vicky. 'She's a lovely baby; how old is she?'

'Just turned six months.' Nancy's face suddenly crumpled. 'This is Mum's only grandchild, and she never saw her,' she said in a broken whisper. 'I feel so awful about it . . . I never even told her I was pregnant. We'd had our differences and . . . I should have told her . . . Luke said I should tell her, but I was too proud. Pride is one of the deadly sins, isn't it?' She wept quietly for a few moments, holding the baby close as if the warmth of the little body brought some comfort.

'They do say that,' Vicky agreed. 'I realize this must be very distressing for you,' she went on, 'but I'm sure you want us to catch whoever killed your mother and we think you may be able to help us. We know so little about her, you see.'

'Yes, I understand.' Nancy dried her eyes and took a few deep breaths to calm herself. 'Of course I want to see her murderer caught,' she said. 'She didn't deserve that, whatever she did in the past.' She looked down at the baby and gently stroked the downy head. 'Emily's falling asleep so I'll put her down and then I'll make some coffee. I dare say you'd like a cup?'

'Thank you, that's very kind.' Vicky was already well primed with caffeine but it would have seemed ungracious to refuse.

'No problem.' Nancy put the baby in a crib by the window and covered her with a light blanket. She went out; while she was absent, Vicky took a quick glance round the room. It was modestly but comfortably furnished, the colour scheme had been carefully chosen and the few pictures and ornaments blended comfortably with their surroundings. There were several framed photographs, one of Nancy, Emily and a good-looking man of athletic appearance and another in which the same man featured in the front row of a local football team. Vicky stood up to take a closer look.

'That was after last season's final,' said Nancy, who re-entered at that moment with a tray, which she put down on a low table. 'My Luke was man of the match so we had to buy the photograph.'

'Of course,' Vicky said warmly, 'and I'm sure Emily will be very proud of her daddy when she's old enough to understand.'

'I hope so.' Nancy poured out two mugs of coffee and gave one to Vicky. 'Luke adores her, but I'm sure he'd like a son next time.' She drank a few mouthfuls of coffee and then said, 'You want to ask me about Mum. I expect you know we'd been estranged for some time.'

'You mentioned when you came to identify her that you hadn't seen her for a while. Her murder must have come as a terrible shock.'

'It did. Luke was at work and his mobile was switched off so I had to leave Emily with a neighbour while I was taken to the morgue in a police car. I just saw her lying there and as far as I remember all I said was, "Yes, that's my mother. Her name's Fenella Tremaine. Will you please take me home now?" I can't imagine what the police or the people in the morgue must have thought of me for not crying or seeming upset, but—'

'It's quite understandable; you were in shock,' said Vicky. 'Perhaps it would help if I told you what we already know about your mother, and then you can fill in the blanks.'

'I'll try.'

'That's fine.' Vicky gave a quick summary of the information that the police had so far gathered about Fenella's relationship with her neighbours and her colleagues at Maxworth's plus the further, more personal, details she and Sukey had gleaned from their interviews with Bradley Donaldson and the nurses at Holmwood Care Home. When she mentioned Fenella's presumed affair with Brian Seaton, Nancy gave a short, sardonic laugh.

'That's doesn't surprise me,' she exclaimed. 'Of course I knew she had affairs. She thought she was being very discreet about them and she never brought them home but as I grew older I learned to recognize the signs. I suppose it was because, like you said, she had a deprived childhood. She must have spent most of her life desperately seeking the love she never got from her own mother. It explains why she was so protective of me, and why she was so down on Luke. She wanted the best for me; she was keen for me to go to university so I did – with hindsight I realize that in those days she made most of my decisions for me – and I know she was hoping I'd marry some classy bloke with loads of money, but things didn't turn out like that. I suppose I should have been more understanding, but while I was at university I became more independent and after I finished my degree I moved out of the house and into a flat of my own. That upset Mum and she tried to persuade me to stay at home, but I couldn't face it . . . I knew I'd feel stifled.'

'A lot of people with overprotective parents feel like that,' said Vicky. 'Tell me how you met Luke,' she said after a few moments of silence during which Nancy sat with closed eyes, having apparently fallen into a reverie.

She opened her eyes with a start and swallowed a mouthful of coffee. 'Sorry about that; I was miles away for the moment. I got a job working in a small art gallery in Clifton. The owner wanted a new shop front and Luke was one of the gang that fitted it. We dated for a long time without my saying anything to Mum, but it got serious so I had to introduce them. He's a lovely chap and he went out of his way to make a good impression. I did so hope she'd take to him, but I should have known better. The next day she called me to say she hoped I wouldn't be seeing any more of such an unsuitable person. She went berserk when I told her we were engaged. We hardly spoke to each other for weeks and she didn't come to the wedding. That was two years ago and I haven't seen or spoken to her since.'

'I take it you never lived with her in Sycamore Park?'

'No. When she finally accepted that I wasn't coming home she sold her house and bought the flat. I visited her there once or twice.'

'Did she mention any of her neighbours, or introduce you to them?'

'She described them as "a pretty mixed bunch", but I certainly never met any of them.'

'Just what did she have against Luke?'

'His working-class background of course. I might have understood if he'd been what she'd have called "common" or "uncouth", but he's anything but; he went to a good school and did well in his exams so he could have gone to university but he simply wasn't cut out for an academic career. He's very practical and good with his hands so he did an apprenticeship. He's done really well – his boss thinks the world of him – and he makes wooden toys as a hobby and sells quite a lot of them at craft markets. He made that.' She proudly pointed to the crib where Emily lay sleeping.

'I've been admiring it; it's lovely,' said Vicky. She referred to her notes. 'You hinted that your mother had several lovers; was one of them a Doctor Ellerman?'

Nancy stared thoughtfully into her mug of coffee. 'Ellerman,' she repeated. 'The name rings a bell. Did his first name begin with M? Maurice? Matthew? No, that's not right.'

'How about Marcus?' Vicky suggested.

'Yes, that's the one.' Nancy snapped her fingers. 'I remember now. They worked for the same company, but I'm pretty sure he wasn't her lover – in fact she once said, "He thinks he's God's gift to women, but I've met his type before and given them the elbow".'

'But he might have tried it on with her?'

Nancy shrugged. 'It's possible. She's . . . was . . . very attractive and she certainly didn't look her age. I suppose he might have tried his luck, but if he did she didn't tell me.'

'Did you know he lived in Sycamore Park?'

Nancy stared in astonishment. 'No kidding? I had no idea.' She frowned and thought for a moment. 'I guess that makes him a suspect, doesn't it?'

'We're following several lines of enquiry,' said Vicky. 'Just one more question. Did your mother drink a lot?'

'Oh yes, she enjoyed a glass of wine or three. I never saw her drunk, though, just mellow . . . and maudlin at times, probably when she'd either dumped or been dumped.' Nancy's eyes clouded again. 'Poor Mum, I should have been kinder to her. You will catch the bastard who did it, won't you?'

'We will,' Vicky assured her. She put away her notebook, finished her coffee and stood up. 'Thank you very much for being so frank. We'll keep in touch.'

'I apologize for troubling you again, sir,' said DC Tim Pringle, 'but we feel there are one or two other things you may be able to help us with.'

'I'll do my best.' John Yardley, in dressing gown and slippers and smelling of aftershave, held the door open for Tim to enter. 'I heard on the news you've made an arrest,' he said when they were both seated. 'No name – just someone "helping with your enquiries", I understand. I hope that isn't what you're going to tell the press about me!' he added with a chuckle.

'We still have a long way to go and a lot more people to interview before we'll be in a position to make an arrest,' said Tim. 'What I'd like to talk about today is the meeting that took place in Doctor Ellerman's flat. You told me –' he referred to his notes – 'that apart from you and Doctor Ellerman, three other people were present, namely Jennifer Freeman, Jared Whittington and Larry Worsley. Is that correct?'

'Quite correct.'

'How long did the meeting last?'

Yardley thought for a moment. 'The question about the accounts was settled very quickly, but then Ellerman offered drinks so we stayed on for a general chat. Whittington and Worsley are Americans, as I think you know. Worsley owns an art gallery and he expressed an interest in one of Ellerman's pictures and got up to have a closer look. Then he went to look at another, and in the end we were all trailing round after him like a load of students in an art gallery.' Yardley chuckled again at the recollection.

'Did you happen to notice a glass-fronted display cabinet, sir?'

'I did, as it happens, but Worsley didn't show an interest in anything in it.'

'Did you happen to look at anything in it yourself – or notice anything of particular interest?'

'Such as?'

'An ornamental dagger, for example.'

Yardley stared at him as if thunderstruck. 'You mean like the one that killed poor Fenella? Good heavens, are you suggesting that Ellerman—?'

'I'm not suggesting anything, sir. Do I take it that your answer to my question is no?'

'I certainly didn't notice anything remotely resembling a dagger, although I didn't really look so that doesn't mean there wasn't one there.' He glanced at his watch. 'Look, if there's nothing else you want to ask me, I do have an appointment in an hour or so and I have some things to attend to first. I'm taking a lady out to lunch, so it's best bib and tucker!'

Tim closed his notebook and stood up. 'That's all for now, sir, thank you very much. Enjoy your lunch!'

After a morning spent mowing the lawn and tending the flowers in the garden behind her cottage, Patsy Godwin took a shower and ate her lunch sitting on her patio while admiring the results of her labours. The flower beds were a colourful mass of blooms, the kitchen garden full of rows of plump onions, beans, lettuces and root vegetables, many ready to be harvested. Henry sat beside her, contentedly cleaning himself while keeping a watchful eye on the birds pecking at the seed containers hanging from the branches of an apple tree laden with rosy fruit. Patsy gave a little sigh of content as she finished her cheese salad and put the empty plate on a low table at her side. The air was warm and still; bees buzzed among the flowers; Henry jumped on to her lap and she idly caressed him for a few moments until her eyes closed and she drifted off to sleep.

She was awakened by the sound of a car pulling up outside her cottage. Moments later the bell rang. She sat up in surprise. 'Now who could that be, I wonder?' she said aloud. 'Better go and see, I suppose.' She stood up, spilling Henry unceremoniously to the ground. She went to the front door and gave a little gasp of surprise and delight.

'Katy!' she exclaimed, giving her cousin a hug. 'How lovely to see you – but why didn't you let me know you were coming this way? We could have had lunch together. New car?' she added, glancing over Kate's shoulder at the red Audi parked outside her gate.

'No, that's not mine, it's . . . that is . . . John Yardley . . . one of my neighbours. I think I mentioned him the day you came to visit me?'

'The day of the murder?'

'Yes, that's right. Anyway, he invited me out to lunch and we went to that pub near where I used to live. He knows this part quite well and he suggested coming back this way and I said I happened to have a cousin living nearby and I thought maybe—' Kate broke off in evident embarrassment. 'I hope you don't mind.'

'Of course I don't mind. Bring him in for a cup of tea.'

Kate hurried back to the car and returned with a distinguished-looking man whom Patsy judged to be in his early sixties. 'I'm so pleased to meet you,' he said as he took the hand she held out in welcome. 'Kate has told me what good friends you two are, and what a comfort you've been over that dreadful murder.'

'Yes, it did shake her up pretty badly,' said Patsy. 'Anyway, do come in. I was dozing in the garden – perhaps you'd like to sit out there and have a cup of tea?' She led the way through the cottage on to the patio and pulled up some chairs. 'Do sit down.'

Henry was crouching near the apple tree, evidently in the hope that an unwary bird would flutter to the ground in search of a fallen nut. At the sound of voices he came to investigate and Kate called him by name. He came running across the grass to greet her; she stooped to stroke him and he rubbed against her legs, purring loudly in appreciation. 'Patsy will tell you that Henry is the most intelligent cat in the world,' said Kate. 'She believes he practically reads her mind!' she added with an indulgent smile.

'He certainly seemed to recognize your voice,' said John. He bent down and tickled one of Henry's ears. The cat stopped purring and backed away, staring up at the newcomer for a few moments without moving. Then he ostentatiously turned round and stalked away. 'He obviously doesn't think much of me!' said John with a chuckle.

'Oh, I'm sure it's nothing personal,' said Kate. 'He's just not used to men.'

# TWELVE

I t was nearly six o'clock and the team had just finished filing reports on their various assignments when DS Rathbone entered the office. 'If you're thinking about going home, forget it,' he said briskly. 'DCI Leach wants us all in his office right away.

The summons came as no surprise. Over mugs of tea and coffee on their return to headquarters the team had been exchanging significant pieces of information they had gleaned from their various witnesses. All had a feeling that, while many questions remained unanswered – including the obvious one, the identity of the murderer – even the most trivial of observations would eventually prove to form part of the overall picture. 'It's like working on a jigsaw puzzle,' Tim Pringle had commented, to nods of agreement all round. 'Now and again you pick up a piece that doesn't seem to fit anywhere, almost as if it belongs to another puzzle and has somehow got into the wrong box. Then you suddenly see its connection with another piece that you haven't noticed before.'

'Right, troops,' said Leach when everyone was settled. 'There are several things to talk about, but first I want to give you the latest report from the CSIs. First of all, they've tested the murder weapon for fingerprints. The only ones they found on the handle were Ellerman's, and there were smudges consistent with it having been used in a stabbing action. It's his knife, of course, so that in itself isn't conclusive although the fact that there are no other prints does strengthen our case against him. However, there could be another explanation for the smudges that he'd be sure to throw up straight away.'

'You mean, sir, he could claim that the killer, having stolen his knife, wore gloves when using it?' Rathbone suggested.

'Exactly, Greg. Now, in one of the bins for recycling glass they've found a quantity of bottles with Fenella's prints on them, which confirms a comment made by one of her neighbours that she was "a bit of a lush". It also explains why she disposed of them at a time when she imagined she'd be unobserved. Nothing new there, but more significantly, the CSIs found traces of blood on the front of the bin, which DNA tests show to be hers. Doc Hanley has already pointed out that as no major artery was severed most of the bleeding was internal; a small quantity had drained down on to the clothing but there were only minute traces on the black plastic bag she was found lying on. However –' at this point Leach leaned back and ran his gaze round his team, who were hanging on every word – 'I'm sure you don't need me to tell you what this means.'

'She was stabbed while she was feeding the bottles through the lid of the bin,' said Mike.

'And the noise of breaking glass would have prevented her from hearing the killer approach,' added Penny.

'Anything else?' Leach glanced round the row of faces. 'Yes, Sukey?'

'We've been assuming up to now, sir, that it was while she was putting rubbish in the skip that the killer stuck the knife in her back, heaved her up by her legs and bundled her over the edge.'

Leach nodded. 'Go on.'

'We know now that isn't the case; she was standing in front of one of the bins feeding in bottles when she was attacked, and the bins are a couple of yards or so from the skip where her body was found. So after he'd killed her the murderer had to pick her up and carry her to the skip.' As Sukey spoke it was as if a film of the killer at work was unrolling before her eyes. Without realizing what she was doing, she stood up and mimed the actions. 'That meant he either had to open the lid of the skip and then go back for her, by which time she'd probably slumped to the ground, or he had to sling her over his shoulder, carry her to the skip, hold the lid open with one hand while heaving her inside. Whichever way he chose, some of her blood was transferred to the bin where the CSIs found it, and when he picked her up he must have got some of it on his clothing. Not a great deal on account of the nature of the wound of course, but maybe that's how it happened.' Feeling slightly embarrassed she sat down to a good-natured round of applause.

'Very well put,' said Leach with a smile. 'And that's where we've lost precious time. By now our man has either disposed of his soiled clothing, or more likely just put it through the wash or sent it to the cleaners. More leg work for the woodentops, I'm afraid.' A hand was raised. 'Yes, Vicky?'

'Excuse me, sir, was the knife in a sheath?'

'Good question, Vicky. I was coming to that. The short answer is that according to Ellerman the knife was in an ornamental sheath when he bought it and that's how it was the last time he saw it – when of course he swears it was in its usual place in the display cabinet. Needless to say, finding the sheath is top priority. Meanwhile, let's hear what all of you have uncovered today. Penny and Mike, you've been to see the two Americans; did they have anything useful to add?'

'Not really, sir,' said Mike. 'They were both at the meeting in Ellerman's flat and they noticed the display cabinet, but neither of them could remember seeing a knife. It seems that like everyone else they were more interested in his art collection.'

'So while everyone's attention was elsewhere, one of the people present could have stolen it?'

'I suppose it's possible, sir.'

'If that was the case, and it was stolen for the express purpose of topping Fenella, the next question is: who had a motive? Of that number, it appears that John Yardley had known her for longer than any of the others so he may be able to shed some light. Tim, you went to have another word with him about the meeting. Did he have anything to add?'

'I asked him if he'd noticed the knife, of course. He seemed genuinely shocked at the notion that Ellerman might have used it to kill Fenella, but he certainly didn't remember seeing it and didn't add anything to what we already knew or have since learned. He was in a hurry to get rid of me though as he was "taking a lady out to lunch".'

'I think you'd better see him again when he's got more time to spare,' said Leach. 'Right, now let's hear Vicky's report.' He listened intently as she recounted her conversation with Fenella's daughter. 'OK,' he said when she had finished, 'from what Nancy said it seems unlikely that Ellerman was one of her mother's lovers so that wouldn't seem a motive for killing her, but there

remains the job rivalry. All the evidence so far still points to him
as our prime suspect. Our top priority is to get our hands on the
clothing he was wearing last Friday.' Leach picked up his phone
and gave a series of instructions. 'Now, Sukey, tell us what
Jennifer Freeman had to say.'

'She more or less confirmed what everyone else has been
saying about the meeting in Ellerman's flat, sir. One little
unexpected scrap of information emerged; she's working on a
makeover for one of the public rooms at Holmwood Care
Home. She's an interior designer, very glamorous and wears
exotic clothes. I have a feeling she's having – or is maybe
about to embark on – an affair with Brian Seaton. She looked
a bit put out, to say the least, to hear that Fenella not only
used to be a visitor there but had probably been having an
affair with him.'

'Well, at least she doesn't have to worry about competition
for his affections,' commented Leach with a wry smile, and there
were grins all round at this touch of gallows humour.

'The things you learn when you turn over stones,' Rathbone
remarked.

'Yes indeed,' said Leach. 'I've left you till last, Greg. I
believe you've been digging into Ellerman's past. What have
you turned up?'

'A certain amount, sir, but I suspect I've only found the tip of
the iceberg. For a start, he claims to have been a widower for
about six years; I've done all the obvious searches but so far as
I can ascertain he's never been married. He told us he lived with
his wife in North Bristol and I tracked him down to a house in
a rather exclusive area close to the Downs where he lived for
several years with a young woman the neighbours took to be his
wife. I spoke to a nice old lady called Mrs Thornton, who lives
next door. She and her husband were already living there when
a couple she referred to as Doctor and Mrs Ellerman moved in
some time after the previous owner left. Mrs Thornton seems a
kindly soul –' Rathbone referred to some notes – 'she said, "I
used to feel rather sorry for Mrs Ellerman as I thought her husband
left her alone quite a lot and now and again I used to invite her
round for coffee and a chat. I supposed he was visiting patients,
which is understandable, and she certainly never complained

about him – on the contrary, she was obviously very much in love with him and I took them for newly-weds. She was what you might call a bit reserved and she never returned my invitations."'

'Just a minute,' Leach interrupted. 'Are you saying that at this time Ellerman was posing as a medical doctor?'

'There's no reason to think he was, sir. Mrs Thornton said she simply assumed that to be the case. She was very surprised when I pointed out her mistake; she admitted that she knew very little about either of them. Incidentally, she never mentioned the Tremaine murder or even asked why we were interested in the Ellermans. She kept on about how she wasn't a nosy parker. "If folks want to tell me anything, that's up to them," she told me. She did, however, go on to say something I think needs further investigation.'

'All right, let's have it,' said Leach impatiently as Rathbone searched for another place in his notes.

'From now on, sir, it's only conjecture on Mrs Thornton's part. Some time after they moved in she noticed that her neighbour had what she called "that sort of look about her" and mentioned to her husband that she thought she might be "expecting". A little while later she was pretty sure, so, in the hope that she might volunteer the information, she issued an invitation for coffee which was politely declined. Reading between the lines – Mrs Thornton is a bit old-fashioned and I had the impression that she found talking about pregnancy with a man rather embarrassing – I think she put the refusal down to morning sickness and said she "quite understood". Anyway, from then on she saw less and less of her presumably pregnant neighbour and when they did happen to meet she thought she looked "rather peaky" and feared things weren't going too well. At this point the Thorntons went on a longish holiday and when they returned the Ellermans had moved out and the house was up for sale. She asked a few of the neighbours where they'd gone but nobody knew anything; all they could say was that they'd seen a removal van with Ellerman directing the men, but there'd been no sign of his wife and in fact she hadn't been seen for some time before that.'

A thought struck Sukey and she raised a hand. 'If they weren't married but just living together, sir, maybe the baby – if there was one – was a problem. I was thinking of Fenella,' she went on in response to Leach's raised eyebrow. 'Her father abandoned her mother when she became pregnant; she blamed the child for ruining her marriage and never forgave her.'

'So what are you saying?'

'Maybe Ellerman told his partner to get rid of the baby. From what I've seen of him I'd say he wouldn't be overjoyed at the prospect of fatherhood. Maybe he insisted on an abortion and she died. He'd have had no compunction in calling himself a widower.'

'How long ago was this?' asked Leach.

'About six years ago according to Mrs Thornton,' said Rathbone.

'He told us he'd been a widower for six years, sir,' said Penny, 'so presumably that's when he moved to Sycamore Park.'

'But why move?' asked Tim. 'He could have told his neighbours his wife had died, shown some decent signs of grief and accepted their sympathy, and quietly got on with life.'

'The flats in Sycamore Park are modest compared to the place he'd just moved out of,' said Rathbone. 'We don't know what he was earning at Maxworth's at the time, but it would have to be a pretty hefty amount to live there. It's an expensive neighbourhood.'

'Get details of his salary from Maxworth,' said Leach, 'and check with a local estate agent about average outgoings for a comparable property. If there's an obvious discrepancy it may have been her money they were living on.'

'Something else has just occurred to me, sir,' said Vicky. 'From what Nancy said about her mother she led quite a colourful life and for all we know she may have had an unwanted pregnancy herself at some time. Supposing Ellerman's partner did have an abortion and Fenella somehow happened to meet her – maybe they were in the same clinic at the same time – and Fenella threatened to expose him. A bit of scandal like that wouldn't do much for his chances of the plum job at Maxworth's that he's hoping to land.'

'But all this happened six years ago,' Rathbone pointed out.

'True, and the job rivalry didn't exist at the time, but when it did, maybe she dropped a hint that she could make trouble for him unless he left the way clear for her.'

Leach was silent for some moments, thoughtfully tapping the file on his desk with the end of his ballpoint pen. 'It's worth looking into,' he said at last. 'Good thinking, Sukey. Maybe that's the motive we've been looking for. Greg, get your team to revisit those of the residents at Sycamore Park who seemed to have been on fairly friendly terms with Fenella. We know she did shopping for at least one housebound lady; she might have been invited in for a chat and let something drop.' He put down his pen and exhaled slowly. 'It's a long shot, but it's worth a try. And call Ellerman in again and question him about the woman he was living with. We know she wasn't his wife but he appears to have cared for her enough to keep souvenirs from trips they made together. If she really is dead we need to know everything about her: her real name, her background, when and where she died, cause of death and anything else that strikes you as relevant.'

'Will do, sir,' said Rathbone.

'I suspect Mrs Thornton might have a bit more to tell us and she'd probably be more at ease talking to a woman. Give her details to Sukey, but certainly keep on digging in other directions.'

Before leaving, Sukey checked her phone and found one missed call. It was from Harry. 'Can't wait to see you this evening. Have picked up a juicy titbit.' She sent a text to acknowledge the call and drove home full of anticipation. She had barely pulled up outside her flat when he appeared. He took her bag from her, together with her shopping, and followed her upstairs.

'What's this juicy titbit you've got for me?' she asked as she slipped off her jacket.

'First things first.' He held her close; for a while she responded willingly, but after a few moments curiosity overcame desire and she pulled away from him.

'Tell me!' she demanded.

'All right, if you insist. I had some spare time this afternoon after doing a report on a planning application not far from Holmwood, so as promised I popped in to see Major Howes. In the event we only had about ten minutes together – some egghead from the local history society was coming to give the residents a talk about the Clifton Suspension Bridge. He asked me if I'd like to go along and listen!'

'It sounds riveting. Did you go?'

'What do you think?

'So what's this titbit the galloping major managed to pass on in the short time he could spare for you?'

'He's suspected for a while that Brian Seaton has a roving eye and he's been keeping an eye on him for the past week or two. One day he came into the residents' lounge in company with a woman whom the major described as "quite an eyeful". He didn't mention her name – or if he did the major couldn't recall it – but he told them that she was an interior designer who was going to give the lounge a complete makeover, by which they understood he meant new curtains, carpets, upholstery and so on. There's a gleam in your eye that tells me you're more interested in the eyeful than in me at the moment,' Harry added with feigned jealousy.

'Too right I am,' Sukey assured him, 'but hang on to "at the moment",' she added, giving him a quick hug and brushing her cheek against his. 'So what else did the major observe?'

'He said with a wink like a dig in the ribs that while the lady was talking colour schemes and waving samples under his nose, Seaton spent more time looking at her cleavage than the samples.'

Sukey punched the air in triumph. 'I'll bet it was Jennifer Freeman of Décor for You!' she exclaimed. 'She lives in Sycamore Park and I had to interview her this morning as part of the enquiry into the Fenella Tremaine murder.' Without giving away sensitive information, Sukey told Harry of her own suspicions about Jennifer's relationship with Seaton.

'Shall I go and see the major again, when he's got more time for a chat?' said Harry.

'Yes, please do. It's hard to see what bearing Seaton's philandering has on our enquiries, and the fact that two of his women live in the same block of flats may be no more than a coincidence, but I keep asking myself whether there's anything in Penny Osborne's theory.'

'You mean that Carla Seaton might have killed Fenella out of jealous rage? But how could she possibly have got hold of the knife if it was in Ellerman's flat?'

'I know it sounds impossible, but I've come across more bizarre connections in the past.'

Harry nodded. 'Come to think of it, so have I. I take it we're not going to talk shop all evening,' he added, pulling her towards him. This time she did not resist.

# THIRTEEN

'I'm really sorry to have to trouble you again, Mrs Thornton.' A pair of surprisingly bright blue eyes set in a wrinkled face smiled up at Sukey through pink-framed spectacles. 'It's no trouble, my dear. Do come in. I was just going to make a cup of coffee; would you like one?'

'Thank you, that's very kind of you.'

'Come this way.' Mrs Thornton showed Sukey into a sunny sitting room overlooking a typically English garden. A white-haired gentleman put down his newspaper and stood up to greet her. 'My husband, Albert . . . Detective Constable Reynolds,' said his wife. 'I'll go and fetch the coffee.' She bustled out of the room.

'What a lovely garden!' Sukey exclaimed as she sat down in the chair Albert Thornton indicated. 'And what beautiful roses!'

The old gentleman beamed. 'They're my pride and joy! Do you like flowers?'

'Oh yes! I don't have a garden – just a few pots on my patio, but roses are my favourites.'

'Mine too. Ah, here's Edie with our coffee,' he added as she entered with a tray, served coffee and biscuits and eventually sat down herself.

'I felt rather guilty not offering coffee to that nice sergeant who came before,' she said shyly, 'but Albert was out playing golf and it didn't seem quite proper . . . the window cleaner was here and he's a real old gossip . . . I didn't want people to think—' She gave a self-conscious giggle as if entertaining a strange man in her husband's absence might arouse comment.

Albert Thornton winked at Sukey over the rim of his coffee cup. 'She reckons she can still turn heads,' he said fondly. Sukey smiled politely and looked forward to passing this gem on to DS Rathbone.

'Now, my dear,' said Edie Thornton, 'you said you'd like to ask me a few more questions about the Ellermans.'

'That's right. Sergeant Rathbone said he thought perhaps you'd be more comfortable talking to a woman.'

'How very thoughtful of him. It's good that Albert's here as well, though. He thinks you might be interested in Mrs Ellerman's car.'

'I'm interested in any information you can give me about either of them,' said Sukey. 'I don't think Sergeant Rathbone said anything about her car.'

'I don't think I mentioned it,' Edie admitted. 'I suppose I noticed that she had one but even if I had told him, I wouldn't have been able to give him any details. I don't know anything about cars, as Albert will tell you.'

'I doubt if she could tell you what car we have, even though we've had the same model for the past ten years,' he agreed with a chuckle.

'So what can you tell me about Mrs Ellerman's car, sir?'

'It was a silver grey Golf and I remember the last three letters on the registration plate were SAD. It struck me from what Edie said about her towards the end of their time here that it seemed somehow appropriate. I'm afraid I can't remember the numbers, but I have a feeling it was fairly new. I've written it all down for you.' He handed Sukey an envelope. 'It's in here.'

'That's a great help; thank you so much!' She put the envelope in her handbag. 'Now, Mrs Thornton, I believe you told DS Rathbone that around the time you thought Mrs Ellerman was expecting a baby she started turning down your invitations to coffee. You said she wasn't looking very well and you thought she might be suffering from morning sickness.'

'Well, I didn't exactly say that,' Mrs Thornton said hurriedly.

'But that's what you thought?'

'Well, yes.'

'You could have been right. And around that time you and your husband went on a long holiday and came back to find the Ellermans gone and the house up for sale. When exactly was that?'

'I'm afraid I couldn't remember the details after all this time.' Mrs Thornton cast a helpless look at her husband. 'Perhaps Albert will know.'

'That's easy.' Her husband went to a bureau and took out a folder. 'It's all in here.' He began flicking through the contents. 'It was a special trip to celebrate our ruby wedding and my retirement; we flew to New Zealand to visit our daughter and her family and we stayed with them for just over two weeks. Then we joined a cruise ship and came back by sea.'

'Oh, it was such a lovely trip, wasn't it Albert?' His wife had been listening with a dreamy smile on her face.

'I'm sure it was.' Sukey was beginning to think Rathbone must have found Mrs Thornton a somewhat frustrating witness. 'But it would help us if we knew exactly when and for how long you were away,' she added.

'A little over six weeks,' said her husband. 'We left here on the fifteenth of March and arrived back home on the thirtieth of April.'

'So it was some time between those dates that the Ellermans moved out,' said Sukey. 'We know that it was around that time that he moved into his present address on his own.'

'On his own? Oh dear!' Edie Thornton's face crumpled in dismay. 'Do you suppose something went wrong with the baby and she died and he just couldn't bear to live here any more?'

'We don't know yet what happened or why he moved,' said Sukey, 'but we mean to find out. Did you happen to ask any of your neighbours if they could tell you the exact date?'

Albert Thornton shook his head. 'I certainly didn't – chatting with neighbours is more in Edie's line.' He turned to his wife. 'You did ask the lady at The Laurels, didn't you?'

Edie nodded. 'You mean Mrs Parr, the music teacher? Yes, I did mention it to her but she couldn't remember exactly. We all thought it was odd, them disappearing like that without a word to anyone, but they'd never been what you'd call neighbourly so—'

'I understand,' interrupted Sukey. 'I get the impression that the Ellermans were younger than most of the people living round here. Is that right?'

'Yes, I suppose so,' said Albert Thornton.

'He was a few years older than her, though,' said Edie.

Sukey put away her notebook and stood up. 'Well thank you very much for the coffee, and for being so helpful. By the way, do any of them still live here besides you . . . I mean the people who were here at the same time as the Ellermans?'

'Oh yes, most of them in fact,' said Albert. He, too, stood up and moved as if to escort Sukey to the door, then stopped and took a pair of secateurs out of his pocket. 'Just a moment,' he said. He opened the garden door, stepped outside and snipped a bud from the nearest rose bush. 'For the lady who loves roses,' he said with a courtly little bow as he tucked it into Sukey's buttonhole.

Back in her car, Sukey called Rathbone. He was out so she left a message giving the details of the car that according to Albert Thornton had been driven by the woman living with Ellerman. 'I managed to get a few other bits of useful information from the Thorntons – mainly from Mister T,' she added. 'I think it's worth speaking to one or two of the other neighbours and that's what I'll be doing if you want to contact me.'

Sukey called first at The Laurels, one of half a dozen similar properties that formed a loop off a road skirting The Downs. She arrived just as a young woman was collecting a little girl carrying a violin case so she waited until the mother had installed the child in her car and driven away before ringing the doorbell, showing her ID and explaining the purpose of her visit.

Mrs Parr invited her into the entrance hall and closed the front door. 'I'm afraid I can't be of much help,' she said. 'We all knew the Ellermans by sight, of course, although Edie Thornton was the only one who had much to do with them. She's a very friendly soul; she called round soon after they moved in to welcome them and offer helpful information about the neighbourhood and so on, but I gather she got the impression that Doctor Ellerman politely told her they had all they needed thank you very much. They pretty well kept themselves to themselves and I suppose we all assumed it was because they were newly-weds and were quite happy to be on their own. And of course they were quite a bit younger than most of us.'

'About how long were they living there?'

'I don't recall exactly. There was an old man – a Mr Armitage, a widower – who'd lived there for years. When his wife died he went to live in a home and the house stood empty for a while.'

'Presumably it went up for sale?'

Mrs Parr thought for a moment. 'No, I don't believe it did – or at least, there was never a For Sale board outside.'

'Perhaps it was sold before the agent got around to putting one up,' Sukey suggested. 'Going back to the Ellermans, would you say they were happy as a couple?'

Mrs Parr shrugged. 'Who can say? He used to be out during the day but now and again I saw them going out together and they seemed all right. I'm out myself quite a lot – I teach music at several schools, so I don't . . .' She spread her slim, tapering fingers in a slightly theatrical gesture that seemed to say 'I have my own life to lead; what other people do is no concern of mine.'

'I know this is going back about six years, but can you remember anything about the time they moved out of the house called The Laburnums?'

'I can't tell you the exact date, but I believe the removal company was Bryant and Wheeler.'

'Thank you; that could be a great help,' said Sukey. 'I don't suppose you remember the name of the estate agent who handled the sale?'

'I do as it happens; it was Melton and Keen. They handle quite a lot of properties round here; in fact we bought this house through them.' Mrs Parr gave Sukey a searching look. 'You told me this is in connection with a murder enquiry. Would that be the woman who was found stabbed in Sycamore Park? It said in the *Echo* that a man has been questioned and released on bail – would that be Doctor Ellerman by any chance?'

'I'm sorry, I can't tell you anything that hasn't been officially released,' said Sukey. She turned to leave. 'Thank you very much for your help.'

Mrs Parr was about to close the door behind her when she reopened it and called her back. 'Just a moment,' she said, 'I've thought of something else you might be interested in. I seem to remember seeing Mrs Ellerman there with another man some time before she and her husband moved in.'

'Someone from the estate agent?' Sukey suggested.

'I don't think so; they came together in his car and they seemed to know each other.'

'Can you describe him or the car?'

Mrs Parr shook her head. 'It was over eight years ago,' she pointed out. 'I had the impression he was quite a bit older than her and he drove an expensive-looking car.'

'Do you remember the colour?'

'I have a feeling it was dark red, but I can't be sure.'

'I see. Well, thank you once again for your help,' said Sukey warmly. She made a few notes before heading for the next house.

'This is intolerable, Sergeant!' Jason Pollard glared across the table at DS Rathbone. 'Isn't it enough that my client has been placed on police bail on the flimsiest of circumstantial evidence without this intrusion into his private grief? Can't you see how distressing this is for him?' He indicated Ellerman, who sat with his hands in his lap and his head slightly bowed.

Penny Osborne, seated beside Rathbone, was struck by the change in his demeanour since the first time she saw him. Then, he had been self-assured to the point of arrogance, even casting flirtatious glances in her direction; later, when caught out in lies and unable to give a convincing account of his movements at the time of Fenella Tremaine's murder, he had become less and less sure of himself.

'Murder is a distressing business,' said Rathbone drily. 'Now, we know that one woman is dead and that your client was closely associated with her. We also know that six years ago he was living in a house in North Bristol called The Laburnums with a woman some years younger than himself. At about this time the woman – whom the neighbours naturally assumed to be his wife – appeared to be pregnant, but looked to a concerned neighbour to be unwell, declined invitations similar to those she had accepted in the past, and in fact was not seen again. Subsequently your client put The Laburnums on the market and moved to his present address in Sycamore Park.'

'My client has already told you that his wife died about six years ago,' said Pollard. 'What possible relevance can her death have to your enquiries?'

'The fact is that your client is lying,' said Rathbone. 'He claims to be a widower, but is unable to produce either a marriage or a death certificate to support the claim and has refused to give us any information about the woman with whom he was living. Moreover, we have not so far found anyone who has seen or heard from her since your client left The Laburnums.' He turned to Ellerman. 'We shall of course find all this out for ourselves, but it would save us a lot of time and trouble if you would tell us the truth.'

Ellerman raised his head and looked directly at Rathbone. 'All right, I admit Julie and I weren't married,' he said, 'but when she died it felt like being widowed. That's all I can say.'

Before Rathbone had a chance to put a further question, Pollard laid a hand on his client's arm. 'Sergeant,' he said sternly, 'are you seriously implying that in addition to suspecting my client of murdering Fenella Tremaine – for which you have failed to establish the slightest vestige of a motive – he also caused the death of the woman he loved?'

Rathbone ignored the interruption. He showed no sign of being moved by what seemed to Penny to be genuine emotion. 'What did Julie die of?' he asked.

'She had a miscarriage.'

'What was her full name and when and where did she die?'

Ellerman made a dismissive gesture. 'That's all I'm saying. Other people will be hurt if this gets out.'

'If there's anything suspicious about Julie's death it most certainly will get out.' Rathbone's tone was harsh and his manner without pity. 'All right, that's all for now.'

At the end of the afternoon the team foregathered as usual in DCI Leach's office for the daily debriefing. When he had heard all their reports he gave a sigh of resignation. 'We've obviously got a lot more work to do. It's a pity Thornton couldn't recall the complete registration number of Julie's car, but at least he's given us something to go on. In any case, if she is dead it will have been sold on, probably through a local dealer. We'll need to trace the man who took her to the house shortly after Mr Armitage moved out. Maybe they were all related and he let the house to her. Greg –' he turned to DS Rathbone – 'did you get any joy from Maxworth's about Ellerman's salary at the relevant time?'

'Not yet, sir, but they're working on it,' said Rathbone with a hint of resignation. 'It was about the time Anton Maxworth was trying to persuade his uncle to computerize the accounts department and things were a bit chaotic.'

'Stone walls at every turn,' said Leach, 'but with just a few chinks to give us hope.' He glanced at the calendar on his desk. 'Friday tomorrow – exactly a week since the night Fenella died. It would be good if we had a breakthrough by the weekend. Keep at it, troops!'

Soon after Sukey reached home there was a call from Harry. 'There's a bit of late news that I think will interest you,' he said. 'Is it OK if I pop round?'

'Of course. Love to see you.' She slipped off her jacket, gently took the white rosebud from the buttonhole and went to find a vase. She had just set it on a low table by the sitting room window when he arrived. 'Look what a handsome gentleman witness gave me as a token of his esteem!' she said teasingly.

'Very nice,' he said. 'Don't you want to hear this hot bit of news?'

'Of course I do, but you might at least pretend to be jealous.'

'Never mind the small talk; this is serious.' He showed her a mock-up of the next day's early edition of the *Echo* and pointed to an item under the headline: 'Car Leaves Road and Hits Wall – Woman Driver Killed.'

Sukey read the report with growing consternation. 'It names the victim as Jennifer Freeman,' she said, 'and the scene of the accident is only a mile or so from Holmwood. There's nothing here to say what time it happened. I know she was going there after I interviewed her yesterday morning; was it on her way there or on her way back?'

'Does it make a difference?'

'It might.'

# FOURTEEN

There was no breakthrough before the weekend. Meanwhile, uniformed police officers continued their search for the sheath that had contained Marcus Ellerman's knife and Rathbone's team continued to hunt for any possible link between him and Fenella Tremaine that might suggest a motive for murder. Regret was expressed by members of the team at the death of Jennifer Freeman, but it was generally accepted that enquiries into the cause of the accident were a matter for the traffic division and of no concern to the CID. Only Sukey had her reservations, which for the time being she shared with no one in the team but Vicky when, together with the rest of the team, they returned to the CID office late on Monday.

'I keep telling myself it isn't feasible,' she admitted, 'but I can't get rid of the feeling that somewhere there's a link. From some of today's headlines, the red tops would certainly like to think so,' she added.

'Link between what?' asked Vicky.

'Remember Penny's suggestion that Carla Seaton might have killed Fenella because of her affair with her husband?'

'And was shot down in flames by the Sarge?' Vicky grinned.

'Yes, well, having met Carla I think we're both prepared to believe she's capable of murder, but it's hard to see how she could have got her hands on Marcus Ellerman's knife, let alone have known when and where she'd have a chance to use it. As for Jennifer Freeman's accident, I know she was going to Holmwood on Wednesday morning after I interviewed her; if it happened on the way there, it's hard to see how Carla could have caused it, but if it was on the way back . . .'

'Well, the boys in traffic division will soon find out if there was anything suspicious about it,' said Vicky. 'It sounds pretty far-fetched to me, but knowing what you're like, you won't let it rest until you find the answer. My money's still on Ellerman as Fenella's killer and Jennifer's accident having nothing to do with the case. Ah, here's the Sarge; I think we're being summoned to the presence.'

'It comes as no surprise,' said DCI Leach when they were all assembled in his office, 'that certain sections of the media are hinting at some kind of ghoulish connection between Jennifer Freeman, Fenella Tremaine and the man we've been interviewing in the latter's murder. "Serial Killer at Large?" is a typical head-line. Needless to say, we've done our best to discourage that sort of speculation; this morning's press release warned against causing panic among women living alone and stressing that we're following a number of leads . . . hundreds of officers working on the case . . . appeals for anyone with information to come forward . . . the usual stuff. It seems from your verbal reports that we've made some progress. Greg, you go first.'

'I checked first of all with the management company at Sycamore Park, sir,' Rathbone began. 'I'd assumed that Ellerman moved into the flat where he's now living when he left The Laburnums, but it turned out that he actually bought the lease on the flat about twelve years ago and lived there for a while – maybe three or four years; I haven't been able to establish the exact dates – and then moved out. Presumably that was when he moved into The Laburnums with Julie, but it turns out he didn't sell the flat, he rented it to a couple who lived there until he went back after her death. Incidentally, he joined Maxworth's at about the time he first moved in.'

'Have you spoken to anyone in Sycamore Park who remembers that far back?' asked Leach.

'Unfortunately not, sir. Only a handful of the people living there now have been there longer than five years.'

'Hm.' Leach tapped his front teeth with his ballpoint pen. 'There's one aspect of Ellerman's character that's been puzzling me over the weekend. He came across at first as arrogant and full of self-assurance, and most of the people we've interviewed have said the same. He also likes to make out he's a bit of a ladykiller, but no one has mentioned seeing him out with a woman, or seen women calling on him. Julie obviously fell for him in a big way – enough to move in with him and get pregnant. Sukey, I believe you've managed to find out a bit more about her.'

'Yes, sir, I went to see old Mr Armitage, the previous owner of The Laburnums. The neighbours thought he'd gone into residential care, but it turns out he's living in sheltered accommodation and still has a degree of independence. It was rather an emotional interview because Julie was his granddaughter and his only living relative. He absolutely doted on her and was heartbroken when she died.'

'So she is dead?'

'Oh yes, sir, but it wasn't from a miscarriage. Julie went to him in great distress one day and told him she was pregnant. She'd expected Ellerman to be delighted, but instead he told her to have an abortion because he didn't want to be bothered with a child. He said in effect it was either that or it was all over between them. The old man was shocked, of course, and tried to persuade her to have the baby and he'd look after them both, but she was completely besotted with Ellerman and said she would go along with whatever he wanted. So she had the abortion, but soon after picked up an infection from it. Unfortunately, she attributed the heavy bleeding and pains to the abortion itself and didn't seek medical attention. A couple of days later she went into toxic shock syndrome, and by the time she got to the hospital it was too late to save her, even with antibiotics. Unsurprisingly, Mr Armitage blames Ellerman for the delay in getting Julie treatment.' Sukey checked her notebook. 'Mr Armitage said, "I couldn't believe what a heartless swine he turned out to be, but he fooled me completely. He came across as a decent sort with a steady job who really cared for Julie."'

'How did Julie and Ellerman come to be living in The Laburnums?'

'Apparently Ellerman said his flat was too small for the two of them and as Julie's grandfather was moving out anyway after the death of his wife he let them live there while they looked for another place, although they don't seem to have spent much time looking. They went on a few foreign trips, which confirms what Ellerman told us. Naturally after Julie died the old gentleman booted Ellerman out and he just gave his tenants notice and went back to his own place. The poor gentleman broke down several times while he was telling me all this and I felt really guilty at upsetting him.'

'You obviously handled it very well to get him to confide in you so much,' said Leach. 'Good work, Sukey. So that's another lie Ellerman has told us.'

'May I say something else, sir?'

'Go ahead.'

'I didn't make any reference to Fenella Tremaine's murder and neither did Mr Armitage, but when I got up to go he said, "Good luck with your enquiries; I hope the swine gets what's coming to him."'

'You think he guessed what prompted your visit?'

'I'm sure of it, sir. It so happens he'd been reading one of the tabloids when I got there.'

'I don't imagine he's the only one. The only reason Ellerman's name hasn't been mentioned in any of the media reports is that one or two editors are still counting the cost of a previous indiscretion. Vicky. Let's hear from you. Was Nancy able to add anything?'

'Not really, sir. If Fenella did have an abortion at any time it would have been some years ago as she was past normal child-bearing age when she was killed. Nancy has no recollection of her mother having her appendix out, which is probably how it would have been explained to a child, but of course it might have happened while Nancy was away at school.'

'In which case it was probably long before Fenella met Ellerman,' said Leach. 'I don't think we need pursue that line any further. Penny?'

'I checked with Sergeant Drury, sir; he's in charge of uniformed at Sycamore Park and he said they've been calling on the residents and enquiring about who was wearing what on the night of the murder. Obviously they're looking for a man, preferably one who corresponds roughly to the description given by Ms Springfield. So far they haven't encountered any opposition; most people claimed they couldn't remember; one or two gentlemen handed over what they thought they might have been wearing and that's been sent to forensics.'

'It'll be a while before we get any results back,' said Leach, 'and to be frank I'm none too optimistic, but we have to keep trying.' At that moment his telephone rang. 'Leach . . . that's great news . . . well done!' He put down the phone. 'That was

Sergeant Drury. Someone has handed in what he's ninety per cent sure is the sheath belonging to Ellerman's knife.'

Five minutes after Sukey arrived home that evening Harry rang her doorbell.

'It's lovely to see you,' she said as she let him in. 'How was your weekend?' Harry had taken his father on a visit to one of his cousins in Lancashire.

'All right. We watched some good cricket but there's something else I'd much rather have been doing.' He set about proving the truth of this statement and she was in no hurry to discourage him. Eventually, when he allowed her to draw breath, she said softly, 'You smell lovely and fresh – have you just showered?'

'As it happens, I have. I needed it after the journey.'

'I think I'll do the same. I won't be long.'

'You do that and then I'll tell you what I've planned for this evening.' His kiss left her in no doubt what plans he had in mind.

Later, as they drank a glass of wine over the remains of a casserole she had prepared over the weekend, he said, 'Have there been any developments in the Tremaine murder?'

'As it happens, there have. It'll be officially announced at tomorrow's press briefing.'

'You mean I have to wait till then?'

'If I tell you, will you promise not to rush home and call your editor?'

He reached across the table and took her hand. 'I promise. I'll make it worth your while,' he added in a throbbing, mock seductive tone.

'How could I refuse such an offer?' she replied, affecting a sexy whisper. Then she went on in her normal voice, 'Oh all right, I trust you. We had a message just before leaving work this evening that a metal sheath that almost certainly belongs to the knife that killed Fenella Tremaine has been handed in by a member of the public, who found it using a metal detector. It was lying under a hedge at the edge of a field a couple of miles away and there's no doubt it's the one because the design matches the carving on the handle.'

'That's brilliant!' said Harry. 'Any chance of getting the name of the guy who found it?'

'I've no idea who it was. It might be revealed at the briefing but whoever it is may prefer not to be identified.'

'True,' he admitted. 'I guess if there are no prints on it other than his and Ellerman's it will pretty well wrap up the case. All right,' he added hastily as she drew a sharp breath, 'I know we have to pretend we don't know the name of your chief suspect.'

'As long as you don't publish it,' she warned him. 'Anyway, forensics will go over the sheath with a toothcomb in the hope of finding prints or other evidence on it, but of course it'll take time. We have to be thankful it hasn't rained since the murder.'

'Plus it's lucky it was made of metal,' Harry commented. 'A lot of those knives come in leather sheaths.'

'We need all the luck we can get,' said Sukey. 'It could have been lying there undetected for ages – and if it had been found, leather isn't the easiest of materials to lift prints from. Just the same,' she added disconsolately, 'even if the only prints we find on it are Ellerman's it won't prove conclusively that he killed Fenella. He'll simply stick to his story that someone stole the knife and wore gloves while using it. Of course, none of the people known to have visited his flat recently is likely to have worn gloves without anyone noticing. Although,' she added after a moment's thought, 'come to think of it he accused Wilkins of stealing it while he was there to do some maintenance job for which he might conceivably have been wearing gloves.' She reached for her notebook. 'I'll mention it to DS Rathbone tomorrow; he might think it's worth checking.'

'It says in our evening edition that a post-mortem on Jennifer Freeman is being held tomorrow,' said Harry. 'You seemed to think the time the accident happened might be important, but why?'

'I'd just like to know if it was before or after her visit to Holmwood, that's all. I think I'll have a word with the traffic department. No,' she said quickly seeing that he was about to repeat the question, 'even if it was when I think it was, I'm not saying anything at the moment. And in any case, if the PM doesn't reveal anything suspicious I suppose I'll just have to forget the whole thing.'

'Well, you can't stop me trying to figure it out for myself. Maybe I'll pay Major Howes another visit.'

'That's up to you.'

On Tuesday afternoon, Patsy Godwin laid aside the *Echo* and Henry immediately jumped on her vacant lap. 'Guess what, they've found the sheath belonging to the knife that killed the woman who lives near Cousin Kate,' she informed the cat as she stroked his glossy fur. 'And there's a bit more about that accident; you know, the one I told you about when another of her neighbours was killed. She was so upset; she rang me up in such distress when she heard about it. She kept on about how awful it was that two single women had suffered such violent deaths and I think she's terrified she might be a third. I wonder if I should go and stay with her for a few days. Yes, I knew you wouldn't like the idea,' she said as the purring ceased abruptly, 'and she does have that nice Mr Yardley to keep an eye on her. Perhaps I'd better not go just yet; I might be in the way! What do you think, Henry?' She gave him an encouraging tickle behind one ear, but it was several minutes before the purring began again.

# FIFTEEN

When Sukey arrived home on Wednesday evening she found a message from Harry. 'If you haven't already spotted the report, you'll be interested to know it concerns the post-mortem on Jennifer Freeman. Call me for details.'

Sukey hastily searched through the pages of the evening edition of the *Echo*. The report, when she found it, merely stated that although the driver had recently consumed a small amount of alcohol, the level in her blood was minimal and there was no evidence of a medical condition that might have caused her to lose control of her vehicle.

She rang Harry immediately. 'I've just got home and picked up your call. The report doesn't say anything significant so what details have you learned?'

'What you've read is all that's been released to the press in advance of the inquest, but it so happens one of the morgue attendants is an old school friend of mine and—'

'And you're going to tell me there's something fishy about the accident?' Sukey interrupted eagerly.

'Not exactly fishy, but Sam did get the impression from a comment the pathologist made to the copper who was there to witness the proceedings that he'd found something he described as slightly unusual and worth mentioning in his report. He didn't catch what the something was, but thinks it will almost certainly come up at the inquest. It's tomorrow, by the way.'

'That early? She's only been dead a week.'

'Which rather suggests the pathologist has had a word in the coroner's ear, don't you think?'

'It certainly looks that way.'

'Is there any chance you can be there?'

'If only!' Sukey sighed. 'There's no way I'd be allowed to take time off from the Tremaine case to attend an inquest on a victim of a road traffic accident just because she happened to be one of Fenella's neighbours. Harry, is there any chance you could be there?'

'I didn't think you'd be able to make it, which is why I asked my editor if I could cover it. He said no at first; said it was a routine job for a cub reporter and he had more important things for me to do. But I hinted that there might possibly be a link with something bigger which could mean a scoop for the *Echo* and in the end he agreed.'

'That's great, Harry. Thanks so much.'

'Any news your end? Have forensics found anything useful on the sheath?'

'Give them a chance. They've only had it for a couple of days. But I did manage to get a word with the traffic division and they didn't find any mechanical defect in Jennifer's car to account for the accident. No other vehicle involved and no witnesses – they think she must have lost concentration and tried to take the bend too fast. They'd had a call from someone who said she'd been at a business meeting and appeared perfectly all right when she left. Indications are he didn't want his name released to the press.'

'Well, that should put paid to all the rumours about a serial

killer,' said Harry. 'Presumably all will be revealed at the inquest
. . . and maybe your hunch will be laid to rest.'

'We shall see.'

'Anyway, I'll come round tomorrow evening and tell you
about it. Shall I bring food?'

'No, that's all right. It's my turn to do the cooking.'

'See you then. Good night. Sleep well. Love you.'

'Love you too.'

As Sukey put the phone down her pulses were tingling with
excitement, but this time it was almost as much in anticipation
of what Harry would have to tell her as the sheer pleasure of
seeing him. 'I'll bet it was Brian Seaton who made that call,'
she said aloud as she prepared her supper. 'There is a link, I just
know there is.'

As soon as the team reported for duty the following morning
they were summoned to DCI Leach's office. 'Chief Superintendent
Baird managed to get forensics to fast-track their examination
of the sheath that was handed in on Monday and they've sent
this preliminary report.' He waved the sheet of paper he was
holding. 'There's no doubt it belongs to Ellerman's knife, but as
far as prints go it doesn't tell us a great deal. The guy who found
it recognized it as soon as he picked it up; fortunately he had
the common sense to wrap it in his handkerchief to avoid further
contamination. He was happy to give us his prints for elims,
which was a great help. The only other identifiable prints forensics
could find are Ellerman's, but indications are that the sheath has
been handled by more than one other person. That's hardly
surprising when you consider its history. He claims to have bought
it in a souvenir shop in India where any number of people might
have handled it before Ellerman decided to buy it. They admit
the same applies to the knife itself, of course, although in that
case the way the prints on the handle are smudged suggests the
killer may have worn gloves. What does that suggest to you?
Yes, Sukey?' he said as she raised her hand.

'Isn't it possible, sir, that another person, knowing of Ellerman's
rivalry with Fenella and believing it could be a motive for killing
her, had a motive of his own for wanting her out of the way. He
– or she, it could conceivably have been a woman – stole

Ellerman's knife and used it to kill her with the intention of incriminating him.'

'You're thinking of Wilkins, the caretaker?'

'Not necessarily, sir. For one thing, he doesn't fit the description of the man Kate Springfield claims to have seen on the night of the murder.'

'We can't be certain the man she saw was the killer,' Rathbone pointed out.

'True.' Leach considered for a few moments. 'We haven't seriously considered the possibility that the killer was a woman,' he began slowly, 'but Fenella wasn't very heavy and it's possible that a strong woman could have picked her up. The only woman who so far as we know had access to the knife in Ellerman's flat was Jennifer Freeman, who died in a car crash last week. Sukey, you've met her. Would you say she was up to it?'

Sukey thought for a moment. 'She was quite a bit taller than I am, but I didn't get much idea of her build. When I met her she was wearing a rather exotic, flowing sort of dress with long sleeves. I suppose she could have been quite muscular, but it didn't show.'

'What's the latest about the accident?'

'According to a report in today's *Echo* the PM made it clear that she wasn't over the limit and had no medical condition that could account for a sudden loss of control. Traffic division told me road conditions were good and they found no mechanical defect in the car. The inquest is being held today.'

Leach raised an eyebrow. 'So soon? Any idea what time?'

'No, sir. Would you like me to find out?'

'If you can get there, I think you'd better go.'

The inquest on the death of Jennifer Freeman was held in a building known locally as the village hall, although the surrounding area, once a small village a few miles from the centre, had long since been part of the conurbation that is now the City of Bristol. Sukey slipped into a seat at the back of the hall; across the aisle she saw Harry but deliberately avoided eye contact. An elderly couple and a few other people whom she took to be Jennifer's parents and friends sat close together in the front row; in the rows behind were a few members of the public. Sitting apart from them were the pathologist, Doctor Handley, a uniformed police officer and a woman whom Sukey recognized as a local GP.

An official called for silence and the coroner, a senior partner in a firm of lawyers, took his seat on the platform and after formally opening the proceedings called Sergeant Killick from the traffic division.

'At three p.m. on Wednesday the thirty-first of July,' he began, 'a member of the public made a nine nine nine call to report an accident on the Portishead-to-Clevedon road. All three emergency services attended; apparently the driver had lost control and hit a tree, causing the car to overturn, trapping the woman driver. The fire service had to cut open the driver's door to enable paramedics to reach her. She was suffering from severe head and chest injuries, a doctor was called and pronounced her dead at the scene.'

'I have read your original report, Sergeant,' said the coroner, 'in which you state that road and weather conditions were good, that the deceased person's car was mechanically sound, that no other vehicle was involved and that in your opinion the driver's loss of control was probably due to the fact that she was taking a bend at too high a speed. Have you anything to add to that?'

'Only that the driver who reported the accident did not actually witness it,' said Killick, 'but he did state that the road was practically empty in both directions at the time. We have appealed for further witnesses, but no one has come forward.'

'Is it possible that an animal had strayed on to the road, causing the driver to brake sharply?'

'There were no tyre marks on the road to suggest that was the case. There is no grazing land along that stretch of the road and we have no reports of any escaped or stray animals in the area.'

'Thank you, Sergeant. You may stand down.' The coroner referred to some papers on his desk. 'I do not propose to cause additional distress to Miss Freeman's parents by asking them to give evidence –' at this point Sukey noticed the couple in the front row turn to each other with clasped hands and bowed heads – 'so I will simply inform the court that Miss Freeman was thirty-eight years old, had held a driving licence for twenty years and had an unblemished record. She had owned the car she was driving for a little over eighteen months and the odometer reading when it was recovered by the police was just over six thousand miles. I now call the police pathologist.' Handley stepped forward and formally confirmed his identity. 'I understand you carried out the post-mortem examination on Jennifer Freeman's body,' the coroner began. 'What, in your opinion was the cause of death?'

'The primary cause was loss of blood from severe head and chest injuries caused as the car rolled over,' said Handley. 'Unfortunately, the position of the driver in the wrecked car was such that it was impossible for the paramedics to reach her in time to stem the flow of blood. By the time the fire service had cut the door open it was too late.'

'You have heard that in Sergeant Killick's opinion the probable cause of the accident was that the driver was taking a bend in the road at excessive speed. Did your examination reveal any factor that might have caused a loss of concentration?'

'I found a trace of alcohol in her blood, but in my opinion the level was insufficient to have such an effect unless she had a particular medical condition which made it advisable to avoid alcohol altogether.'

'Did you find anything else in her system that might have affected her competence to drive?'

'I found evidence that she had recently ingested six-hundred milligrams of quinine.' At this statement, Sukey saw the GP in the front row stiffen slightly, as if in surprise. 'The drug is sometimes taken to relieve night cramps, but I would be surprised to hear that such a large dose had been prescribed.'

'Thank you, Doctor Handley. You may stand down. I now call Doctor Mavis Sullivan.' The slim, grey-haired woman whom Sukey had already recognized stood up and confirmed her identity 'I understand that you are the late Jennifer Freeman's doctor. How long has she been your patient?'

'Ever since she and her family moved to the area – about fifteen years.'

'What was her general state of health?'

'She was a very fit young woman who came to the surgery very rarely.'

'When was the last time you saw her?'

'In June last year, when she had an infection for which I prescribed an antibiotic. I have not seen her since.'

'Did you ever advise her to avoid drinking alcohol?'

'No. I never saw any reason to do so.'

'Did she ever complain of night cramps?'

'No, never.'

'Have you at any time prescribed quinine for her?'

'Certainly not. It used to be prescribed, as Doctor Handley stated, to relieve night cramps, but recent advice is that it has not proved effective except in a few cases, and because of possible side effects we are advised not to prescribe it except in cases of malaria – which of course are comparatively rare in this country.'

'What, in your opinion, are typical side effects of quinine?'

'Among other things it has been variously thought to have caused confusion, nervousness and in some cases difficulty in hearing.'

'If Miss Freeman had suffered from night cramps, had heard that they could be relieved by quinine and decided to treat herself without consulting you, could she have bought it over the counter at a pharmacy?'

'The drug is normally available in three-hundred-milligram capsules, for which a prescription is required. I understand that small, single doses in an injectable form may be bought from some pharmacies over the counter, but I have never prescribed them or advised any of my patients to use them.'

'Thank you Doctor Sullivan. You may stand down. Doctor Handley, would you kindly return to the witness stand? I have one further question,' he continued after Handley complied. 'During your examination of Miss Freeman's body, did you observe any sign of injections?'

'No, sir. It is something I look for as a matter of routine in such cases and I found none whatsoever.'

After a few minutes' consultation with an official, the coroner announced that the inquest would be adjourned until a later date. Among the people making their way to the exit, Sukey spotted Jennifer's assistant, Hazel. She appeared to be alone; Sukey wondered what would become of Décor for You after the death of its proprietor.

Harry was waiting for her outside. 'So you managed to get clearance,' he said. 'Is there something I don't know?'

'I merely put forward the suggestion that Fenella's killer might have been a woman, and that Jennifer was the only woman known to have had access to Ellerman's dagger.'

'You don't seriously think Jennifer was the killer?'

'No, of course not.'

'Any theories about the quinine?'

'Maybe. I need time to think.' And despite Harry's most beguiling efforts, Sukey would say nothing further either then or later that evening.


# SIXTEEN


When Sukey reported for duty the following morning she found DS Rathbone in pessimistic mood. 'Another week gone without a breakthrough,' he grumbled. 'I take it no one has anything significant to report?' he added, casting his eye over the team with a visible lack of optimism.

Everyone but Sukey shook their heads. 'I attended the inquest on Jennifer Freeman, Sarge, as instructed by the CIO,' she said.

'I suppose we have to clutch at any straw,' said Rathbone. 'Don't tell me some dramatic revelation supported your suspicion that she might have killed Fenella. That'd be too much to hope for.'

'Not exactly, Sarge, but the inquest was adjourned and I have a feeling the coroner may be asking for further enquiries to be made.'

'For what reason?'

'On account of certain medical evidence, Sarge.'

'Can't you be more specific?'

'I've done my report, Sarge. I've emailed it to you, DCI Leach and the rest of the team.'

Computers were hastily checked. Rathbone scanned the report, picked up the phone and called DCI Leach. 'May Sukey and I see you right away, sir? She sent a report . . . it should be in your in-box . . . good . . . thank you, sir.' He put down the phone.

'He's reading Sukey's report and we're all to go to his office in fifteen minutes.'

'It so happens I had a call from the coroner shortly after speaking to you, Greg,' said Leach when the team assembled in his office. 'He wants us to find out how Jennifer Freeman came to ingest such a large dose of quinine. I think he suspects that some person deliberately introduced it into either food or drink without her being aware of it . . . someone who not only had access to the drug but knew the possible side effects.'

'That would suggest someone with medical knowledge who had a grudge against her, wouldn't it, sir?' said Penny Osborne.

'I suppose you're thinking of the woman who runs the care home, Carla Seaton?' said Leach. 'We suspect that she knew her husband was having an affair with Fenella Tremaine, but it appears not only unlikely but virtually impossible that she had access to Ellerman's knife or even knew of its existence, so we can rule her out as a suspect in that case. If, as Sukey and Vicky suggest, Seaton was either having or intending to have an affair with Jennifer, that's a different matter altogether. It's possible that quinine is prescribed for one of the residents at the care home; Carla Seaton is a qualified nurse and is no doubt in charge of all medication.'

'So she had a motive for causing her death and access to the means of bringing it about, sir,' said Penny eagerly. 'It occurred to me—'

'Let's not get too carried away,' Leach admonished. 'Even if we assume that Carla, as the most likely person to have had access to quinine, was the person who administered it to Jennifer, there's no proof that she intended to cause her death. And besides, although we know Jennifer had arranged to visit Holmwood on the day she had that fatal accident, we don't know how long she stayed or whether she had anything to eat or drink while she was there. Yes, Sukey?' he added as she raised a hand.

'According to traffic division, the accident happened shortly before three o'clock and the direction she was travelling in suggested she was heading from Holmwood back to base, sir.'

'And your point is?'

'It would be the normal time for her to be on that part of the road if she had been invited to lunch there. And there's the anonymous call from a man who said she'd been at a business meeting. I think it's more than likely that Brian Seaton made that call.'

'What makes you think that?'

'The day I interviewed Jennifer she was about to leave for a meeting with him because she had a contract to renew the décor in the main lounge and she said the Seatons were having second thoughts about their choice. She had arranged to call in with some fabric samples; her assistant offered to take them as she had another errand in the same direction, but Jennifer insisted on going herself.'

'Which suggests a personal as well as a business reason for the call,' said Leach thoughtfully. 'I wonder if it was Seaton or his wife who asked to see more samples. If he was hoping to get Jennifer into bed it was hardly likely he'd plan to do it in his own home with his wife around. You're suggesting that it was Carla Seaton who persuaded her to stay for lunch with the express purpose of doping her with quinine?'

'She might have been keeping an eye on him for some time and suspected him and Jennifer of being more than business associates. Vicky and I learned from the nurses we interviewed at Holmwood that it wouldn't have been the first time he'd strayed. They weren't prepared to say whether Carla knew about Fenella although we think she probably did.'

'So she'd have been keeping a close eye for signs that he was up to his old tricks,' said Rathbone. 'Just the same, sir, if she was planning to kill Jennifer, she could hardly have chosen a more unlikely way of doing it.'

'Maybe murder wasn't what she had in mind,' said Leach. 'Maybe the intention was simply to make her feel ill. If it was Seaton who issued the invitation to lunch I don't suppose Carla was best pleased, but if she was going to administer quinine she'd have had to think pretty fast. Sukey, is there any means of checking whether Jennifer did actually have lunch with the Seatons?'

'I could ask Hazel, her assistant, whether she knew about it. She was at the inquest but wasn't called as a witness.'

'Do that. Yes, Mike?'

'It's difficult to see how anyone could get Jennifer to swallow anything containing that amount of quinine,' said Haskins. 'The capsules would have to be opened and the powder extracted. I believe it tastes very bitter; she'd have been bound to notice it.'

'True,' Leach agreed. 'It's obvious we have to look into this more deeply. Sukey and Vicky, you've got a foot in the door at Holmwood Care Home. Go and kick it wide open.'

'Décor for You. Hazel Norton speaking.'

'Ms Norton, this is DC Sukey Reynolds, Avon and Somerset CID.'

'I remember you. You came to interview Jennifer on the morning of the day she died.' The voice was staccato, tinged with suspicion. 'What do you want?'

'I noticed you at the inquest so you are aware that it was adjourned and for what reason. We have been asked to make some enquiries. May I ask you a few questions?'

'What questions?'

'When Jennifer left the showroom after I interviewed her on the day of her death she was, I understand, on her way to the Holmwood Care Home. What time was her appointment there?'

'Eleven o'clock. She said the Seatons were having second thoughts about their choice of fabrics and she took some fresh swatches to show them.'

'Did she mean both of them were having doubts, or just Brian Seaton?'

'I understand he made the call but said it was his wife who was having a rethink.'

'Did Jennifer have a further appointment that morning, or were you expecting her to come straight back after the business was concluded?'

'There was no other appointment in her diary and I expected her back, but she rang me about twelve o'clock to say she'd been invited to stay for lunch. She said Carla Seaton had apologized for being . . . "a bit unpleasant" I think were the words she used, and by way of making amends issued an invitation for lunch.'

'What was your reaction to that?'

'I was surprised, to say the least. After her first visit, Jennifer told me that Carla Seaton was a miserable sour-faced cow who didn't deserve such a nice husband and I said, "Perhaps she was just having a bad hair day," but I don't think Jennie was prepared to make excuses for her.'

'She found Brian Seaton easier to get on with then?' said Sukey, who found herself mentally endorsing her own first impression.

'To be honest, I think she fancied him and from one or two things she let drop she believed it was mutual.'

'Do you think they were having an affair?'

There was a pause before Hazel said, 'She came back from her first visit to Holmwood full of enthusiasm; she said it was going to be a pretty lucrative contract if we got it. When Seaton rang to say they accepted our estimate she went to Holmwood to take detailed measurements. After that visit she was on a bit of a high; I thought the order was in the bag and then she announced out of the blue that the Seatons had changed their minds and wanted to look at some different fabrics so she had to go back to Holmwood again.'

'I was there when she told you,' said Sukey. 'I remember you offered to do it as you were going to be in the area.'

'And she insisted on going herself,' said Hazel. 'It was then that I had the feeling there was something going on between her and Seaton and I got worried. The fact is, she had a relationship that was serious and lasted quite a long time, but it ended about a year ago. I don't know what went wrong; she was pretty cut up about it at the time because I think she hoped it was going to turn into something permanent, but it seemed like she was getting over it. I didn't want her to be hurt again.'

'You've obviously known her for quite a while. Did she confide in you?'

'Not a great deal.'

'Did you ever hear her say anything about taking quinine for night cramps?'

'On the contrary, she didn't like taking any sort of drug if she could help it, not even an aspirin for a headache. When she had an infection and her doctor prescribed an antibiotic she was in two minds whether to take it. And if it was the quinine that caused Jennie to lose her concentration,' Hazel continued in a sudden blaze of anger, 'then that woman somehow managed to get it into her with the deliberate intention of causing her death!'

'I advise you not to repeat that to anyone,' said Sukey. 'Meanwhile, thank you for the information.' She put down the phone and turned to Rathbone. 'Yes, Sarge, Jennifer did have lunch with the Seatons and Hazel believes Carla could have murdered her.'

'OK, so we tick that box,' he replied.

'So shall Vicky and I go to Holmwood now?'

'Not for the moment.' He got to his feet. 'While you were talking to Hazel we had a call from reception. We have a new witness in the Fenella Tremaine case – Douglas Cowell. He's in interview room three.'

The new witness was a well-built man in his early thirties with dark, neatly cut hair and steel-grey eyes. Rathbone took a seat opposite him with Vicky on his right and Sukey on his left. Rathbone performed the introductions before saying, 'Mr Cowell, I see from your business card that you are a professional body-guard. You say you have information concerning Fenella Tremaine. Do we understand that she hired you to protect her?'

Cowell gave a faint smile and shook his head. 'The fact is, Sergeant, guarding bodies isn't exactly a full-time occupation and I need something else to fill in the gaps. Here's my alternative business card.'

'Douglas Cowell, Private Investigator.' Rathbone read aloud. 'I won't ask you to explain how you manage to keep these two plates in the air without dropping one of them,' he said drily, 'but if you have any information that may help in our investigations, please tell us.'

'A couple of months ago,' Cowell began, 'I was approached by a woman who suspected her husband of having an affair. I followed him and before long I observed him in what appeared to be compromising situations with a woman. I took photographs and gave them to my client.' He took an envelope from his pocket and handed it to Rathbone. 'The dates and venues are on the back of each shot.'

The three detectives studied the pictures in silence for a couple of minutes. Then Vicky said, 'Fenella Tremaine and Brian Seaton. The first was taken at the end of June, the second a week later and the third about ten days before Fenella was murdered. Were these the only meetings you observed?'

'Yes.'

'The last one – the one in the restaurant – doesn't appear to have been very relaxed,' Rathbone remarked.

'That was my impression,' said Cowell. 'In fact, the body language suggests that he was trying to dump her and she was pleading with him not to.'

'Which confirms what those two other witnesses told us,' Sukey mouthed at Vicky behind Rathbone's back.

'What was the name of your client?' asked Rathbone.

'Mrs Carla Seaton. I delivered the pictures to her, she appeared satisfied, paid my fee and as far as I was concerned that was the end of the matter.'

Rathbone returned the photographs to the envelope. 'We need to keep these as evidence,' he said. 'We'll give you a receipt.'

'No problem,' said Cowell.

'It's nearly two weeks since Fenella Tremaine was murdered,' Rathbone continued. 'Why haven't you come forward earlier?'

'I've been in Europe on bodyguard duty. When I'm in England I check the papers every day to see if there's anything relevant to one of my enquiries. If I'm sent abroad I make a point of catching up when I come home.'

'I see. Well, sir, thank you very much for your help. We have not, of course, recorded this interview, but my colleagues will prepare a statement based on the information you have given us and we'd be most appreciative if you would sign it.'

'No problem,' Cowell repeated. 'Glad to be of help.'

# SEVENTEEN

The two detectives showed their IDs to the woman who opened the door to Holmwood Care Home. Her white overall had the monogram HCH embroidered on the pocket. 'We'd like to see Mr and Mrs Seaton,' said Rathbone.

The woman hesitated. 'I'm not sure if they're available,' she said doubtfully. 'If you'd care to . . .'

She waved a hand at some chairs in the small reception area

behind her, but without giving her time to finish Rathbone said, 'Then we'll wait until they are. Just inform them we're here, please.' He sat down and beckoned Sukey to an adjacent chair.

The woman scurried away. Several minutes ticked past before Carla Seaton appeared. Her face was flushed and to Sukey's experienced eye she appeared agitated. 'I intend to lodge a complaint, Sergeant,' she began. 'This constable and her female colleague –' she gestured in Sukey's direction without taking her gaze from Rathbone – 'gave my husband and me a firm undertaking that they found nothing to complain of in our treatment of Mrs Donaldson and were advising her son that we had no case to answer. Perhaps,' she went on, 'you are here to offer an apology for harassing my staff . . . or perhaps that's too much to hope for,' she added with a slight curl of her lip.

Rathbone stood up and Sukey did the same. 'If you wish to make a complaint about our officers' previous visit I suggest you put it in writing to the Chief Constable,' he said. 'It so happens that we are here today on an entirely different matter.'

'What matter? Has there been another complaint?'

'Is your husband available?'

'My husband is busy. I assure you I am perfectly capable of dealing with any matter you wish to raise.'

'I'm afraid it's essential that we speak to both of you.' Rathbone made shooing movements with his hands to indicate that she should lead him and Sukey to her husband. She clicked her tongue in annoyance, but after a moment's hesitation she complied.

'They want to see us both,' she snapped as she flung open the office door and slammed it shut behind the detectives when they had entered. 'They wouldn't tell me anything. It's nothing short of harassment . . . you must write to the Chief Constable!'

'Suppose we wait to hear what they've got to say,' Seaton suggested. He was plainly startled by the unexpected arrival of the police, but managed to summon a smile and invited them to sit down. He sat behind the desk and his wife took a chair beside him. 'What can we do for you, Sergeant?'

'We are looking into the circumstances of the road accident that took place shortly before three o'clock on the afternoon of Wednesday the thirty-first of July, in which Ms Jennifer Freeman was fatally injured. We understand she paid you a visit on the morning of that day.'

Husband and wife exchanged glances before Seaton said, 'That is correct. She was here on business. We read about it in the papers . . . a very tragic accident.'

'Ah yes, on business,' Rathbone repeated, with emphasis on the last word. 'After the report of the accident appeared in the press we received an anonymous call from a man who stated that she had been at a business meeting, but gave no details.' He fixed a penetrating gaze on Seaton. 'Would that have been you, sir?'

'My husband is not in the habit of making anonymous telephone calls,' said his wife.

'Perhaps he'd care to answer for himself.' Rathbone turned back to Seaton. 'Sir?'

'I assure you, Sergeant, that the call did not come from me,' Seaton replied firmly. 'I can confirm that Ms Freeman had an appointment here at eleven o'clock on that day to show us some fabric samples. We have awarded her firm a contract to replace the curtains and reupholster the chairs in the residents' lounge.'

'How long did the meeting last?'

Seaton hesitated, but his wife was quick to answer. 'Approximately an hour.'

'Until about midday?'

'About then, I suppose.'

'Did she have another appointment?'

'She might have done. She didn't say.'

'Did you offer her any refreshment while she was here?' asked Sukey.

Carla shot her a disdainful look before saying, 'We had coffee in the office while we were discussing the details of the contract.'

'Who made the coffee?'

Carla made an impatient gesture. 'One of the domestic staff.' She turned back to Rathbone. 'Really, Sergeant, what on earth has all this to do with Ms Freeman's tragic accident?'

'How did Ms Freeman take her coffee?' asked Rathbone. 'With milk and sugar?'

Seaton looked enquiringly at his wife, who said, 'I don't remember. What difference does it make?'

'So the business discussion ended at approximately midday. What happened next?'

'Ms Freeman put her samples away and was preparing to leave when Carla asked her if she would like to stay for lunch,' said Seaton.

'Was this an impromptu invitation on your wife's part or had you agreed on it beforehand?'

'Carla said nothing about it in advance, but of course I was more than happy to endorse it.'

'We already know about the invitation,' said Sukey. 'I spoke to Ms Freeman's assistant this morning and she told me about it. She said Carla Seaton had apologized for being "a bit unpleasant" at an earlier meeting and had invited her "by way of making amends". What do you think she meant by "a bit unpleasant", Mrs Seaton?'

Carla made what seemed to Sukey a conscious effort to convey a conciliatory attitude. 'You must understand,' she said, in milder tones, 'that I have a very demanding and responsible position and there are times when I tend to get a little short-tempered. I apologized for any apparent discourtesy on my part during our initial discussions and I wanted to make it clear there was nothing personal intended.'

'Of course there wasn't; it was a very nice gesture on your part, dear,' said her husband.

'All the more unfortunate that it had such a disastrous sequel,' Rathbone remarked. 'Do you remember what food you served?'

'We had the same menu as the residents. Do you want me to check?'

'Yes, please.'

Seaton consulted his computer. 'We had shepherd's pie with fresh vegetables, followed by fruit salad and cream.'

'What about drinks?'

'We offered her a sherry, but she declined. Then she caught sight of a bottle of Campari on the sideboard and said, "Oh, my favourite poison! May I have that?"'

'Did she drink it neat or with soda?'

'She had a splash of soda, but she said, "Not too much, I like the bitter flavour."'

'How many drinks did she have?'

'She accepted a second Campari, but after that she drank only water.'

'I see. That confirms the pathologist's findings that the level of alcohol in her blood was well below the legal limit. You may have heard that the inquest was held yesterday and the coroner was naturally anxious to establish the precise cause of the accident.' Rathbone paused briefly to give the Seatons an opportunity to comment, but neither of them spoke. 'Since certain questions remained unanswered, it was adjourned pending further enquiries, which is why we are here. Mrs Seaton –' at this point he fixed his gaze directly on her – 'among your residents there must be many who are prescribed medication by their doctors. Who has charge of the drugs – the patients?'

She appeared surprised, and to Sukey almost relieved, by the sudden change in the line of questioning. 'Certainly not,' she said crisply. 'All prescriptions are handed to me or my husband and we order the drugs from a local pharmacy.'

'And they are delivered to you here?'

'Yes. As a qualified nurse I take responsibility for all drugs. I keep them under lock and key and dispense them to the patients in accordance with their doctors' instructions.'

'You give them to each patient yourself?'

'Either I do it personally or I instruct another suitably qualified member of staff. In any case, we have to make sure that patients actually take their medication. Some of them are a bit vague so we have to keep an eye on them,' she added.

'By the way –' the tone was deceptively casual – 'do any of your residents complain of night cramps?'

'None of them has complained to me.'

'My mother used to be disturbed by cramp in her legs,' said Sukey. 'Her doctor prescribed quinine tablets; she said they were a great help.'

'Current medical opinion advises against the use of quinine for cramp,' said Carla.

'So it hasn't been prescribed for any of your residents?'

'Definitely not.' She glanced pointedly at her watch. 'Have you any further questions?'

'Thank you,' said Rathbone. He stood up. 'That's all for

now. We'll see ourselves out,' he added as Seaton half rose from his chair.

'Do you think Seaton was telling the truth when he denied making that anonymous call, Sarge?' asked Sukey as they went back to their car.

'I do, as it happens, although like you I thought he seemed the most likely person. Could it have been one of the residents?'

'It's possible, I suppose,' said Sukey, mentally resolving to check with Harry if he had spoken to Major Howes recently, 'but what would be the point unless the caller suspected something?' A thought struck her. 'So far we've only seen female staff; I wonder if there are any male employees here?'

'There's probably an odd-job man, or a gardener. Speaking of which . . .' Rathbone pointed across the front garden to where a man was hoeing one of the flower beds.

Sukey stopped in the act of clipping on her seat belt. 'Shall we go and have a word?'

'Later, when we come back.'

'When are we coming back?'

'As soon as we can get hold of a search warrant.'

'So what's new?' asked Vicky as Sukey settled down at her computer.

'Plenty,' Sukey replied. 'Let's grab some lunch when I've finished my report and I'll fill you in with the details. The plot is definitely thickening.' She finished her report, emailed it to DCI Leach and the rest of the team, and then made two phone calls, one to Harry and the other to Hazel Norton. She sat back and flexed her arms. 'Ready when you are,' she said to Vicky. They made their way down to the canteen and joined the queue. 'What sort of a morning have you had, by the way?'

'Fascinating,' said Vicky. 'Penny and I had the task of checking on Cowell's photographs and it seems Seaton used the same hotel on several occasions, and not just with Fenella. She had at least one predecessor; there may have been more but the receptionist we spoke to has only been there about eighteen months.'

'Carla obviously had reason for her suspicions,' said Sukey. I wonder if she ever tackled him about it.'

'Probably. And no doubt he shed tears of contrition and promised to be a good boy—'

'Until next time,' Sukey finished as Vicky paused to take a bite of her bacon sandwich. 'I believe that, knowing his track record, she saw Jennifer as her next potential rival and unexpectedly saw a chance to get even.'

'So you believe she did sneak the quinine into Jennifer's drink?'

'I reckon so, although like DCI Leach I doubt if she had murder in mind. I think it's more likely she was hoping Jennifer would become disorientated and make a fool of herself in front of Brian. I checked with Hazel and she said Jennifer always drinks strong black coffee without sugar, which of course tastes very bitter. I dare say there was some comment about it – maybe Jennifer said that was why she liked it – and Carla hit on the idea of inviting her to lunch knowing they had Campari in the drinks cupboard. She was probably going to offer it anyway, banking on its bitter flavour concealing the bitterness of the quinine she was planning to put in it. Jennifer played into her hands by asking for it.'

'Carla must have a razor-sharp brain to concoct her plan so quickly.' Vicky finished her sandwich and began tackling her portion of chocolate gateau. 'So what happens next?'

'We go back to Holmwood with a warrant and check for quinine.'

On the way back to the canteen, Sukey's mobile rang. 'Is that DC Sukey?' It was a woman's voice and it sounded familiar.

'Speaking. Who's calling?'

'This is Barbara Melrose. I'm calling from Holmwood Care Centre. I've just overheard something I think you should know about.'

'What is it?'

'The Seatons have been having a flaming row. Something about quinine tablets prescribed for old Mrs Donaldson. He said, "Why didn't you tell them?" and she said, "What was the point? The old lady's dead." Then he said, "What became of them?" and she said, "What is this? Are you accusing me of bumping off your latest floozie? I'm not staying here to listen to this rubbish." I thought she was about to come out of the office any second so I hurried into the residents' lounge just across the corridor.'

'Where are you calling from?'

'I'm in the nurses' room. Sally's here with me.'

'Did she overhear the Seatons as well?'

'No, I told her about it and she said I should call you straight away.'

'Absolutely right. Now listen, when's the next time Mrs Seaton will unlock the drugs cabinet?'

'About seven o'clock, when the patients have their evening meal.'

'Right. Can you and Sally between you manage to keep an eye on the drugs cabinet and let us know at once if Mrs Seaton goes to it before the usual time?'

'Will do.'

'Cheers.'

When she got back to the office she hurried over to Rathbone's desk and reported the call. 'Right,' he said. 'I've got the warrant. Let's go!'

# EIGHTEEN

'What in the world do you want now?' demanded a furious Carla Seaton, leaping to her feet as Rathbone and Sukey entered the office. 'Haven't we suffered enough harassment and inconvenience already? And how dare you come marching in here without even having the courtesy to knock at the door?'

'Sorry, this is no time for formalities,' said Rathbone. 'We have a warrant to search the premises and I must ask you to remain in this room for the time being. We have no wish to cause unnecessary disturbance to your residents,' he went on, 'and we see no need to enter the lounge or their private rooms for the time being. Where is your husband?'

At that moment Brian Seaton entered in an obvious state of agitation. 'Whatever's going on?' he gasped. 'There are a dozen police officers waiting outside the front door.'

Carla grabbed hold of his arm and shook it. 'These two detectives are back . . . they want to search the place . . . they've got a warrant . . . tell them it must be a mistake, we've got nothing to hide.'

'Please, both of you, sit down.' said Rathbone. He held out a hand. 'Mrs Seaton, please give me the key to your drugs cabinet.'

For a moment Sukey thought she was going to defy him, but after a brief hesitation she opened a drawer in the desk, took out a key attached to a bright red tag and gave it to him. 'The cabinet is in a locked cupboard; this opens both of them. If you're expecting to find a supply of Class A drugs you're wasting your time,' she added with an attempt at bravado. 'Everything in there is perfectly legitimate and properly accounted for.'

'We shall see.' He gave the key to Sukey. 'Let the officers in and ask them to wait while you find our contact. You know what to do. Then come back here.'

'Right, Sarge.' Barbara Melrose had told her the exact location of the nurses' sitting room and she was waiting there when Sukey entered. 'Right, the search party's downstairs,' she said, ignoring the curious glances from two other occupants. 'I'll take you to the officer in charge.'

Back in the entrance hall, Sukey introduced Barbara to Sergeant Drury. 'Nurse Melrose will show you round,' she informed him. 'DS Rathbone says there's no need to search the residents' lounge or any of their private rooms for the time being. Here's the key to the drugs cupboard. DS Rathbone and I are interviewing Mr and Mrs Seaton in their office. If you find anything, let us know straight away.'

'Will do.'

Leaving them to it, Sukey returned to find Rathbone sitting in a relaxed position with his legs crossed. When she entered he sat upright and indicated the chair beside him. She sat down and looked across at the Seatons, who sat side by side behind the desk. He was toying nervously with a glass paperweight while she sat as if turned to stone, her face expressionless.

'Right,' said Rathbone, 'we want answers to some of the questions we asked this morning, and this time we want the truth. Mrs Seaton, do you recall DC Reynolds mentioning that her mother's doctor had prescribed quinine tablets to relieve her night cramps?'

'I can't say I do,' she replied.

Rathbone turned to Sukey. 'Perhaps you would refresh Mrs Seaton's memory.'

Sukey opened her notebook and read out the references to quinine, ending with Rathbone asking whether it had been prescribed for any Holmwood residents. 'And what did Mrs Seaton reply?' he asked.

'She replied "definitely not".'

'Mrs Seaton, I'm asking you once again,' said Rathbone, 'has quinine been prescribed at any time for any of your residents?'

Carla Seaton passed a hand over her forehead and appeared to be searching her memory. 'I suppose it's possible at some time or another,' she said vaguely, 'but it would have been quite a while ago. It is still used in the treatment of malaria – but as you can imagine we don't have many cases of that here,' she added with a touch of sarcasm. 'And as I think I told you, it is no longer prescribed for night cramps.'

'As you think you told us,' Rathbone repeated, slowly and with emphasis on each individual word. Carla's colour rose as she realized her mistake. She took a handkerchief from her pocket and wiped her mouth, where Sukey had already noticed beads of sweat on the upper lip. Rathbone pulled his chair forward and planted his elbows on the desk. Sukey could not see his face but from past experience she could visualize his steady, penetrating gaze. Carla's hands were shaking. 'First you claim not to remember any reference in our previous interview to quinine being prescribed for the relief of night cramps,' he began, 'and in the next breath you point out that you had already informed us that its use for that purpose has been discontinued.'

Carla shifted in her seat and clasped her hands together in an attempt to steady them, but even her voice was shaking as she stammered, 'I have a lot on my mind; I can't recall every detail of every conversation.'

'Wouldn't it be more accurate to say that you were telling a deliberate lie?'

'No, I was not lying. I simply made a mistake.'

'Because the last time quinine was prescribed for a patient was such a long time ago?'

'I suppose so.'

'We may have up to thirty residents at any particular time,

Sergeant,' Brian Seaton interposed. 'Sometimes they are here for
only short periods of respite care and then return home. And
their average age is about seventy, so one way or another there
is a considerable turnover. It is not reasonable to expect me or
my wife to carry all their details in our heads.'

'Quite so, sir,' said Rathbone briskly, 'but I presume you keep
a file on each resident?'

'Naturally. All the files are on our computer.'

'We'd like to see the late Mrs Donaldson's history, please,
Mr Seaton.'

'Mrs Donaldson? So that's what this is about! Her son put
you up to this!' After wriggling uncomfortably under Rathbone's
questioning, Carla now managed to summon up a display of
righteous indignation. 'Despite your assurances that no blame
whatsoever attached to us, Bradley Donaldson has made some
trumped-up excuse to bring you back here to make our lives a
misery and disturb the peace of our establishment. What's he
accusing us of? Having caused her death by mismanaging her
medication? It's absolutely monstrous! Brian!' She rounded on
her husband. 'Shut down the computer and call Mr Goodall.
We're answering no more questions without consulting our
solicitor.'

There was a knock at the door. Sukey opened it and an officer
entered, carrying in gloved hands two clear plastic bags. 'Sergeant
Drury told me to bring these to you right away, Sarge,' he said.
'This –' he held up one of the bags – 'was in a special waste
bin along with a load of similar items.' Sukey recognized a foil
strip of the type used by used by pharmaceutical companies to
pack capsules containing drugs. 'One of the staff told us it was
a load of out of date or out of use pills and stuff waiting to be
destroyed. The packet in this other bag was with paper waiting
to be recycled.'

Rathbone took the bags, turning them while he scrutinized
their contents through the plastic. 'This strip held quinine
sulphate three-hundred-milligram tablets,' he read aloud.
'According to the label on the packet, identical tablets were
prescribed for Mrs Angela Donaldson in February this year.' He
turned back to the couple behind the desk and said, 'I suggest
you call your solicitor from police headquarters. You will

probably wish to nominate one of your senior staff to deputize for you during your absence.'

There was a brief consultation between husband and wife before Brian said, 'Barbara Melrose is our most senior nurse. Shall I go and find her?'

He half rose from his seat, but Rathbone said, 'No thank you, sir.' He turned to the officer. 'Find Nurse Melrose, pass on Mr Seaton's instruction and tell her where we're going. Inform Sergeant Drury and tell him to let me know immediately if you find anything else.'

'Will do, Sarge.'

At police headquarters Brian and Carla Seaton, with their solicitor, Hedley Goodall, sat side by side at a table in an interview room. Opposite them sat DS Rathbone and DC Sukey Reynolds. After the completion of formalities, Goodall said, 'Sergeant, I have had a full and frank discussion with my clients and they assure me that while they deeply regret the death of Ms Jennifer Freeman they categorically deny any responsibility for it.'

'Thank you, sir, your comments are noted,' said Rathbone. 'Perhaps, so that you should be fully informed, I'll ask DC Reynolds to read you an extract from this afternoon's interview with your clients in their office at Holmwood Care Home.' After Sukey read the exchanges referring to the use of quinine in the treatment of night cramps, Rathbone turned to the Seatons and said, 'Do you agree this is an accurate record of what was said?' They exchanged glances and nodded. 'Please speak aloud for the tape.'

After they had both reluctantly muttered, 'Yes,' Rathbone continued. 'I have here –' he held up a file that lay open on his desk – 'a report of the proceedings at the inquest on Jennifer Freeman that was held yesterday afternoon. Do I take it that neither of you attended?'

'We didn't even know the inquest was taking place,' said Brian.

'Have you read any reports of the proceedings?' Both the Seatons gave negative replies. 'Then you may be interested to know that as certain questions remained unanswered it was adjourned pending further enquiries.'

'May we know what questions?' asked Goodall, as neither of his clients showed any reaction.

'The post-mortem examination revealed a significant quantity of quinine in Jennifer Freeman's system – a drug that had never been prescribed for her.' At the mention of quinine, Sukey noticed Carla stiffen. 'As we have just heard,' Rathbone continued, 'it was once the practice to use it as a relief for night cramps but as you, Mrs Seaton, told us it is no longer recommended, chiefly because – as an experienced nurse – you are no doubt well aware that it has been known to cause certain side effects such as disorientation and confusion. That's true, isn't it?'

'Yes,' she replied through tight lips.

'Now, let me remind you of some further exchanges between us, this time from this morning's interview. Sukey?' Once again, Sukey read out her transcript of the relevant passages.

The Seatons listened in silence. When Sukey had finished, Rathbone said, 'Quinine has a bitter taste. You, Mr Seaton, informed us that Jennifer Freeman had expressed a fondness for bitter drinks, among them strong, black, unsweetened coffee. And you, Mrs Seaton, suddenly invited Jennifer to stay for lunch by way of apologizing for having been "a bit unpleasant" during a previous discussion. I put it to you that, hoping she would ask for Campari as an aperitif, you saw an opportunity to spike her drink with quinine with the deliberate intention of causing some of the known side effects.'

'That is a preposterous statement,' said Carla indignantly. 'Why on earth do you suppose I wanted to harm her?'

'I'll come to that in a minute. As you anticipated, Jennifer did ask for Campari with, according to your husband, a splash of soda. Which of you poured the drinks?'

'I did,' said Brian Seaton.

'And did you hand Jennifer's drink to her immediately?'

Brian Seaton hesitated for a second and glanced at his wife. Sukey read a desperate plea in her expression; in his was a dawning look of apprehension. 'I'd like an answer please,' said Rathbone.

With an obvious effort, Brian Seaton turned from his wife's face and looked directly at Rathbone. 'I poured the drinks – Jennifer's Campari and a couple of sherries for us – and put them on a tray.' His voice had a slow, almost mechanical quality, as if he were reliving the scene. 'Jennifer was looking out of the window admiring the garden. She had her back to us. I was about to take the tray and put it on the low table beside her when Carla said, "You forgot to return Mrs Lear's call. You'd better do it now."'

'And is that what happened?'

'Yes.'

'What was the nature of the call?'

'It was to a lady wanting to talk about her mother who has been ill for some time.'

'Where did you make the call?'

'In the office.'

'How long were you away?'

'I suppose we were talking for almost ten minutes.'

'And when you returned, what did you find?'

'Carla and Jennifer were sitting on the sofa with their drinks and chatting.'

'So you were out of the room for almost ten minutes,' said Rathbone. 'How far is the drugs cupboard from the room where the drinks were being served?'

'It's next door.'

'Next door,' Rathbone repeated. 'That would have given you plenty of time, wouldn't it, Mrs Seaton, while your husband was out of the room and Jennifer's back was turned, to take out the pack of quinine tablets which you happened to know were still there, break open a couple of three hundred milligram capsules of the drug and slip it into her drink, knowing it would at worst enhance the bitter taste for which Jennifer had expressed a liking?'

Before she had a chance to reply, Goodall intervened. 'On behalf of my client I strongly object to this line of questioning,' he said. 'What you are implying is pure supposition on your part and I advise her not to answer.'

'All right,' said Rathbone. 'Let me turn to the empty drug packet which, according to the label, contained quinine tablets prescribed for Mrs Donaldson, who died several months ago. Leaving aside your assertion that quinine had not been prescribed for any of your residents for a long time, can you explain why the empty packet came to be with a quantity of material waiting to be recycled?'

'I came across it a few days ago in the drugs cupboard. Due to an apparent oversight it had not been thrown away.'

'I see. Were any of the tablets left over?'

'No, it was just an empty packet.'

'You're quite sure of that?'

'Quite sure.'

'Now, Mrs Seaton –' Rathbone made a point of referring to the open file in front of him – 'let me return to your earlier question concerning your motive – or lack of it – for wishing to harm Jennifer Freeman.' He paused for a moment before saying, 'I believe that you have in the past had occasion to suspect your husband of being unfaithful to you?'

Once again, Goodall intervened. 'Really, Sergeant, what relevance has my clients' private life to do with the present enquiry?'

'It has every relevance, as I propose to show in a moment.' He turned back to Carla Seaton. 'It is true, is it not, that you once employed a private detective, who found evidence that confirmed your suspicions?'

Carla bit her lip and lowered her eyes; her husband took her hand. 'Yes, it's true,' he said. 'It was unforgivable and I bitterly regret it, but she did forgive me and I promised it would never happen again.'

'But you didn't really trust him to keep that promise, did you Mrs Seaton? In fact, you suspected that he had already started – or was about to start – another affair, this time with Jennifer Freeman. You saw an opportunity to cause her harm, even so far as to affect her control of her vehicle on the drive home—'

'Sergeant Rathbone, I cannot allow you to intimidate my client with these accusations for which you have so far not produced a shred of evidence,' said Goodall angrily. 'In the circumstances I must insist that you either charge her or release her and her husband immediately.'

Rathbone turned to Sukey. 'Constable Reynolds, you informed me that shortly after our visit to Holmwood this morning you received a telephone call from one of the employees. I take it you took a careful note of what you heard.'

'Yes, Sarge.'

'Read it back, please.'

As Sukey read out Barbara Melrose's report of the angry exchanges she had overheard between her employers, the Seatons sat rigid with horror. As the call ended, Carla let out a sudden scream of despair. 'All right, I admit it . . . I did lace her drink . . . I once saw the effect quinine had on a patient and I hoped it would do the same for Jennifer Freeman . . . but all I was hoping was that she'd just become confused and disorientated . . . and make a fool of herself in front of Brian . . . so help me God, I never meant to cause her death!' She rounded on her husband and screamed, 'This wouldn't have happened if only you'd loved me just a little!' To everyone's astonishment, and to Brian Seaton's obvious embarrassment, she clung to him, sobbing uncontrollably. After a moment's hesitation, he put his arms round her and held her close.

# NINETEEN

Sukey arrived home on Friday evening physically exhausted and mentally drained. She dropped her bag and jacket on the sitting room floor, sank into an armchair and closed her eyes. She felt a sudden need for Harry's company; the news of the Seatons' arrest would be released to the press within a few hours and she was tempted to call him and unload some of the conflicting emotions that, knowing it was part of her job to view the case objectively, she had been fighting to keep under control. From past experience she knew she could rely on him not to release any details before the official announcement, yet she still hesitated.

She became aware of feeling empty, having had little to eat since her lunchtime sandwich. Reluctantly, she dragged herself out of the chair with the intention of foraging in the kitchen for something quick and easy to prepare. As she did so, she noticed the light on her answering machine indicated that she had a message. It was with a surge of relief that she heard Harry's voice.

'Hi,' he said, 'I hear things have been popping. Call me ASAP.'

He replied after two rings. 'Where have you been? It's after nine o'clock. Your mobile's switched off . . . I was getting anxious.'

'I've only just got in,' she said. 'Sorry about that; I left my mobile on silent but I forgot to check it. Anyway, how did you know things were popping, as you put it?'

'Aha, we news hounds have our sources. Is it all right if I come round so we can compare notes? Have you eaten, by the way?'

'Not a lot,' she admitted, touched by his concern. 'I'm too tired to face anything that calls for too much effort so I was just about to have some soup with a bit of bread and cheese. Come and chat while I eat it.'

'With you in ten minutes.'

He was there in five. His eyebrows rose at the sight of the empty can. 'Don't tell me you've run out of your wonderful home-made soup!' he said in mock disgust.

'No, of course not. There's plenty in the freezer but it would take too long to defrost. Do you want some of this – there's enough for two?'

'No thanks, Dad and I had dinner a couple of hours ago.'

'Huh! All right for some.'

'It has been known to be the other way round,' he reminded her. 'Would a drop of wine make you feel any better?'

'It might.' While he fetched a glass and poured her wine, she ladled soup into a bowl and put bread, butter and cheese on the kitchen table. 'You can tell me what you've heard while I have this.'

'Enough to make me keen to know more. Major Howes is my source, by the way. I've been in to see him a couple of times and told him we suspect Brian Seaton of having it away with Fenella Tremaine. He reads all the crime reports in the press and knowing I'm with the *Echo* he loves to chat about them. Mostly he asks me questions, but this afternoon he called me in great excitement to say Holmwood was swarming with police and the Seatons had been arrested. I called my editor and he told me to get over there right away. Is it true?'

'Harry –' Sukey paused with her spoon in mid-air – 'I can imagine the rumours that have been flying around, but please don't publish anything before the official press statement.'

'How long do we have to wait?'

'Only till tomorrow.'

'Fair enough . . . but as you can imagine I'm dying to know

the inside story. You can let me have a little advance information, surely? In the strictest confidence, of course,' he wheedled.

'So you can have your story all ready to file while your rivals are still writing theirs, I suppose.'

'So what's wrong with that? Come on, love, you know you can trust me. I might even be able to offer some helpful suggestions. It wouldn't be the first time, would it?'

'True,' she admitted. She put her spoon down, took a mouthful of wine and cut a slice of cheese. 'All right, here's what happened. Acting on information received, we – that is DS Rathbone and I – interviewed the Seatons this morning about Jennifer Freeman's visit to Holmwood the day of her accident. We weren't satisfied with everything they told us, but there was no evidence to justify taking them in for further questioning.'

'What was the "information received"?'

'Sorry, I can't tell you that.'

'Would it have anything to do with the quinine found in Jennifer's body? I was at the inquest, remember?'

'So you were. Well, it was significant enough to make Rathbone apply for a search warrant and we went back in the afternoon with a posse of uniformed.'

'Which is what the dear old major called to tell me,' said Harry. 'He also rang again later to tell me that the place was buzzing with rumours that the Seatons had poisoned one of their residents! Some of them are feeling pretty alarmed.'

'Well, at least I can assure you there's absolutely no truth in that,' said Sukey. 'There's no need for any of the residents to worry.'

'So where did they get the idea about poison?'

'Things lose nothing in the telling, but I assure you there's no threat to anyone at Holmwood.'

Harry gave a deep sigh of frustration. 'I can see you mean to play it close to your chest,' he said resignedly. 'I suppose that should go some way to reassuring them, except that the latest news is that the Seatons have been brought back and everyone's frantic to know what's been going on.'

'I'm afraid they'll have to wait until the evening edition of the *Echo* tomorrow – or they may see it on the TV lunchtime news.'

'But we are talking about the death of Jennifer Freeman, aren't we?'

'Yes, I can tell you that.' Wearily, Sukey finished her frugal meal and went back to her wine. 'It'll be official in the morning. Both the Seatons have been arrested, charged in connection with her death and released on bail.'

'What are the charges? Attempted murder by quinine?'

'That's all I'm telling you for now,' said Sukey firmly. 'I don't suppose it triggered any helpful suggestions, by the way?'

He thought for a moment and then shook his head. 'Nothing comes to mind, but I do have one further question,' he said. 'What about the anonymous phone call that was mentioned at the inquest? Presumably it was Seaton who made it?'

'He denies it very firmly and we're both inclined to believe him. We're working on the possibility that it was another male employee at Holmwood. We saw a man working in the garden and there might be a handyman as well; that's something we have to look into.'

She emptied her glass and he held out a hand. 'Another?'

'No thanks.' She put down the glass and suddenly and inexplicably burst into tears.

He was at her side in a moment, holding her close and gently stroking her head while for a few minutes she sobbed her heart out. When she finally calmed down she groped in her pocket for a tissue, but he was ready with a clean white handkerchief and waited patiently while she mopped away the tears. 'Want to talk about it?' he whispered.

'It's not a pretty story – in fact it's typical of some of the cases the tabloids enjoy picking over,' she said huskily. 'It would be a relief to tell you about it, but I think I'd like a coffee. My throat's pretty dry.'

'That's hardly surprising. I'll make the coffee and we'll have it in the sitting room. You go and sit down and I'll bring it in.'

'I'd rather stay here with you.' For the moment he had become her link to normality and she had a sudden crazy fear of letting him out of her sight.

'Whatever you say.' He got up and filled the kettle. When they were settled in armchairs they sat in silence for a few minutes. Then he said, 'Before you say anything, I give you my solemn promise that what you tell me is not for publication without your express permission, OK?'

'OK. Thanks for that.' She put down her cup, reached out and took his hand. 'Like I said, there's nothing particularly unusual about the Seatons' story; in fact it's a classic case of an older and, to be honest, not particularly attractive woman who'd more or less given up hope of love and marriage being swept off her feet by a sexy man who pretended to be in love with her so he could get his hands on her money. It was listening to her desperate outpouring of mingled guilt and humiliation that I found so distressing.'

'Why did you have to listen to it? Aren't there – what d'you call them? – family liaison officers who specialize in that kind of thing?'

'There are, and one will be assigned to them but there was no one available immediately. Her solicitor applied for bail for the two of them and stayed with them while they were waiting for a decision. He suddenly asked to speak to DS Rathbone to say Carla Seaton had begged for a private word with me. Why she asked for me particularly I've no idea.'

'She obviously thought you'd be more likely to understand than Rathbone.'

'I guess so. I don't think I was feeling particularly understanding at the time but I could hardly refuse. She was obviously in a highly emotional state after being charged and said she wanted to explain what drove her to put the quinine in Jennifer's drink. She swore she never meant to kill her. At one point she seemed on the point of collapse and a doctor was called. He wrote a prescription for a sedative but he thought it would help her if she first had a chance to get it off her chest.'

'So you got lumbered?'

She gave a wan smile. 'You could put it like that.' She took a deep breath, fearing for a moment that more tears would come, but she fought them back. 'In this job we inevitably come up against some pretty distraught individuals, but I've never seen anyone so upset as Carla Seaton. Somehow it really got to me.' Her voice wavered and she broke off for a moment to steady herself. 'The background to the story is very simple,' she went on. 'Carla and her father, who was a doctor, owned and ran

Holmwood for a number of years. There was money in the
family and they invested quite heavily to bring it up to a very
high level of care and accommodation so there was always a
waiting list. The father died unexpectedly of a heart attack at
a comparatively young age and Carla inherited the business. She
had done nursing training so she carried on single handed with
the help of an old friend, also a doctor. It seems she offered him
a share of the business but for some reason he declined. Then
along came Brian Seaton, son of one of the residents – who
died long ago, by the way – who'd offered Carla a sympathetic
ear when she was not only grieving for her father but struggling
to run the business side of Holmwood. He became her right-hand
man and she became increasingly dependent on him. Then one
day, out of the blue, he declared himself passionately in love
with her and asked her to marry him. She fell for it hook, line
and sinker; before long she had put control of all the finances
in his hands.'

'Are you saying he'd been squandering it? Is Holmwood in
financial trouble?'

'It seems not. I understand his father spent all his savings on
the fees at Holmwood and he found himself on his uppers after
paying for the funeral. He saw the chance of landing a cushy
job with money to spend on whatever woman took his fancy, but
to be fair to him he's only been spending peanuts pursuing his
. . . hobby, you might call it.'

'He sounds a nasty bit of work just the same,' Harry commented.
'So how long before the cracks began to show?'

'Not long, according to Carla. He became less and less attentive and she began to notice his "wandering eye" as she put it.'
Sukey drained her coffee and held out her mug. 'Any chance of
a refill?'

'Sure.' He brought it and sat down again. 'You're right, it's a
pretty classic story,' he agreed, 'but I'm not sure I understand
why you should feel so distressed.'

'You might if you'd been there. Carla was distraught, almost
beating her chest and sobbing things like, "He couldn't help
the way he was . . . and I forgave him . . . I'd have gone on
forgiving him forever if only he'd loved me just a little." It was
pitiful . . . it went straight to my heart and it was all I could

do not break down and weep with her. It was a relief when the news they'd been granted bail came through and they were sent home.'

There was a silence while she drank her second cup of coffee. He took the empty cup from her and then gently squeezed her hand. 'Well, at least you don't need to worry about my intentions,' he said, keeping his tone light.

'How d'you mean?'

'If you've got a fortune stashed away I'm not aware of it, so you can be sure I'm sincere when I tell you I love you. And I hope –' he cupped her face with his free hand and turned it towards him – 'that's true for you as well.'

'Oh Harry!' She was on the verge of tears again. 'Of course it is!'

'Then let's have no more of this nonsense. We'll talk again soon; what you need now is a good night's rest.'

She gave a wan smile. 'You can say that again. It's going to be a busy weekend – for me at any rate. Good night, Harry. Thanks for putting up with me.'

He gave her a gentle kiss. 'I'll always be here for you, my love,' he whispered. 'Good night. Sleep well.'

# TWENTY

'Hi, everyone!' Rathbone greeted the team the following morning with unusual gusto. 'I hope you've all had a good night's rest. We've got plenty of leads to follow up. The game's afoot, as the saying goes.'

'Been brushing up your Shakespeare, Sarge?' said Vicky artlessly. 'Doing a Henry the Fifth, urging us into battle?' she added as he momentarily looked blank.

'Never mind the literary allusions, Vicky,' he said, with a swift change of mood. 'You and Sukey, Tim and Mike are to go to Holmwood this morning and find out who made that phone call, and why it was anonymous. While you're there, get statements from all the members of staff – and don't put up with any interference from the Seatons. Remind them that bail conditions can be reviewed if necessary. Understood?'

'Yes, Sarge,' they replied in chorus.

'Have you a job for me, Sarge?' asked Penny.

'You're coming with me to DCI Leach's office. We're going to spend some time reviewing the Ellerman case in the light of what we learned yesterday and since you were among the first to suggest a possible link between the two deaths, you can sit in. You might even have something useful to contribute,' he added magnanimously.

'Thank you, Sarge,' said Penny with enthusiasm.

'OK. We know that Brian Seaton had a number of affairs before the one with Fenella Tremaine, and was almost certainly planning to shag Jennifer Freeman if he hadn't already done so. Carla Seaton knew about the last two, but she adores her husband and is obviously prepared to forgive him and do everything in her power to keep him. She swears she never intended to bring about Jennifer's death and it's difficult to see how she could have got hold of the knife that killed Fenella, let alone contrive to be at the scene at the precise moment that murder was committed. But we all know that seemingly impossible things sometimes have a rational explanation and we have to explore every avenue, so the rest of you get going.'

After a brief discussion on the way to the car park, the four agreed to split into pairs using separate cars. 'In case one of us comes across a lead that takes us away from Holmwood,' Mike explained when he put forward the suggestion.

'What's the betting they're planning to sneak off to a pub for lunch?' said Vicky. 'I vote you and I book a pool car.'

'Why not?' said Sukey. By the time she and Vicky had picked up a car and driven to Holmwood, the others had already arrived and were waiting in reception, where Carla Seaton was angrily demanding whether they were ever going to be allowed to go about their business in peace.

'Isn't it enough that my husband and I find ourselves in this dreadful predicament,' she hissed in a stage whisper to avoid being overheard, 'without our staff being subjected to constant harassment?'

'I assure you, madam,' said Mike courteously, 'there is no

question of your staff being "harassed" as you put it, but it is essential that we put certain questions to them. We suggest that you return to your office and continue to run your business and allow us to go about ours as the law requires.'

'Oh, very well,' she said crossly, 'but be assured our solicitor will be informed of everything that goes on while you are here.' She swung round and left the four detectives exchanging glances.

'I think she got the message,' said Vicky. 'Right, where do we start?'

'I called Nurse Barbara Melrose before we left and asked her to make a complete list of the staff and split them into males and females,' said Sukey. 'Apart from the gardener and possibly a handyman, I know there are several male care assistants. They may be more comfortable being interviewed by Tim and Mike. I've a feeling they're not all native English speakers so we'll have to be patient.'

'That makes sense,' said Tim. 'You and Vicky have been here before, so you lead the way.

They went up to the nurses' office, where Barbara was waiting for them. 'I've made the lists as you asked, but not all the staff are here at the moment,' she said, handing out sheets of paper. 'They work shifts; the night shift ends at eight thirty and consists of a skeleton staff in case of emergencies, which thankfully don't happen very often. Last night there were just three on duty – two women and one man. I've asked them to stay on so perhaps you'd speak to them first so they can get home.'

'Were they all on the night shift the day of Jennifer Freeman's accident?' asked Sukey.

Barbara nodded. 'Not everyone is willing to work nights so they're all volunteers and they do a four-week stretch. After that they go back to daytime working.'

'Fine.'

'It so happens at the moment that two residents have just moved out and their rooms will be unoccupied for a couple of days,' Barbara went on, 'so you can use them to conduct your interviews. Do feel free to come back here when you've finished and help yourselves to coffee.'

'Many thanks. We'll get started right away.'

Less than half an hour later the detectives were back in the nurses' room comparing notes. The statements from the two female care assistants tallied in one significant respect; they had both noticed occasional signs of tension between Brian and Carla Seaton and put it down to what one of them called his "overfamiliar way of talking to other women". However, neither of them related it specifically to Fenella Tremaine and they didn't treat it seriously. 'It was a lot of gossip,' the older of the two explained. 'Some people read too many of those silly magazines.'

'The chap we interviewed hasn't been working here long and didn't seem to have a clue what we were on about,' said Mike.

'So, nothing much there to help us forward,' agreed Tim. 'Let's hope the day shift comes up with something a bit more useful.'

An hour later the four returned to the nurses' room to refresh themselves with coffee. 'How did you two get on with the female staff?' asked Mike.

'As before, we found a general agreement that relations between the Seatons often appear strained,' said Vicky. 'One of the carers, a middle-aged woman called Flo Baxter, was determined to make the most of her chance to talk to the police and she claimed to have been passing the office door one day when she heard raised voices. She admitted she had stopped to listen but couldn't hear what they were saying. She went on by and a few seconds later Brian came "storming out looking like thunder" as she put it so she was pretty sure they'd been having a run-in.'

'She assumed that Carla had been having a go at him about the Tremaine woman,' said Sukey. 'You know, "the body in the bin" as the *Echo* calls it,' she went on, quoting from her notes. 'When we asked what made her think it was about that, she said, "Well, we all guessed he'd been having it off with her but had dumped her. We even thought Carla might have been the one who topped her and I for one wouldn't put it past her. She's a hard-featured so-and-so. And then when she and Brian were arrested after the other woman died it seemed pretty obvious." Poor Flo, she couldn't understand why the two of them weren't banged up on the spot. At this point,' Sukey went on with a chuckle, 'Vicky informed her in no uncertain terms that we need evidence, not malicious gossip, to justify an arrest.'

'She was a bit miffed at that,' grinned Vicky. 'She muttered something like "that's all the thanks you get for trying to help the police".'

'I'm afraid none of the women we've seen so far came up with anything new,' Sukey sighed as she gratefully accepted the mug of coffee Mike handed to her, 'but from that smug look on your and Tim's faces, I've a feeling you've had more luck.'

'I wouldn't go so far as to say we're feeling smug,' said Mike, 'but we think we may have come up with something. We've spoken to a couple of male care assistants; they didn't come up with anything new – in fact, they both pooh-poohed the gossip about the Seatons' marital problems as "women's talk" – but we had more luck with George Goodbody, the handyman. And we also solved the mystery of the anonymous phone call. That was Loopy Larry.'

'The gardener,' Tim explained. 'That's what some of the staff call him. He's what you might describe as a "simple soul"; he's a retired postman and George says he sees himself as a kind of one-man neighbourhood watchdog. Keeping an eye open for suspicious behaviour is something he got in the habit of doing while he was on his rounds. Every time he hears or reads about a local incident – even something comparatively trivial like a purse being pinched from a woman's shopping bag – he rings Crimestoppers claiming to have information. It's seldom anything useful and the people manning the line have learned to recognize his voice and don't bother reporting his calls unless it's about something serious.'

'So what about this particular call?'

'All he said when we asked him about it was that he saw the picture of the wrecked car in the *Echo* and noticed the registration number. He was pretty sure it was the one he saw on the day of the accident, but he didn't say in his message that the driver had been to a meeting at Holmwood. He was afraid it might somehow get back to the Seatons and he'd lose his job; he's got an invalid wife and he needs the extra money to supplement his pension. We showed him Jennifer Freeman's picture, but he didn't recognize her.'

'Well, that's one loose end tied up,' said Sukey. 'But you've obviously got something more interesting up your sleeves, so spill it.'

'It's more to do with the Tremaine murder,' said Mike. 'George suggested we talk to a woman called Minnie who comes in three times a week to do the cleaning. She works for an agency and she's reported as saying that another woman from the same agency saw the picture in the *Echo* of the murder weapon – the knife with the fancy handle – and got quite het up about it. She's known as Aggie; George says she "looks sort of foreign" but her English is very good and she told Minnie she'd seen the knife but she wouldn't say where. According to George, Minnie tried to persuade her to talk to the police but the mention of the word seemed to terrify her. She's probably had a bad experience in her own country.'

'So she's hardly more reliable than Loopy Larry,' said Vicky, with a degree of scepticism.

'Not so fast,' said Mike. 'Minnie works for an agency that calls itself, would you believe, Clean as a Whistle. I rang them to try and get the names and addresses of the people Aggie cleans for, but the woman I spoke to refused to give the information over the phone.'

'Maybe some of her employees are illegals,' suggested Sukey.

'That occurred to me when she wouldn't budge even when I repeated my name and rank. Either that, or she didn't believe I was really a copper. Anyway, I've spoken to the Sarge and he's told us to get over to the office and demand the information. We've seen all the blokes so that's where Tim and I are off to now.' He finished his coffee with a flourish and stood up. 'See you later, girls!'

Sukey and Vicky interviewed the remaining people on their list without learning anything new, thanked Barbara for her cooperation and returned to headquarters for a canteen lunch. They were back in the CID office filing their reports when Tim and Mike returned. 'Where's the Sarge?' he asked.

'Over there, and he's not exactly a happy bunny.' Vicky pointed in the direction of the drinks machine, which Rathbone was feeding with coins. He filled a mug and was drinking from it as he crossed the room towards them.

'Any luck?' he asked brusquely.

'We interviewed the woman who owns the Clean as a Whistle Domestic Agency, Sarge,' said Mike. 'She's a Mrs Joyce Shilling;

age about fifty, smartly dressed, well spoken and businesslike. She gave us this bit of publicity she distributes from time to time.' He handed Rathbone a small laminated sheet, which he read and passed round. 'She tried to explain her reluctance to talk to me over the phone by saying she thought I might be a competitor trying to pinch some of her staff,' Mike added.

'*Tried* to explain?'

'We're not sure we believe her,' said Tim. 'She was a bit vague about the people she employs to stuff these flyers through letter-boxes so we suspect some of them may be illegals, but of course that wasn't why we were there. Anyway, she didn't know anything about any of her staff getting excited over the knife in the Tremaine murder but –' here he paused for effect – 'one of the people Aggie cleans for is Doctor Marcus Ellerman.'

Rathbone finished his drink and wiped his mouth with the back of his hand. 'Well that's a fat lot of help!' he grumbled. 'If all Aggie's got to tell us is that she saw the knife in Ellerman's flat, it adds nothing to what we already know.'

'There's a bit more, Sarge. Aggie – that's short for Aghami, by the way – helps out with the cleaning at Holmwood from time to time if Minnie's away or if they need an extra pair of hands for any reason, so she's probably heard the gossip about Fenella Tremaine and Brian Seaton. She failed to turn up on Thursday and Friday last week at the places where she was supposed to clean and she hasn't called in to report sick. Mrs Shilling has had to arrange for another cleaner to cover for her, which happens from time to time. We duly sympathized, thanked her for her help and left a number for her to call if anything else occurred to her.'

Rathbone chewed his lower lip in silence for a few moments. 'Let's think this through,' he said slowly. 'Everyone at Holmwood knew about Brian Seaton's affair with Fenella Tremaine. Aggie cleans there and she also cleans for Ellerman so it's quite likely she knew Fenella lived in the same block of flats. Supposing she mentioned this to Carla one day when she was cleaning the office; maybe she'd already told her about the artefacts like the elephant cushion covers and the knife, perhaps because she recognized them as coming from her own country.'

'Sarge, you're not suggesting that Carla asked Aggie to steal the knife so that she could sneak round at dead of night to stick it in Fenella's back?' said Sukey incredulously.

Rathbone made a slightly despairing gesture. 'I grant you it's pretty far-fetched,' he admitted, 'but supposing Carla has some kind of hold on Aggie – knows something about her that she wants to keep secret, something to enable Carla to put pressure on her to "borrow" the knife on the pretext that she'd like to have a look at it. It would explain Aggie's reluctance to speak to us. It's the first link, albeit a tenuous one, between the Tremaine and Freeman deaths. We know Carla is responsible for the latter, and she had reason to hate both of them. So the first thing we have to do is find out why Aggie let some of the clients down. Was Ellerman one of them, by the way?'

'No Sarge, she cleaned for him as usual on Wednesday. The ones she missed were on Thursday and Friday.'

'I take it you have the full names and addresses of both these women?'

'Yes, Sarge.' Mike handed a slip of paper to Rathbone, who passed it to Sukey.

'You and Vicky, get round to Aggie's place ASAP and see if you can find out why she's been absent from work. She has a reputation for being scared of the police, so if she's there tread carefully. And then go and talk to Minnie. They may have exchanged more information. Tim, you and Mike find out from the agency if Aggie cleaned at Holmwood around the time of the Tremaine murder and if she did, go back and put a few questions to Carla.'

The first address was a house in a somewhat down-at-heel Victorian terrace. Beside two of three bell pushes beside the front door were cards bearing the names Edmond and Boyden. The one at the top was blank, so they tried that first and waited, but there was no response.

'I didn't hear a bell ring,' said Sukey. 'Maybe it's out of order. We'd better knock.' They hammered on the door and eventually it was flung open by a bald-headed man in carpet slippers, who glared at them with red-rimmed, watery eyes.

'What the hell's the idea of making all that racket?' he demanded. 'What d'you suppose we've got bells for?'

'We want to speak to a lady called Aggie who we understand lives here; we tried the top bell but there was no reply. DCs Armstrong and Reynolds, Avon and Somerset CID,' she added, showing her ID. Vicky did the same.

The man peered at the two badges and said curtly, 'Don't know anything about her, never see her, can't help you,' and made to shut the door, but Vicky put a firm hand against it.

'You can at least show us which flat she lives in,' she said, and he reluctantly held the door open to let them in.

'First floor, door on the right,' he said. He responded to their thanks with a grunt before disappearing behind his own door.

They knocked several times on Aggie's door without success. 'Maybe she's been taken ill,' said Vicky. 'D'you think we should go in?'

'That lock doesn't look very strong,' said Sukey. They exchanged glances and nodded. 'Let's go for it.'

The lock gave easily to their combined weight. They found themselves in a fair-sized bed-sitting room, one corner of which was fitted out with basic kitchen facilities. A toilet with a shower and washbasin were hidden behind a folding door. It was sparsely furnished with a single bed, a table, two chairs and a chest of drawers. The bed was made up and a few items of clothing were hanging in a built-in cupboard, but there was no sign of the occupant.

'No jacket, no shoes and no handbag, so presumably she went out as usual and never returned,' said Vicky. 'I don't like the look of this.'

'We'd better report to the Sarge,' said Sukey. She took out her mobile but it rang before she could key in Rathbone's number. She listened for a moment and then said, 'I was about to call you, Sarge, to say we're at Aggie's flat; she's not here and according to a not very helpful neighbour she hasn't been seen lately.' She waited again, then said, 'Right, Sarge, will do.' She ended the call and met Vicky's enquiring glance. 'The body of a woman has been found on waste ground about a mile from Sycamore Park,' she said. 'No ID as yet. We're to wait here until uniformed arrive and then call in for further instructions.'

# TWENTY-ONE

While they were awaiting the arrival of the uniformed officers who had been dispatched to secure Aggie's flat, Sukey and Vicky put on plastic gloves and made a further, more detailed search of the room. There was a small refrigerator containing a packet of prepared salad, an unopened packet of cheese, butter substitute and a half litre bottle of milk. Sukey took out the milk and examined it.

'The best-before date was yesterday,' she said. She unscrewed the cap and gave the bottle a gentle shake. 'It's curdled. The salad's past its sell-by date as well.'

'And according to what Mrs Shilling told Tim and Mike,' said Vicky, 'she cleaned for Ellerman as usual on Wednesday and hasn't been seen since. This doesn't look good for her – or for him either. It looks as if we're going to have to pay him another call.'

'Are you thinking what I'm thinking?' said Sukey,

'You mean, is Aggie the dead woman who's just been found near Sycamore Park?'

'That's my gut feeling.'

'Mine too. Let's see what else we can find. It's just occurred to me,' Vicky went on as they moved around the flat, 'when we were questioning Ellerman about people having access to his flat, he remembered Wilkins the caretaker had been in to do something to a window – in fact he immediately accused him of being Fenella Tremaine's killer – but he never mentioned a cleaner—'

'And we asked him if he had one, but he never gave us an answer.' Sukey put a hand to her eyes as an awful possibility suddenly occurred to her. 'Oh dear, was that a fatal blunder on our part?'

'Let's hope not.' Vicky, who had obviously had the same thought, clutched her friend's hand and they were both silent for a moment before she said, 'There's nothing we can do about it now, so why don't we just get on with the task in hand?'

A few toiletries were neatly arranged on the chest of drawers and a string of beads hung over the corner of a small mirror. Vicky picked it up and said, 'I don't think much of her taste in jewellery, do you?'

She handed it to Sukey, who studied it for a moment and said, 'This isn't jewellery, it's a rosary.' She held it out and showed the crucifix. 'I had a friend at college who was Roman Catholic and she had one very similar to this.'

'You're right. I hadn't noticed.' Vicky took back the rosary and replaced it carefully on the mirror. 'So she's a Christian. I wonder if that's why she's so scared of the police. Maybe she's from a strict Muslim background and she's afraid someone from their mosque will ask us to look for her. Isn't it a fact that they consider converting to Christianity a capital offence?'

'So I've heard. It's true in some very strict families as well, even if they live in Western countries.' Sukey thought for a moment, frowning. 'Tim and Mike were speculating about her possibly being an illegal,' she said slowly as if thinking aloud, 'but I seem to recall that in the flyer he showed us Mrs Shilling claims that all her cleaners are fully insured and trustworthy. She also mentions "full key security" which suggests that some cleaners need access to places when the client is absent – such as business people like Ellerman. She'd be mad to make that sort of claim if she employed illegals.'

'You're right,' Vicky agreed, 'so there must be some other reason why Aggie's so reluctant to talk to the police.'

'Perhaps she's running away to avoid an arranged marriage,' Sukey suggested, 'or like you said, she may be afraid of being the victim of an "honour" killing by someone in her own family.'

They continued to search for a few more minutes without success. Presently they heard a car draw up outside; Vicky, who happened to be by the window, said, 'Here are the woodies,' and Sukey hurried down with the intention of admitting the two uniformed officers before the irascible downstairs neighbour had a chance to object to the disturbance. He had, however, already seen the police car and was on the doorstep demanding to know what the hell was going on.

'It's a fine state of affairs when a man can't read his paper in peace,' he grumbled.

'Nothing for you to worry about, sir,' said one of the officers as they followed Sukey up the stairs. 'We're just a little concerned for one of your neighbours and we'll come back and have a word with you in a few minutes.'

'He told us he knows nothing about her and never sees her,' Vicky informed them when they were back in Aggie's flat.

'We'll get a statement from him anyway when we've secured the place and we'll try and contact some of the other residents before we go.'

'We think they're out, but we'll have to leave you to it,' said Sukey. 'It seems we have another murdered woman on our hands.'

'You reckon it might be this one?'

'We hope not, but we have a hunch it might be.' She took out her mobile and called Rathbone, who gave her directions to the latest crime scene.

The rendezvous point for the police vehicles was in a side road bordering an uneven area of about an acre of rough land which, PC Jenks informed them, was known locally as Fiddler's Patch. 'In the good old days they had a maypole here and the girls used to dance round it while a local chap played the fiddle,' he explained.

It lay between the middle-class area close to Sycamore Park and a working-class estate with a handful of shops including a small general store, a greengrocer, a takeaway fish shop, a pharmacy and a post office. There was also a bus stop. A well-trodden footpath, obviously used as a short cut by local residents, led directly across it. According to PC Jenks, while most of the people on the estate were good citizens, law-abiding, hard-working folk who kept their properties in good order and their children under control, a few families were generally regarded by the majority as 'neighbours from hell' and were the subject of regular complaints about antisocial behaviour. 'Quite a few have form and there's a lot of fly-tipping goes on – mostly old tyres, unwanted mattresses and other stuff they can't be bothered to take to the tip,' Jenks went on, 'but as far as I know none of them's been done for GBH.'

'Speaking for myself, I wouldn't fancy walking over there after dark,' Vicky observed. 'I take it she's the one who found the body.' She nodded in the direction of a middle-aged woman clutching a shopping bag, who was apparently being comforted by a woman constable.

'That's right. She's pretty shocked, which is natural enough. She keeps on saying "nothing like that's ever happened round here before". I can confirm that; we've never been asked to patrol here at night and we've had no reports of muggings. Quite a few people living on this side use it in the daytime to walk across to the shops or catch the bus.'

Two CSIs were already in attendance and had laid out stepping boards from the road and along the side of the footpath to a tangle of bramble bushes. A short distance away Rathbone was conferring with the pathologist, Doctor Handley; DC Penny Osborne stood a little apart from them with a handkerchief to her mouth. 'Are you OK?' Sukey asked her, concerned at the young DC's pallor.

Penny swallowed hard and pushed the handkerchief into her pocket, looking faintly embarrassed. 'It's . . . she looks sort of greenish . . . and there's a nasty smell when you get close. And the flies . . . they've laid their eggs in her eyes . . . it's just horrible! The Sarge says that means she's been there some time . . . she's begun to decompose.' She gave herself a little shake and squared her shoulders. 'Don't worry, I'll be fine. Thanks for asking.'

Seeing Sukey and Vicky, Rathbone beckoned them over. 'You've come at the right moment,' he said. He too had been holding a handkerchief to his face and the pathologist had put on a mask. 'The CSIs have just finished taking their shots and Doc Handley's about to have a closer look at her. I should warn you, she's in a pretty poor condition.'

The dead woman lay face upwards, almost hidden behind the brambles. Her eyes were closed and her features appeared relaxed, the lips slightly parted. 'You might think she'd just fallen asleep,' said Sukey softly, 'except for the pong and . . .' There was no need to say more; the ugly bruises round the slender throat told how the woman had died.

'I reckon you're right about her origins, Sukey,' said Vicky.

Sukey nodded. 'Her colouring and cast of feature could be Middle Eastern or possibly Indian. She looks quite young; she can't be much more than twenty.'

Meanwhile, Handley had finished his examination and was peeling off his protective gloves. 'What can you tell us, Doc?' asked Rathbone.

'First impressions are that the cause of death was manual strangulation, but I can't be sure till I get her on the slab. From the state of decomposition I'd say she's been dead three or four days. I'm surprised it's taken so long for anyone to find her – I'd have thought a dog walker would have spotted her long before this. The smell's enough to attract any dog.'

'According to the local copper it's not an area much used by dog walkers,' said Rathbone. 'It's not safe to let them off the lead; there's too much litter lying around, especially broken glass. The woman who found her is interested in wildlife; she thought she saw a rare butterfly flitting around the brambles and went over to investigate.' He gave a wry grin. 'The poor dear staggered back and threw up on the spot, as you may have noticed.'

Handley grinned. 'I'm not surprised. I noticed your young DC nearly did the same.' He closed his bag. 'I'll be off now. I'll let you know when I'm ready to do the PM.' He made his way back to his car, ducking under the blue and white tape barrier with which uniformed officers were enclosing the area, despite the protests of a few women with shopping bags. 'Sorry, ladies,' Jenks apologized, 'I'm afraid this is a crime scene so you'll have to go the long way round to the shops.' One or two hurried away, grumbling and complaining that they were going to miss their bus, but the rest remained behind to watch what was going on and were soon joined by others.

'Amazing how word gets around,' commented Rathbone. 'I didn't think it'd be long before *they* got wind of it,' he added resignedly as a van with *Bristol Echo – Your Favourite Newspaper* painted on its side slid into the gap left by Handley's car. The driver got out and began plying Jenks with questions. A second man with a camcorder hovered at his elbow.

Rathbone took out his mobile. 'Now Handley's finished I'll call for a hearse,' he said. 'While we're waiting for them to come and take her to the morgue you can bring me up to date.' He listened in silence to their report and then said, 'It certainly begins to look as if that's Aggie's body and from what you say we may have a problem finding her next of kin. If it is her it means Ellerman's well and truly back in the frame. Yes?' he said as one of the CSIs approached holding out his camera.

'Found this in some soft earth just under the brambles, Sarge,' he said. 'We thought you'd like to see it before we take a cast.'

Rathbone inspected the picture. 'Looks promising,' he said. 'We'll come and have a look.' Together with the two DCs he studied the impression of a man's shoe, clearly visible in the soft earth. 'It's a good, clear print – size ten or thereabouts so it's almost certainly a man's and from the depth of the impression he was carrying a heavy weight. At a guess, I'd say he'd left his car over there, where our lot are parked.' He handed the camera back. 'Nice work, Andy. Anything else?'

'Nothing along the path itself; the grass has worn away and the ground has been trodden too hard to show prints. The grass and stuff has been trodden down between the path and the place where the body was found, but we didn't find anything useful.'

'Well, the shoe print is pretty distinctive, so let's hope that'll be enough to nail the bastard,' said Rathbone with considerable feeling. 'Here's the hearse . . . now the ghouls are in for a treat.'

The four detectives waited in a respectful silence as the body was lifted on to a stretcher, covered and taken away. The moment they had gone Rathbone and his team returned to the road to face the reporters, who plied them with questions. 'All I can tell you at this stage is that the body of a woman has been recovered from the area known as Fiddler's Patch,' he said. 'She has not yet been identified and a statement will be issued in due course.' To the knot of curious onlookers he said, 'I advise all you good people to return home and leave us to get on with our enquiries.' Followed by the three DCs he returned to the rendezvous point, ignoring the barrage of further questions. 'See you back at HQ,' he said to Sukey and Vicky as he and Penny got into their car.

'I've got a feeling this is going to be a long day,' said Sukey as she and Vicky prepared to follow them.

Rathbone had evidently alerted DCI Leach on the way back to HQ and as soon as the team reassembled they went straight to his office.

'OK, Greg, what have you been able to find out about the dead woman?' Leach began.

'So far, not a great deal I'm afraid, sir,' said Rathbone. 'We think she's probably a woman known as Aggie, possibly of Middle Eastern or Indian origins, who works as a cleaner for an outfit called Clean as a Whistle and hasn't been seen for several days with no explanation. Tim and Mike have interviewed her employer and we hope she'll be willing to go to the morgue to see if she can identify the dead woman, but I gather they haven't yet been able to contact her again. It was pure chance she was in her office earlier today – she isn't normally there on a Saturday but she had some admin jobs to catch up on. Mike will give you the latest.'

'We tried her number about an hour ago, as soon as we'd seen the body,' said Mike. 'There was no reply – just a recorded message to say the office was closed till Monday morning. We checked in the personal directory under Shilling, but the only one turned out to be a reverend gentleman who was most affronted at the notion that his wife might run a domestic agency. Our Mrs Shilling must have a landline, so we assume she's ex-directory.'

'So no hope in that direction until Monday,' said Leach resignedly. He turned to Sukey. 'I gather you and Vicky have been to Aggie's flat. What did you find there?' He listened attentively while Sukey gave their report. 'Do you think there's reason to think the dead woman is Aggie?' he said when she had finished.

'Yes we do, sir, and we think it's significant that she hasn't been seen since she cleaned for Marcus Ellerman on Wednesday.'

'What about the other woman – the one called Minnie who told the handyman about Aggie getting het up over having seen the knife? Have you spoken to her?'

'Not yet, sir,' said Vicky. 'We have her address and we planned to call on her after leaving Aggie's place, but then DS Rathbone told us about the body on Fiddler's Patch and instructed us to go straight over there.'

'I see.' Leach doodled on his pad for a few moments. 'You think Aggie's a Catholic; maybe Minnie can tell you what church she goes to. If so, go and see the priest and ask if he knows her well enough to identify her. And if all else fails, maybe Minnie would be willing to help with the ID if Mrs Shilling refuses.'

'Well, you were right about it being a long day,' said Vicky as, the meeting over, she and Sukey went back to their car. 'Let's hope Minnie isn't quite as fierce as Aggie's neighbour.'

Minnie's address was a bungalow in a development of retirement dwellings about a mile from Holmwood, set in pleasant gardens with a small lake in the centre of a circular lawn. The name beside the bell push was Jackson and the door was opened by a man of about seventy, with white hair, clear hazel eyes and an upright bearing that to Sukey suggested a military background. 'Yes?' he said enquiringly.

'We apologize for troubling you,' said Sukey, 'but we're from Avon and Somerset CID and we need to speak to Mrs Minnie Jackson.'

'Police eh?' he said as he inspected their IDs. 'You'd better come in.' He closed the door behind them and led them into a cosy combined sitting and dining room where a table was laid for a meal. 'I hope this won't take long – we're just about to have our supper. The wife's in the kitchen. Min!' he called, 'you're wanted by the police. What've you been up to?' he added, winking at the two detectives.

'Police?' A pleasant-looking woman of a similar age to her husband emerged, holding a tea towel. She looked enquiringly at the two detectives. 'Why do you want to speak to me?'

'We think you may be able to help us with some enquiries and we'd like to ask you a few questions,' said Sukey. 'It will only take a few minutes. Perhaps you'd like to sit down.'

'I'll help if I can.' She handed the tea towel to her husband and sat down on the sofa. 'Go and turn the gas down under the potatoes, Vic.' He disappeared for a moment and then returned and sat beside her. They exchanged slightly anxious glances before looking back at the detectives. 'All right, I'm ready,' she said.

'We understand you're employed by Clean as a Whistle cleaning agency and that you do a regular cleaning job at Holmwood Care Centre,' Sukey began.

'That's right. Three mornings a week for a couple of hours – Mondays, Wednesdays and Fridays. I've been doing it for several years.'

'I've been on at her several times lately to give it up,' her husband interposed. 'It isn't as if we need the money.'

'I enjoy chatting to the people there . . . and it gives me something to do while you're playing golf,' she retorted. She turned back to Sukey. 'What do you want to know?'

'We're enquiring into the death of a young woman whose body was found today on a piece of wasteland known as Fiddler's Patch. We have reason to believe it may be that of a woman employed by the same agency who hasn't been seen for several days. We understand that her name is Aggie, and that she has at some time spoken to you about the knife used to kill Fenella Tremaine.'

Minnie turned pale and clutched her husband's hand. 'Oh, no! I told her . . . I begged her to tell you about it,' she said shakily, 'but for some reason she was too scared. She wouldn't say why.' She took a paper tissue from her pocket and dabbed her eyes. 'Do you really think this dead woman might be Aggie?'

'We can't be sure,' said Vicky. 'We need formal identification, but we have no idea how to contact her next of kin. As the two of you have been seen speaking together several times we're wondering if you can help us.'

Minnie shook her head. 'I'm sorry, I've no idea. She's always been quite cagey about her family. I know she's a Catholic – I've an idea she goes to the Sacred Heart church in Westover. Maybe the priest there could help you.'

'Thank you, that's very useful; we'll certainly go and see him after we've spoken to you,' said Sukey. 'Now, about the knife, did Aggie give you any idea where she saw it?'

'None at all,' said Minnie. 'Actually, it wasn't the knife itself, but the sheath. She saw a picture of it in the *Echo* with the report that it had been found and got very agitated; she said she'd seen it, but when I asked her where or when that was she clammed up. I told her she should report it at once, but the mention of the police seemed to scare the pants off her.'

'What day was this?' asked Vicky.

'It was . . . let me think . . . yes of course, it was Wednesday of last week. She was helping out at Holmwood that morning – two of the residents had left and their rooms had to be thoroughly cleaned ready for the next people to move in so I was extra busy. The report in the *Echo* was on the front page of the midday edition – it's delivered to the home every day. She must have picked it up off the hall table; she came rushing to the room where I was working with it in her hand. She was shaking and looking quite shocked.

'And that's really all you can tell us?'

Minnie shook her head in evident regret at her inability to help further. 'I'm afraid so.'

'We understand she did her regular cleaning job last Wednesday, presumably after she left Holmwood. Do you remember what time that was?'

'It must have been about a quarter to twelve. She said she had to catch the bus that stops just by the gate. Now I come to think of it, I had a feeling she wasn't all that keen to go to her next job.'

'Do you know where the next job was?'

'I'm afraid not – Mrs Shilling at the agency will tell you.'

'Could you give us a description of her?'

Minnie half closed her eyes and thought for a moment. 'I think she may be either Indian or from one of the Arab countries because of her colouring. Straight black hair, sort of coffee-coloured skin. Rather pretty in fact. Slight build, about my height.'

'Age?'

'Somewhere in the late teens, at a guess. Does that mean . . .?'

'All we can say at the moment is that your description fits that of the dead woman in some respects,' said Sukey. 'We shall of course do our best to trace her next of kin, but if we are unable to do so and her priest can't help, would you be willing to come with us to the morgue to see if you can identify her?'

'Oh dear . . . I'm not sure if I could . . .' Minnie faltered, clearly shocked at the suggestion.

'You don't have to answer right away,' said Vicky. 'We just want to know how you feel about it if we can't trace anyone close to her.'

'Of course she will,' her husband said firmly. 'It's your duty,' he told his wife, seeing her look of horror at the prospect. 'I hope it won't be necessary, but if it is I'll come with you. We owe it to the poor woman to do whatever we can. And I'm sure,' he added, turning back to the detectives, 'we both hope you'll find the person who killed her.'

'We will,' Sukey assured him.

# TWENTY-TWO

'Whatever the Jacksons were having for supper sure smelt good,' said Sukey with feeling as she and Vicky returned to their car. 'It seems like forever since we had anything to eat – I'm starving!'

'Me too,' Vicky agreed. 'I wonder if there's a pub anywhere near the church where we could pop in for a snack before calling on the priest.'

Sukey glanced at her watch. 'It's ten past seven. We'd better locate the church first and then decide. I've got a feeling we drove past it on our way to Aggie's flat.'

They found the church without difficulty. There was only one car in the parking area and she pulled in beside it. 'It doesn't look as if there's a service on,' she said. 'Perhaps that's the priest's car. He may be inside; let's try the door.'

The door was unlocked and they cautiously pushed it open and stepped inside. The scent of incense hung in the air and the sanctuary lamp glowed red in a side chapel. Slanting rays of the late evening sun through the stained glass window above the west door laid a multicoloured mosaic of light on the aisle. 'It's beautiful, isn't it?' Sukey said softly.

'Sure is,' Vicky agreed. There appeared to be no one about, but after a moment they heard the murmur of voices. 'There's obviously someone here. Shall we go and investigate?'

Sukey put a finger to her lips and ushered her to the door. 'We'd better wait outside,' she whispered. 'I don't think we should interrupt.'

'Interrupt what?' Vicky asked as Sukey closed the door carefully behind them.

'I'm not exactly sure, but something's just occurred to me. Let's go and have a look at the notice board.' They studied the information on the board; below the name of the priest in charge and the list of services was the time for hearing confessions. 'From six to seven on Saturdays,' Sukey read aloud. 'I thought that might be what those murmurings were about.'

'In that case it's a good job we didn't go barging in,' said Vicky. 'The presbytery's next door – I saw the notice on the gate as you drove in. There's sure to be a housekeeper; why don't we find out what time Father –' she glanced back at the board – 'Father Burke is likely to be finished. He's running late as it is,' she added. 'It's almost half past seven.'

'That's not a bad idea,' Sukey agreed.

The housekeeper was a plump woman with short, straight grey hair and a bloom on her rosy complexion that owed nothing to make-up. 'You'd better come in and wait; he should be back any minute,' she said after they had explained the reason for their call. 'I hope your business won't take too long; the poor man had to go without a proper lunch because . . . ah, here he is,' she added, her face lighting up with pleasure at the sound of a key in the lock. 'These two ladies are from the police, and they think you might be able to help them,' she explained in response to his inquiring glance at Sukey and Vicky. 'Just ring the bell when you're ready for your supper, Father.'

'Thank you, Mavis,' he said with a smile and she hurried away.

Father Burke, a tall, striking figure with strong features, ushered them into a book-lined study and pulled up a couple of chairs for them before sitting down behind his desk. 'How may I help you?'

'We're enquiring into the disappearance of a woman known as Aggie – which we believe is short for Aghami – but we don't know her surname,' Sukey began. 'We have been told she worships at your church.' Reading from their notes, the two detectives gave Father Burke all the information they had about Aggie and their reasons for believing she might be the woman found dead on Fiddler's Patch. He listened at first with careful attention, then with dawning recognition and finally with concern.

'This is very distressing news. Poor woman.' He made the sign of the cross. 'May she rest in peace, whoever she is.' He reflected for a moment before saying, 'Your description could certainly apply to a young woman who comes to hear Mass in this church from time to time, although I'm afraid I don't know her name or anything about her. She seems very shy and retiring . . . almost, I would say, withdrawn. She sits at the back of the church and leaves as soon as the service is over. She doesn't come to confession so I have never had an opportunity to speak to her. I'm afraid I know nothing of her family or where she comes from.'

'We're doing our best to trace them,' said Vicky, 'but we haven't much to go on at present except that, as we explained, for some reason she is afraid of the police. Her handbag – if she had one – is missing, but we hope it will turn up, in which case it may contain some clues to her identity.'

'I certainly hope so,' said Father Burke, 'and if there's anything at all that I can do to help, don't hesitate to ask.'

'If all else fails, we may ask if you would be willing to come to the morgue to see if you can identify her,' said Sukey, and he gave a grave nod.

'Of course.'

'I guess we'd better update the Sarge,' said Sukey as the door of the presbytery closed behind them.

'OK, you do that,' said Vicky. 'I'm going to update Chris; he's been sending me texts for the past hour wanting to know when I'm going to be home.' She spoke on her mobile. 'Hi, we've had one hell of a day with no time to eat and we're both famished. Sukey's just checking with the Sarge and I know we're hoping we can sign off. Looks like it,' she added as Sukey gave her a thumbs-up, 'yes, glory be, we're on our way home. See you soon. And rustle up something special, there's a love . . . What? Hang on a minute, I'll ask her.' She turned to Sukey. 'He wants to know if you'd like to join us for a meal.'

Sukey shook her head. 'That's very kind, but I've sent Harry a text to say I'm on my way home and to get something out of the freezer. The Sarge says Tim's been trying to contact Ellerman but he's not answering his phone,' she went on. 'He's checked with the SIO, who says we might as well go home and try again tomorrow. And seeing as we can't get much further until we talk to him, with any luck he's away for the weekend and we can all have tomorrow off.'

'In our dreams!' said Vicky as they headed for home.

'Harry and I had planned a romantic evening together,' Sukey sighed. 'I'm beginning to wonder what possessed me to join the CID.'

Vicky laughed. 'I guess we all have moments like that – especially when there's nothing really interesting to get our teeth into.'

When Sukey reached home, Harry was waiting for her. He gave her a quick hug and then held her at arm's length for a moment, studying her face with concern. 'Darling, you look exhausted,' he said. He ran his fingers through her hair and gently kissed her on the brow. 'Come and relax with a snifter.'

'That's exactly what I need,' she said, sinking gratefully on to the sofa.

'I guess it's the Fiddler's Patch murder that's kept you so late,' he said as he handed her a glass of red wine and sat down beside her.

'Right first time – and with the usual caveat.'

'Don't worry, I know better than to try and pre-empt the official statement,' he assured her. 'On the contrary, I might have a bit of info for you. Major Howes rang me this evening and it's possible what he was saying could be of interest to your people.'

'I'm not sure my brain is capable of taking in any more stuff this evening,' she said wearily. 'At least, not until I've had something to eat. What are we having, by the way?'

'Lasagne, and it won't be ready for fifteen minutes so I'll tell you anyway. Major Howes saw the report in this evening's *Echo* and he couldn't wait to tell me he recalled overhearing a conversation between two women – a carer and a part-time cleaner. He's certain they mentioned Fiddler's Patch; he isn't sure, but he thinks they were talking about buses to Holmwood. He's wondering if by any chance one of them could be the murder victim.'

Sukey took a long pull at her wine before saying, 'I don't suppose Major Howes gave a description of the . . . either of the women?'

'Aha, so it rings a bell. And you nearly let drop which of the two you think might be of interest, didn't you?'

'*Touché*,' she admitted. 'Don't tease, Harry; this might be very important.'

'All right. Howes went on to say that the cleaner wasn't one of the regulars but one who comes in as a relief from time to time. He's never spoken to her but from her accent and her colouring he thinks she might be Indian or Pakistani. This means something to you, doesn't it?'

Sukey nodded. 'Yes, I'm afraid it does,' she said sadly.

'You think you know the identity of the dead woman, don't you? All right,' he said hastily, seeing that she was about to protest, 'I'm not going to ask you any more questions now . . . but if there's anything you think a dedicated news-hound can do to help I hope you'll bear me in mind.'

'I will,' she promised. 'Now, what about that lasagne?'

At about the time that DCs Sukey Reynolds and Vicky Armstrong were interviewing Father Burke, Patsy Godwin was relaxing in her sitting room with her feet up and Henry blissfully purring on her lap. She had been watching a quiz programme that had just ended and she reached for the remote and switched off the television. She put her feet on the floor, dislodging Henry, who ceased purring, sprang from her lap and turned on landing to give her a reproachful glare.

'There's no need to look at me like that,' she teased him. 'You know it's supper time so you'd have had to move anyway.' The cat immediately made for the kitchen; Patsy was about to follow him when the telephone rang. 'Oh bother, who's that?' she muttered as she picked up the instrument. 'Hullo? Oh Kate, lovely to hear from you. How are . . . hang on a minute, stop gabbling . . . what's that? Another murder? Good Heavens! Where?' She listened for a few seconds and then broke in. 'Look, just try and calm down and tell me quietly . . . what? You mean now?' Patsy glanced at the clock. 'I was just about to have my supper and I'm not sure if I . . . oh, I see, you've had yours. Well, all right then, for a couple of nights . . . how are you going to get here? . . . Oh, that's very good of him. See you in about an hour then. Bye.'

She turned off the phone and went into the kitchen where Henry was sitting expectantly beside his empty food bowl. 'You'll never guess what's happened,' she informed him as she spooned food into the bowl. 'Your Auntie Kate is having kittens – haha! – because a body's been found about a mile from where she lives and she's babbling on about a serial killer and she's afraid to stay another night in Sycamore Park so she wants to come and

stay with us for a few days.' At the mention of Kate's name
Henry briefly looked up from his food. 'You like your Auntie
Kate don't you? She's got a soft spot for you as well – you'll
have a choice of laps.'

She ate her ham salad followed by fruit yogurt and then went
upstairs to check that all was in order in her little guest room.
She put out clean towels and was on her way downstairs when
the front doorbell rang. Kate stood there, ashen faced and trem-
bling. Behind her was John Yardley, carrying a small suitcase.

Kate flung her arms round her cousin. 'Oh Patsy, it's so good
of you to have me at such short notice,' she said breathlessly.
'And dear John has been wonderful – he dropped everything to
bring me.'

'I was glad to be of service,' he said with what struck Patsy
as uncharacteristic gravity.

'Come in, both of you. You can leave that down here for the
moment,' she added, pointing to the case. 'I've made coffee –
would you like some?'

'Coffee would be lovely, thank you.' They followed her into
the sitting room; as they entered, Henry emerged from the kitchen
and Kate held out a hand. 'Come and say hullo to your Auntie
Kate!' she cooed. The cat stared for a moment and then deliberately turned and went back into the kitchen.

Patsy burst out laughing. 'I think he won't talk to you because
John's here. I do believe he's jealous! Never mind him, just sit
down while I fetch the coffee and then you can tell me all about
this latest murder. I see you've brought the *Echo* – is the story
in there?'

While her guests drank their coffee, Patsy scanned the account
of the discovery of the body. 'This area they call Fiddler's Patch,
Kate,' she said. 'Where is it, exactly?'

'It's an acre or so of wasteland a short distance from Sycamore
Park,' said Kate. 'There's a footpath across it; a lot of people
use it as a short cut to the shops and the bus stop . . . I used to
use it myself, but now John takes me if I need to go shopping.'
She gave him a grateful glance and he nodded and patted her
hand.

'It's always a pleasure,' he said.

'Just think, if I was still having to walk that way, it might have been me who found . . . it . . . her!' Kate shuddered at the thought. 'The minute I read about it in the paper I rang John . . . I was terrified . . . afraid to leave the flat. It was his idea that I ring you.'

'I hope I did the right thing?' he said with a glance at Patsy. 'Of course you did,' she assured him. 'More coffee?'

'No, thank you; I'll be going now. Goodbye for now, Kate. Try not to worry; you're in good hands.'

She grasped his hand and smiled up at him. 'You're such a good friend, John,' she said huskily. 'You know, Patsy,' she said when her cousin returned from seeing him to the door, 'He's trying to be sensible and reassuring for my sake, but I'm sure he's as worried about this latest murder as I am.'

'I'm not surprised,' said Patsy. 'I expect a lot of people are – I'm beginning to feel that way myself. Ah, here's Henry,' she added as the cat emerged from wherever he had been lurking. Perhaps he'll talk to you now his rival's gone home!'

# TWENTY-THREE

Sukey awoke on Sunday morning feeling relaxed, happy and at peace with the world. She raised herself on one elbow to check the time; it was just eight o'clock and she lay back on her pillow with a little sigh of contentment. Harry stirred and mumbled sleepily, 'Do we have to get up?'

'Not yet,' she whispered in his ear, 'it's Sunday and we both have a day off.' She snuggled down beside him and closed her eyes, enjoying the smooth warmth of his body and the regular sound of his breathing. She was dozing off when her phone rang.

'Don't answer that,' Harry grunted from beneath the duvet.

'I'd better,' she said resignedly. 'There might have been some development in the Fiddler's Patch murder I should know about.'

'If it's your bossy sergeant, tell him you're not available,' said Harry, by now wide awake. 'He said you weren't needed till tomorrow, remember?'

The phone continued to ring and she picked it up. 'Hullo . . .

sorry Sarge, I was asleep . . . what? . . . where? . . . all right, give me time to get dressed.'

'Something tells me your day off is off,' said Harry as she hung up. 'At least, you're not going anywhere without some breakfast.' He got out of bed and pulled on trousers and a sweat-shirt. 'I'll fix you something while you're getting ready.'

'Bless you.' She blew him a kiss on her way to the shower, emerging five minutes later vigorously towelling her body dry before brushing her damp chocolate-brown curls into shape. By the time she was dressed Harry had brewed coffee and put cereal, toast, butter and marmalade on the kitchen table.

'So what's going on?' he asked as she sat down, shook corn-flakes into a bowl and added milk.

'Uniformed reported that Ellerman returned home around midnight,' she told him. She polished off the cereal, buttered a slice of toast and spread it thickly with marmalade. 'I'm to rendez-vous with Rathbone and Vicky at Sycamore Park. We're going to pull him in for questioning because—' She broke off and clapped a hand to her mouth. 'Oh, gosh, I shouldn't be telling you this!'

'It's the least you can do in return for supplying your need for nourishment,' he retorted as he filled a mug with coffee, topped it up with milk and put it front of her.

'I suppose I should be thankful the *Echo* doesn't have a Sunday edition,' she said resignedly. 'Harry, you won't . . .?'

'You know you can trust me,' he assured her. 'I haven't let you down yet, have I?'

'That's true,' she admitted, 'but in this case it really is very important there are no leaks. There's been an awful stink over another case – nothing I was involved in, thank goodness – where stuff got into the papers that wasn't supposed to be published and there's a suggestion that someone in the police fed them with information incriminating a suspect who turned out to be innocent and is now threatening to sue.'

'Don't worry,' said Harry. 'Our editor has hammered all this into us until he's blue in the face – he's just as anxious as you are that we don't blot our copybook.'

'Make sure he keeps it that way.' She finished her food, drank the last of her coffee and put on her jacket. 'I have to go now; I'll be in touch when I get back.'

'Have a good day. See you later, darling.' He gave her a quick hug and a kiss before pouring coffee for himself and putting more bread in the toaster. 'I'll clear this lot away before I go home. Dad'll be pleased to see me – he'll probably suggest golf and lunch at the club.'

'Have a nice day then. Bye.'

There was little traffic about and within fifteen minutes she had reached the mobile police station that had been stationed close to the Sycamore Park flats ever since the discovery of Fenella Tremaine's body. She found Rathbone drinking coffee and talking to Sergeant Drury.

'Ellerman came back shortly after midnight, put his car in the garage and went straight to his flat,' Rathbone informed her. 'The light came on after a few minutes and went out about half an hour later. We know he hasn't left the building again because Sergeant Drury has been keeping an eye on the front entrance and young PC Dandridge has been covering the back. Not that we have any reason to suppose he'll be thinking of leaving. It's possible, as he was out all day yesterday, that he hasn't heard about the discovery of the body.'

'Even if he had, he'd hardly do a runner,' Drury remarked. 'That would be as good as an admission of guilt. He's a cocky devil; he's managed to cover his tracks so far so maybe he thinks he's done it this time. I gather you and Vicky have a good idea who the victim is, but haven't found any definite proof of identify?' he added, turning to Sukey.

'Not yet, Sarge. We hope to get more information tomorrow from the owner of the cleaning agency where we think she worked.' As she spoke there was the sound of a car approaching. She glanced out of the door of the van. 'Here's Vicky.' She felt her pulse quicken with excitement. Her initial resentment at having to leave the warm bed she had shared with Harry was forgotten.

'Morning all,' said Vicky as she entered the van. 'Do I take it we've got some real evidence against Ellerman at last, Sarge?'

'Let's just say that uniformed have found a couple of witnesses who remembered seeing a woman answering to the description of the murder victim entering A block some time after midday on Wednesday. One of them – a semi-invalid lady who spends quite a lot of time sitting by her front window – told PC Dandridge she'd seen her before at about the same time on previous Wednesdays and she quite often sees her leave an hour or so later, but—' Rathbone broke off to take a mouthful of coffee.

'But she didn't see her leave this time?' Vicky anticipated.

'Exactly. And not only that, the same lady often sees Ellerman leave at around nine o'clock in the morning; she says he doesn't normally come home during the day, but on this particular Wednesday she happened to spot him returning at about half past eleven, which she says was unusual.'

'She's almost too good to be true,' Sukey chuckled. 'I assume she's a reliable witness and not some ditzy old dear with a vivid imagination?'

'On the contrary, she's a dedicated supporter of Neighbourhood Watch and Dandridge often drops in for a chat with her. Anyway, we already know from Mrs Shilling that Aggie cleans for Ellerman so it looks like Wednesday was her regular day, which ties in with what Minnie told you and Sukey. That's something Mike and Tim will have to confirm when they see her tomorrow.'

'From what Minnie told us, Sarge' said Sukey, 'Aggie was in a pretty agitated state after reading the report about the dagger sheath being found and wasn't all that happy about her next job, so maybe she already had reason to think Ellerman had something to do with the Tremaine murder. But,' she added after a moment's reflection, 'if she was that scared, why not make some excuse not to turn up?'

'There could be more than one reason,' Drury pointed out. 'Maybe she needed the money and was afraid she'd lose her job if she failed to show. But if it was Ellerman she was scared of because she'd seen the dagger in his flat, why didn't she show any sign of it at the time of the Tremaine murder? It was the lead story in the *Echo* for days; that was two weeks ago and so far as we know she didn't get upset over that.'

'Maybe she hadn't heard about it,' said Vicky. 'Maybe she doesn't normally see the *Echo*. It could have been pure chance that she spotted the report on the front page of the paper she saw at Holmwood.'

'Or maybe she read about it when she was on her own, so no

one saw her having a wobbly . . . but I guess you could be right,' Drury admitted with a shrug.

'Anyway,' said Sukey, 'going by what the witness saw from her window she went straight to Ellerman's place after leaving Holmwood.'

Rathbone nodded. 'I think we can take that as fairly certain. It's frustrating that Mike and Tim won't be able to speak to Mrs Shilling until tomorrow to ask whether Aggie was supposed to clean for anyone else after Ellerman on Wednesday. Their understanding is that it's only the Thursday and Friday clients who reported her non-appearance, but they'll need to check.'

'At least this should put paid to any possibility of the Seatons' involvement,' said Rathbone. 'Unless,' he added sardonically, 'Seaton was making a play for Aggie so Carla decided to nip things in the bud, jumped into her car, followed Aggie's bus with the intention of grabbing her and throttling her in broad daylight at the earliest opportunity.'

There were chuckles all round at what they were agreed was an unlikely scenario and they set off to call on Marcus Ellerman.

'This is an outrage!' exclaimed Jason Pollard. 'On behalf of my client –' he indicated Marcus Ellerman, who was sitting on the sofa beside him – 'I object most strongly to the high-handed manner in which you have come barging into his home on what should be a day of rest and relaxation without giving him a word of explanation.'

They were in Ellerman's sitting room; he had answered the door at their third ring, unshaven and still in his dressing gown. Sukey guessed from his flushed cheeks and apparent sensitivity to the light that he was suffering from a hangover – an impression confirmed by the fact that he swallowed two aspirins while awaiting Pollard's arrival.

'The only explanation your client allowed us time to give,' said Rathbone, 'was that we wanted to ask him some questions about the woman whose body was found yesterday about a mile away. His first reaction was to try and shut the door; when prevented from doing so—'

'By force,' Ellerman interrupted.

'I put my foot in the door and threatened to arrest him on the spot if he refused to cooperate,' Rathbone explained, still speaking to Pollard. 'There was no question of excessive force; we merely pushed past him when he declined to admit us. He then refused to say another word without your presence and immediately contacted you. And I should like to express our appreciation of your very prompt response, sir, and we apologize for causing you what is undoubtedly a considerable inconvenience.'

'Humph,' Pollard grunted with little sign of being mollified. 'I hope you have good reason for this intrusion.'

'We believe we have. We are investigating the suspicious death of a young woman whose body was found yesterday on a piece of wasteland known as Fiddler's Patch.' He turned to Ellerman. 'You have lived here for a considerable time, so I assume you are familiar with that area? We understand quite a few of the locals use it as a short cut to the shops.'

'Of course I know *of* it, but I'm hardly familiar with it,' said Ellerman disdainfully.

'So at least you know where it is?' said Rathbone patiently.

'I've driven past it many times but I've never walked across it myself.' Ellerman's tone was dismissive. 'Who is this woman anyway, and what has her death got to do with me?'

'We have reason to believe she may be an employee of the Clean as a Whistle cleaning agency. We understand that your flat is regularly cleaned by a lady from that agency – is that right?'

Sukey noticed that at the mention of the agency Ellerman gave a slight start and his belligerent attitude appeared to soften. He hesitated for a moment before saying, 'I have a contract with the cleaning agency you mention, yes. The lady who cleans my flat is employed by them.' He spoke slowly with a hand to his eyes, as if groping in his memory for something half forgotten.

'Do you happen to know her name?'

'Good heavens no – why on earth should I? In fact,' he went on, this time with renewed confidence, 'she comes when I'm out; I'm in my office all day Monday to Friday and that's why I agreed, subject to the usual assurances about the woman's honesty and so forth, to allow the agency to supply her with a key.'

'Are you telling us that you have never set eyes on this woman?'

'Haven't I just said so?'

'Do you at least know which day she comes to clean your flat?'

'I can always tell when she's been by the state of the place.' He put a hand to his forehead again and winced. 'I think . . . yes, that's right . . . I'm pretty sure Wednesday's her day. Excuse me, I need . . .' Walking a trifle unsteadily, he left the room.

It was some time before he returned and sat down. Before Rathbone could speak, Pollard said, 'Really, Sergeant, even if the dead woman turns out to be the same woman who cleans my client's flat, it seems clear from what he has told you that he cannot possibly be involved in her death, nor have any motive for killing her. As you can see, he is far from well and I am therefore advising him not to answer any more questions. On his behalf I am asking you and your colleagues to leave.' He stood up, and then sat down again as Rathbone put up a hand.

'Not so fast, sir. I have further questions for your client. His indisposition doesn't appear to be serious and if he refuses to answer we shall have no alternative but to arrest him.'

Ellerman and Pollard exchanged shocked glances and then looked back at Rathbone. 'And your reason for this assertion, Sergeant?' said Pollard as Ellerman mopped his brow with a handkerchief, apparently bereft of speech.

Ignoring Pollard, Rathbone leaned forward and fixed Ellerman with a penetrating gaze. 'Doctor Ellerman, we have a witness who saw you return to your flat around midday last Wednesday, contrary to your usual practice. The same witness also observed a young woman – whom she has seen on a number of occasions entering the building shortly after midday on Wednesdays – arriving at her usual time. We therefore feel it is safe to assume that she arrived while you were there. She normally leaves a little over an hour after her arrival, but it appears that on this occasion she did not do so. And –' Rathbone paused for a moment, as was his normal practice before delivering his most telling point – 'that young woman has not been seen alive since.'

Ellerman's jaw dropped and he put both hands to his temples and closed his eyes for a moment. 'Oh my God!' he gasped.

He cast an appealing glance at Pollard, who stood up, took him by the arm and drew him to his feet. 'Is there somewhere we can talk?' he said in an urgent whisper.

'In my study,' Ellerman replied.

Pollard turned to Rathbone. 'Sergeant, I insist that you allow me some time to confer with my client.'

Rathbone spread his hands in a conciliatory gesture. 'By all means. We've got the bugger rattled,' he said with satisfaction as the two withdrew, closing the door behind them. 'He didn't bargain for witnesses – there aren't many people around at midday. I wonder what cock-and-bull yarn he'll come up with.' He rubbed his hands together with satisfaction. 'What's the betting he'll give us a good reason to take him back to the station on suspicion and interview him again, this time under caution?'

# TWENTY-FOUR

Marcus Ellerman showed no reaction as DS Rathbone, seated between DCs Sukey Reynolds and Vicky Armstrong, switched on the tape and reminded him that he was being interviewed under caution. When asked if he understood he answered 'Yes' with more than a hint of arrogance as if, Sukey thought, what he would really have liked to say was, 'Of course I understand – do you take me for a halfwit?'

'When I questioned you an hour or so ago about the arrangements you have for cleaning your flat,' Rathbone began, 'you stated that this service has been carried out every Wednesday for the past few weeks by an employee of the Clean as a Whistle agency. You also went on to say – or at least to imply – that you had never seen the woman who does the work because she has a key to your flat and cleans it in the daytime, that is, during your absence. Is that true?'

Ellerman glanced at his lawyer, Jason Pollard, who was seated beside him. 'May I point out, Sergeant,' said Pollard, 'that my client has already admitted inadvertently making a slightly misleading statement due to a temporary lapse of memory.'

'And may I point out,' said Rathbone in a voice that held a hint of steel, 'that the question I have just put to your client was a perfectly straightforward one to which I require a straightforward answer.' He turned back to Ellerman. 'Do you admit to having made that slightly misleading statement –' he made quotation marks with his fingers – 'as your legal adviser puts it?'

'All right, yes . . . I did say that at first,' Ellerman admitted, 'but that was before—'

'Before you were confronted with evidence that proved you were lying?' Rathbone interrupted.

'I was not deliberately lying,' Ellerman retorted angrily. 'As I've already explained, I made a simple mistake . . . I so rarely return home during the day that for the moment I simply forgot. As you know, I'm not feeling very well this morning,' he went on a little peevishly, putting a hand to his forehead as if appealing for sympathy. Behind Rathbone's back, Sukey and Vicky exchanged glances. 'Your unannounced arrival caught me on the hop,' he continued. 'I suppose it just slipped my memory.'

'You so rarely return home during the day,' Rathbone mocked. 'Most people tend to remember anything out of the ordinary, but that doesn't seem to apply in your case. Are you saying your brain can only deal with routine, run-of-the-mill events?'

'I have a very responsible job which requires me to deal with a great many important matters,' Ellerman retorted, evidently stung by the implication. 'Multitasking is something I have to do all the time. As I've just said, your visit so early in the morning was totally unexpected and I spoke without thinking.'

'Ah yes, we caught you on the hop, didn't we? A rather thin excuse for such an obvious error, especially from a man holding a senior position in an industrial company, don't you think?'

'No comment,' said Ellerman after a quick glance at Pollard.

'Doctor Ellerman,' Rathbone continued, 'I put it to you that there was a particular reason why you went back to your flat that day . . . a very urgent reason connected with this.' He picked up a newspaper that was lying on the shelf beside him and passed it across the table. 'For the tape, I am showing Doctor Ellerman the front page of the *Bristol Echo* dated Wednesday the seventh of August. It carries a picture of the sheath belonging to the knife used to kill Fenella Tremaine, found the previous day by a member of the public. Did you see this report?'

Ellerman gave the paper a cursory glance before tossing it back. 'I don't read the local rag,' he said disdainfully.

'Can I take that as "no"?'

'If you like.'

'I am told that the *Echo* is highly regarded for its coverage of regional business affairs and local politics and is read by many people of your standing,' said Rathbone.

Ellerman shrugged. 'That's as may be. I prefer something with a bit more substance, such as the *Financial Times*.'

'Do you recognize the object in the photograph?'

'No comment.'

'Doctor Ellerman, you have previously admitted ownership of the knife used to kill Fenella Tremaine – a knife that you claim was stolen. The detailed workmanship on the sheath in this illustration is identical in design to that on the handle of your knife. Are you suggesting there is no connection between the two?'

'No comment.'

'The report accompanying this picture says that the sheath was recovered in Corley Woods. Do you know the area?'

'I've heard of it.'

'Have you ever been there?'

'Not that I remember.'

'Today is the eleventh of August and the seventh of August, the date this report appeared, was last Wednesday. Wednesday is the day your cleaner comes to clean your flat. Witnesses have told us that in the morning of that particular Wednesday she saw this report and appeared very upset by it. She then appeared uneasy about going to her next job – something the witnesses are convinced was in some way due to the picture of the sheath. Have you any idea why this should be so?'

'None whatsoever.'

'Well I have.' It was clear to Sukey from his tone that Rathbone was beginning to lose patience with Ellerman's evasive replies. 'The woman's next job was to clean your flat, and in the circumstances it is not unreasonable to draw the conclusion that this was the cause of her anxiety. I put it to you,' he went on, leaning forward and thumping the table with his fist to emphasize each point, 'that having used your knife to kill Fenella Tremaine you had the problem of disposing of the sheath. To leave it in one of the skips was out of the question and to discard it in the immediate neighbourhood was also too risky. Sycamore Park and the surrounding area was obviously where the police would begin their search, so you decided to wait for a few days and then find a suitable opportunity to dispose of it some distance away – such as in Corley Woods, for example. Meanwhile, you had to keep it somewhere in your flat – out of sight, naturally, possibly in a drawer in your study – before disposing of it. You saw that report and realized that your cleaner had probably seen it as well. She might even have noticed the knife in the display case before you used it to kill Fenella and thought nothing of it at the time . . . but it suddenly struck you that if she happened to be of a prying nature she might have come across the sheath in the course of her cleaning duties and put two and two together.'

'Really, Sergeant,' said Pollard angrily, 'all this is pure supposition on your part.'

'If you will allow me to finish I think I can show beyond any reasonable doubt that it is the only possible explanation of the woman's reluctance to enter your client's flat on that particular day. Or perhaps,' he turned back to Ellerman, 'you can offer another reason. Have you perhaps made unwelcome advances to her?'

'Certainly not!' said Ellerman indignantly.

'So we have to think of an alternative explanation, which I put it to you is this: even if she had not found the sheath, this report would have reminded her where she saw the actual knife, wouldn't it?'

'Sergeant Rathbone, once again I must object to this line of questioning,' Pollard interrupted a second time before Ellerman had a chance to reply. 'You have not produced a shred of evidence that my client murdered Fenella Tremaine, neither can you even be certain that the woman whose body was found yesterday on Fiddler's Patch and the woman who cleans my client's flat are one and same. People disappear every day for a variety of reasons.' He turned to Ellerman. 'I advise you not to answer that question.'

'Well, Doctor Ellerman?' said Rathbone, ignoring the interruption.

'No comment.'

'All right, let me ask you another question. What was your

reason for coming home at lunchtime on Wednesday, contrary to your normal practice?'

'I've already given you the reason.'

'That was while we were in your flat, so repeat it for the tape, please.'

Ellerman affected exasperation by taking a deep breath and rolling his eyes upwards. 'All right, I'd been working in my spare time for a couple of weeks on research into a small company that I thought Anton Maxworth might be interested in taking over. I'd almost finished but I was anxious to get it out of the way. Things were quiet that particular morning so I decided to take my lunch hour at home and try to get it off my back.'

'Is that the reason you gave your PA or any of your colleagues for unexpectedly leaving the office in the middle of the day?'

'I'm not the office boy and I don't have to account for my every movement,' Ellerman retorted. 'I told her I was going out and would be back after lunch to deal with anything that cropped up in my absence.'

'Was Mr Maxworth aware of what you were doing?'

'No. I didn't see the point of mentioning it until I was ready to put the idea before him.'

'Doctor Ellerman,' said Rathbone, 'I put it to you that the reason you have just given me for returning home at lunchtime on Wednesday is a completely spurious one. Your real motive was to confront the woman who, you feared, might have seen this report –' he made stabbing movements with the newspaper in Ellerman's direction – 'and so be in a position to give evidence which could prove that you were Fenella Tremaine's killer. It was a risk you couldn't afford to take so you invented an excuse to leave the office and return home.'

'That's not true,' Ellerman shouted. It was his turn to bang a fist on the table.

'You were there when she arrived,' Rathbone pursued. 'She was already apprehensive about coming to your flat but, being fairly confident that you would be at work as usual, she was prepared to take the risk – probably because she needed the money and could not afford to lose her job. I can imagine her reaction when she saw you there. She must have been terrified . . . her worst fears were realized . . . no doubt she screamed and tried to run from the flat . . . but you didn't dare let her go because she knew too much . . . you had to silence her . . . and so you strangled her and later disposed of her body on Fiddler's Patch.'

'No!' Ellerman leapt to his feet; the uniformed officer standing on guard behind him moved forward to restrain him, but Pollard intervened by putting a hand on his arm. Reluctantly, Ellerman sat down, pulled out a handkerchief and wiped beads of sweat from his forehead with a shaking hand. 'You've got it all wrong,' he said. 'It wasn't like that.'

'So tell me how it was,' said Rathbone, 'and try telling the truth for a change.'

'I need to use the toilet first.' Rathbone nodded to the uniformed officer, who escorted Ellerman out of the room.

As soon as they returned Pollard said, 'Sergeant Rathbone, before we go any further I wish to confer with my client. May I also remind you that my client has had very little to eat this morning and he is still feeling slightly unwell. I therefore request a break from questioning so that he may take a rest and have some nourishment.'

'Very well, Mr Pollard,' said Rathbone. 'Interview suspended at twelve o'clock.' He switched off the tape. 'We'll resume questioning your client in three hours' time.' He left the room, accompanied by Sukey and Vicky.

'He's going to be a tough nut to crack, by the looks of it,' said DCI Leach after he had listened to Rathbone's report. 'Uniformed are going over his flat with a tooth comb,' he went on. 'So far, none of the shoes they found appear to match the impression taken from the crime scene, but he takes the same size so he probably disposed of the ones he was wearing the day he killed the cleaner. We've got his toothbrush and one or two other personal items for DNA samples to be compared with DNA taken from the dead woman. It'll take time for the results to come through, of course – the Super will no doubt put in the usual request for fast-tracking – so if we can't get a confession out of him within a reasonable time we'll simply have to bail him again.'

'We're doing our best, sir,' said Rathbone. 'We know from past experience that Pollard's a wily old bird and given half a chance he'll play the sympathy card – accuse us of bullying a sick man.'

'Sick?' queried Leach.

'He was well and truly hung-over, sir,' said Sukey.

'He had to go to the loo to throw up,' Vicky added, 'and then used body language in an attempt to rouse sympathy.' She gave an impromptu impression, to which Leach responded with a slightly raised eyebrow. 'It was really quite funny, sir.'

'I hope you didn't let your amusement show, or that would give him another excuse to have a go at us,' said Rathbone in some alarm.

'It's all right Sarge, we did keep our faces straight,' Sukey assured him.

'DS Rathbone has a point so just be on your guard, all of you,' said Leach. 'Now, we have to do everything possible to contact the dead woman's relatives. I've spoken to Doc Handley and an actual mug shot, even after she's been cleaned up, might be distressing, so I'm sending an artist round to the morgue to produce a recognizable impression without showing the effects of decomposition. That should be ready to release tomorrow, so I'll talk to the press in the morning and bring them up to speed. And naturally we'll ask them to publicize our appeal for anyone who can help with ID to come forward.' He turned to Rathbone. 'Make sure you get more details from him of his so-called project . . . the name of the company he's claiming Maxworth's might be interested in and what work he's done on it. It's possible that's something he's dreamed up on the spur of the moment to account for coming home during the day. And send a couple of your DCs to check whether he's telling the truth about leaving the office without explanation on Wednesday.'

Rathbone made a note. 'Will do, sir.'

'I've arranged for one of our whiz-kids to check his computer.' Leach glanced at his watch. 'You'd better go and grab some lunch before you tackle Ellerman again.'

'D'you reckon he did it?' said Vicky as she and Sukey sat down to a sandwich lunch in the canteen.

'It's funny you should ask,' said Sukey. 'Common sense and logic tell me that having eliminated Carla Seaton from suspicion of committing the two previous murders – which was a pretty long shot anyway – Ellerman is the only one with motive and opportunity. I feel as if we're in a dark room and pressing all the right buttons but the lights won't come on.'

'You're right.' Vicky bit into her tuna sandwich and chewed thoughtfully for a moment. 'But if he didn't do it, who did? We've interviewed scores of witnesses and haven't come across a single lead pointing to anyone else who might have a motive for killing Fenella Tremaine. We're fairly confident that the Fiddler's Patch victim is Aggie, but supposing she isn't?'

'In that case,' said Sukey despondently, 'we're back to square one.'

## TWENTY-FIVE

Despite being subjected to several more hours of questioning by successive teams of detectives, Ellerman refused to change his story. As there was no possibility of seeking further information either from his colleagues at Maxworth Engineering or from Mrs Shilling at the cleaning agency until their respective offices reopened on Monday morning, DCI Leach had no option other than to order that he be detained pending further enquiries. Jason Pollard put in a strong plea for bail, pleading that his client was unfit to spend a night in the cells and insisting on a doctor being summoned. After a considerable delay a somewhat disgruntled doctor appeared, examined Ellerman and said that in his opinion there was no medical reason why he should not remain in custody overnight. Pollard's request was therefore refused and the team was told to go home and report for duty as usual the following morning.

It was a little after eight o'clock when Sukey returned home. She had been indoors barely ten minutes when Harry rang her bell. 'I didn't think it'd be long before you showed up,' she said resignedly as she opened the door. 'I suppose you'd better come in.'

'Well, there's a nice way to greet your beloved,' he said reproachfully. He held her close for several moments before releasing her and saying, 'What you need is a stiffener.'

'Oh yes, please.' She sank into an armchair and shut her eyes. 'This case is an absolute nightmare; we're ninety-nine per cent sure we've got our man but we haven't been able to nail him yet. He's as slippery as an eel; we've all been having a go at him in relays for several hours and getting nowhere. Thanks love,' she added as he put a glass of wine into her hand and sat down beside her. 'And now I suppose you're going to try and winkle some extra information out of me. I wouldn't bank on it . . . as it is I've already said too much.'

Harry chuckled. 'Your problem is you just can't resist my winning personality. Do I take it the slippery customer you're referring to is Doctor Marcus Ellerman?'

'No comment.'

'All right. Let me tell you what I have found so far and you can fill in the blanks.'

'In your dreams!'

'We'll see. Now, I and my fellow news-hounds already know that your people have, shall we say, shown a lot of interest in Marcus Ellerman ever since the discovery of Fenella Tremaine's body. No, we haven't had any leaks and my editor would cut off his right arm rather than pay for info,' he assured her as she was about to interrupt. 'Just the same, we do have a very effective bush telegraph and we're pretty sure that your sergeant's recent visits to Ellerman weren't social calls.' He broke off for a moment to take a generous mouthful from his own glass of wine. 'Right, fast forward to yesterday afternoon when a woman's body – as yet unidentified so far as we know – is found on a patch of waste ground not much more than a mile from where Ellerman lives. Am I right so far?'

'Since the media flew to the scene like wasps to a picnic there's no point in denying it,' Sukey admitted. 'I take it you were there?'

'I'm asking the questions. What about the ID or lack of it?'

'I suppose there's no harm in answering that,' she said after a moment's thought. 'A description of the dead woman will be given at tomorrow's press briefing and you'll all be asked to appeal for information from anyone who thinks they may know her identity. An artist's impression will be circulated as soon as it's been made.'

'No mug shot; I imagine that means the face has been beaten to a pulp or she's started to decompose,' said Harry.

'No comment,' said Sukey. 'Look, I've just said you'll get more information first thing tomorrow. Can't you wait till then?'

'I haven't finished telling you what I already know,' said Harry.

'All right, clever clogs; get on with it.'

'You think the dead woman is Marcus Ellerman's cleaning lady who hasn't been seen since she went to his flat as usual on Wednesday. He was there at the time, contrary to his usual practice, and he's been at HQ all day helping with your enquiries into her disappearance.' He could not resist a smirk of triumph at Sukey's look of mingled astonishment and dismay, at which she gave him a thump on his free arm.

'How the hell did you figure that out without inside info?'

'Easy – I followed a hunch and went round to Sycamore Park after leaving Fiddler's Patch. It was pretty obvious something was afoot, what with CSIs going in followed by uniformed making off with a load of stuff including a laptop – Ellerman's no doubt since there is now a seal on his flat – and curious onlookers hanging around gawping and chattering. They were falling over themselves to tell me what one of the residents had seen from her window. The neighbourhood watch network at Sycamore Park is pretty slick, I can tell you.'

'Let's hope they'll be as helpful in getting an ID for the Fiddler's Patch victim,' said Sukey. She drained her glass and held it out for a refill.

'Oh, I'm sure they'll be a great help,' he said as he topped up both their drinks. 'By the way, has Ellerman been freed on bail or banged up for the night? The *Echo* has a reporter hanging about outside HQ and he'd like to know so he can go home.'

'I'm afraid he'll just have to hang about . . . and I wish it was a snowy night in winter instead of mid-August,' said Sukey with feeling.

'You hard-hearted woman. What happened to the milk of human kindness?'

'It's curdled . . . and I'm not saying another word – except that I'm ready for some food.'

'Me too. Why don't I go out for some fish and chips? Or would you rather have a pizza?'

'Fish and chips please.'

\*    \*    \*

On Monday morning, as soon as the press briefing was over, the team were given their orders for the day. In view of Ellerman's intransigence DCI Leach decided to lead the first session of questioning himself, with Rathbone's support and DC Penny Osborne sitting in to observe. DCs Mike Haskins and Tim Pringle were sent to the Clean as a Whistle agency in search of further information about Aggie, while Sukey and Vicky were instructed to go to Maxworth Engineering and interview Ellerman's PA.

On returning to headquarters at lunchtime the team were once again summoned to DCI Leach's office. 'You will not be entirely surprised,' he began, 'that we have been unable to shake Ellerman; DS Rathbone and I did our best to trip him up, but we got nowhere. He insists that on arriving home on Wednesday he merely exchanged a couple of words with "the girl" and went straight to his study to work on his project. He's already agreed that she seemed what he called "a bit jumpy" when he walked in, but simply put it down to the fact that she was surprised to see him. So,' Leach continued wearily, 'unless any of you have come up with something to justify applying for an extension, we'll have to bail him again. It seems our only hope at the moment is for his DNA to be found on the woman's body or clothing, but barring a miracle it will be days or even weeks before we get a result. Tim and Mike, I'll start with you. How much was Mrs Shilling able to tell you about Aggie?'

'Quite a lot, sir,' said Mike. 'She was a bit cagey at first and waffled on about confidentiality as if she was Aggie's lawyer, but when we told her why we needed the information and gave her a description of the Fiddler's Patch victim she was horrified and only too willing to help us in any way she could.'

'You think she recognized Aggie from the description?'

'Undoubtedly, sir. Her full name is Aghami Hussein; she's been working for Clean as a Whistle for about three months and all the clients speak very highly of her. She told Mrs Shilling when she signed on that she didn't want any of her family – or the police – to know where she was, which explains why Mrs Shilling hesitated at first about giving us any more information.'

'So I take it she went ahead and answered all your questions?'

'Yes, sir. She began by confirming that Aggie didn't have any more jobs after she'd finished at Ellerman's flat so she assumed she'd gone home. When a client rang on Thursday morning to complain that she hadn't turned up Mrs Shilling thought she must be ill as she'd never missed a job before. It wasn't until the same thing happened on Friday that she became concerned; she called Aggie on her mobile but there was no answer.'

'If she was so concerned, why didn't she say so when you went to see her on Saturday?'

'It's a quite complicated – and all too common, I understand – situation among some immigrant families, sir. Aggie comes from a Muslim family who settled in this country – quite legally, it appears – when Aggie was about twelve. She went to the local comprehensive school where she made friends with a girl from a Catholic family and secretly became a Christian, but of course didn't dare tell her own family. When she was fourteen her father told her he'd arranged for her to marry his cousin, a very wealthy man much older than her. She didn't dare defy her father, but she was revolted by the idea because she knew the man and found him repulsive. The next day at school she told her friend and begged her for help. The friend told her own parents; knowing that forced marriages are illegal in this country they wanted to contact Social Services in the hope that they could arrange for her to be taken to a women's refuge, but she was terrified at the suggestion; she had brothers who were strict Muslims and would, she knew, be determined to seek her out and force her to return home. And if they knew she'd become a Christian she was certain they would kill her.'

'Where was the family living at the time?' asked DCI Leach.

'Mrs Shilling isn't sure, but she seems to remember hearing her mention Hackney.'

'Hackney – that's in East London.' Leach made a note. 'That's a useful starting point for tracing her family.' He turned to DS Rathbone. 'Get one of your team to send her details to the local police, Greg.'

'Will do, sir.'

'Presumably she was at school in the area. How come she ended up in Bristol?'

'It seems she was desperate to get away from London to be out of the reach of her family, sir,' said Tim. 'Her friend's parents had relatives in Bedminster – a Mr and Mrs Franklin – and they arranged for her to stay with them for a while. Happily they took to one another straight away – the Franklins had no children of their own and she filled a gap in their lives. They found a place for her at a local school and eventually they offered her a permanent home.'

'As she was a minor they should have informed us, but I suppose she managed to persuade them not to,' Leach remarked. 'How long did she live with them?'

'Until she left school, sir.'

'How old was she then?'

'Just turned eighteen. It seems she was hoping to go to university but Mr Franklin, an engineer with a company making water treatment equipment, was unexpectedly moved to an overseas job and she was suddenly faced with the prospect of losing her home. The Franklins were very good to her; they helped her find somewhere to live and gave her some money. According to what she told Mrs Shilling she used to help with all the domestic chores and it was Mrs Franklin's idea that she should look for work as a cleaner and study part time to get some kind of qualification. We've checked a few local adult education colleges but we haven't come up with anything in that direction so far.'

'She seems to have been very frank with Mrs Shilling,' Leach commented.

'She was obviously pretty low when she applied for the job, sir, and was probably desperate for someone to confide in. Underneath her no-nonsense, businesslike manner, Mrs Shilling struck us as a very kind, sympathetic human being. She showed us the letter Mrs Franklin had written testifying to Aggie's honesty and reliability as a cleaner. It included the name of her doctor and a copy of her latest school report. Everything seems to be in order.'

'She's registered with a doctor eh?' said Leach, his expression lightening for a moment. 'That's good news. He should be able to help us with an ID.'

'Sorry sir, no luck there I'm afraid,' said Mike. 'She only saw a doctor once in all the time she lived with the Franklins and he died two years ago. No one else at the practice can even remember what she looked like.'

'What about the Job Centre? Presumably she signed on when she was looking for work. Did she have a National Insurance number?'

'Everything's in order, sir. She knew where her father kept her passport and somehow managed to get hold of it. She actually showed it to Mrs Shilling as proof of her ID.'

Leach nodded. 'There was no passport in her flat and her handbag is missing so it's probably in that along with her purse and her mobile.'

'Yes, it'd be a great help if that turned up,' Leach remarked. 'You mentioned in a previous report that Aggie caught a bus from outside Holmwood to her next job. Did you check on that?'

'I did, sir,' said Tim. 'It's route four-oh-two. We've contacted the bus company and asked them to check if any of the drivers noticed a woman answering Aggie's description travelling on their bus around one thirty on Wednesday.'

Leach nodded. 'Well, at least we have a clearer picture of Aggie's background, although I don't see that it does much to strengthen our case against Ellerman. Sukey and Vicky, let's hear from you.'

'I'm afraid we aren't going to be of much help either, sir,' said Sukey. 'We spoke to Ellerman's PA, a Mrs Nuttall. She confirmed that Ellerman left his office a little after eleven on Wednesday morning, saying he might not be back but to call him on his mobile if anything urgent cropped up. He didn't say where he was going, which didn't surprise her.'

'She was careful not to say anything critical about him,' said Vicky. 'However, she made it clear that the relationship between them is strictly a business one and that he neither volunteers, nor is she interested in, anything he does outside the office.'

'You're saying she thought he might have had some sort of assignation?'

'That was our impression, sir.'

'He does fancy himself as a ladies' man,' Rathbone remarked with a hint of mockery.

'So she knew nothing about this so-called project he was supposed to be working on?'

'No, sir,' said Sukey, 'but he did return to the office at about four, saying he needed to pick up some papers he'd left behind as he wanted to read them during the evening. We asked her if he seemed at all agitated, but she said he appeared perfectly normal.'

Leach thumped his desk with his fist in an uncharacteristic gesture of frustration. 'Either the man's completely without human feelings or . . . I hate to admit this, but I'm beginning to wonder if he's telling the truth after all. The girl's history has made me think . . . supposing her brothers had managed to track her down . . . found out where she lived and been lying in wait for her when she got home. Or maybe they'd been shadowing her, found an opportunity to grab her . . . bundle her into a car . . . she'd probably have put up a struggle and they accidentally strangled her while attempting to subdue her. We can't be a hundred per cent sure that she never left Sycamore Park the day she went missing . . . not even the nosiest of neighbours spot everything.'

'Surely, sir, someone would have noticed a couple of young men of Middle Eastern appearance hanging around near Aggie's flat?' said Rathbone.

'They could have found the route she regularly took home and chosen the time and place carefully, Greg. Get your team to find out everything they can relevant to Aggie's regular movements.'

'Will do, sir.'

'Meanwhile,' Leach went on, 'there's some stuff from Ellerman's flat to go through. The techies have hacked into his laptop, so you'll have to trawl through everything on there. You might find something to help us get into his head.'

'You think he might keep a diary, sir?' said Mike.

'That's for you to find out. Uniformed also brought out a carved wooden box that was tucked away at the back of a cupboard. It looks Indian – probably another bit of kitsch that his wife insisted on buying. They think there's something inside it but they haven't been able to open it. There must be a secret catch somewhere – one of you should be able to find it.' Leach made a few notes and closed his folder. 'Right, that's it for now.'

# TWENTY-SIX

'**I**'ve seen these things before,' said Vicky as she examined the elaborately carved wooden box that Rathbone handed over. 'So see if you can get into it,' he said curtly.

'I'll do my best, Sarge.' He gave a dismissive grunt and strode over to the drinks machine. 'I do believe this case is getting him down; he seems to be on an even shorter fuse than usual,' Vicky commented with a nod in his direction. 'I have a feeling,' she went on, turning her attention back to the box, 'that you have to slide this bit one way . . . or maybe the other . . . no, perhaps it's this bit . . . ah, that's it . . . and then press something . . . voilà!' There was a faint click as the lid sprang open. 'Right, what have we here?'

'A bunch of dried rosemary,' said Sukey, peering over Vicky's shoulder. 'For remembrance,' she said softly. 'What else?'

'Picture postcards,' Vicky lifted out the items while she spoke and passed them one by one to Sukey. 'The Colosseum . . . the Eiffel Tower . . . the Brandenburg Gate. Nothing written on them except dates so I suppose she bought them as keepsakes in places they'd been to.'

'Quite a few photographs, all of the two of them,' Sukey remarked. 'They're sitting on an elephant in this one.' She turned the picture over. 'She's written "The two of us on a howdah in India – the best holiday ever".'

'And to think that awful man made her abort their baby and they both died,' said Vicky. 'I wonder he can sleep at night.'

'He's kept all these mementoes of her, so he must have loved her in spite of everything.' Sukey felt a constriction in her throat as she put the photos to one side. 'What next?'

'Theatre programmes,' said Vicky as she unfolded them. 'They saw *The Merchant of Venice* at Stratford and *The Applecart* in London. She's written "My birthday treat" on one and "Our anniversary – exactly a month since our first date" on the other. A few admission tickets to art galleries and so on. And the last thing is this.' She took out a small, leather-bound volume. 'It's a diary.'

'Is it hers?'

'I suppose it must be.' Vicky handed it to Sukey. 'You look through it. I don't want to . . . I'm beginning to feel . . . intrusive.'

'One of us has to.' Sukey took the diary and opened it at the first page. 'Yes, according to this it belonged to Julie Ellerman, which means she obviously considered herself as good as married to him.' She turned over the pages. 'She seems to have started it about the time she met Marcus . . . or at least when they began the relationship. There's an awful lot about him . . . once or twice she refers to him as "darling Marc" . . . and goes on about how wonderful he is. Poor girl, she was obviously besotted . . . little did she know what was coming to her.' Sukey read through a few more pages without comment. 'Hang on a minute,' she said suddenly. 'This looks interesting.' She held the diary out to Vicky, who took it with some reluctance. 'Read that.'

'Jay drove me to The Laburnums today to measure up for curtains,' Vicky read aloud. 'He's got a lovely new car – an Audi – and he's so proud of it. He's such a dear and he thinks the world of me, in fact he once asked me to marry him. He got quite upset when I told him about Marc. In fact he said some quite nasty things about him. When I told him how happy my darling makes me he kept saying I hadn't known him long enough to be sure. Of course I'm sure, I said, the first time I met Marc I just knew he was the only one for me. Poor old Jay gave up after that, just said he'd always be there for me if I needed him.' Vicky handed the diary back to Sukey. 'It's hardly surprising that Jay – whoever he is – fancied her. From the pictures of her she was quite a dish.'

'She'd have been a lot better off with him; he sounds a really nice guy,' Sukey commented, turning over a few more pages. 'She then goes on at some length about how lovely it was of Gramps to let her and Marcus live in the house.'

'Gramps – that must be the old boy you went to see.'

'That's right – Mr Armitage. He didn't have a good word to say about Marcus Ellerman either. Hang on a minute; I've just remembered something. There was this lady who lives across the way from The Laburnums.' Sukey trawled through her memory. 'She's a Mrs Parr, a music teacher. She mentioned seeing a couple turn up at The Laburnums one day before the Ellermans moved in. She was sure the woman was Julie, but the man with her looked a lot older than Ellerman so it couldn't have been him. He was driving what she described as "an expensive-looking car" and she thought it was red but she couldn't say what make it was.'

'So perhaps it was this man she refers to as Jay,' said Vicky thoughtfully. 'That could be short for Jason.'

'Or Jacob or James,' Sukey suggested. 'There's a man called Jared living in the same block as Ellerman . . . but it can't be him; he's far too young. I've just had a thought; I wonder if she told darling Marcus about this other man who wanted to marry her. Maybe he would know who he is. If we could track him down he might know something we could pin on Ellerman.'

'You mean something to link him with Fenella Tremaine . . . something to suggest a motive for killing her?'

'It's possible, don't you think?'

'But even if Ellerman does know who Jay is he's hardly likely to incriminate himself by telling us,' Vicky objected, 'and if Jay does know something, why hasn't he come forward?'

'Good question, but I think DCI Leach should know about this.' Sukey was flicking through the remaining pages of the diary as she spoke. When she came to the last entry she caught her breath.

'What is it? Vicky asked.

'She wrote, "I can't believe it. Marc doesn't want the baby. He says he couldn't live with a squalling brat in the house and if I don't get rid of it he'll move out. Gramps says he'd look after me and the baby and find somewhere for us to live, but I can't face life without Marc so I've decided to do as he says." Well, that confirms what old Mr Armitage told me.' Sukey closed the diary and replaced it in the box with the other items. 'I'm pretty sure the Sarge will be interested in this.'

Vicky shrugged. 'If you say so, but I'm still not convinced that it helps us. We already know what happened to her.'

'I'm inclined to agree with Vicky,' Rathbone commented after reading the entries in the diary that Sukey pointed out to him, 'but I'll show it to DCI Leach anyway.'

'This is definitely worth following up,' said Leach after reading the relevant passages for himself. 'This man, Jay, might, as you are obviously hoping, hold a key piece of info that will help us pin the Tremaine murder on Ellerman – and consequently provide a strong motive for Aggie's murder as well. On the other hand, he may know something that could clear Ellerman altogether, which would be frustrating but it's a possibility we have to face. He hasn't been released from custody yet, so question him again and see what he has to say about it.'

'Doctor Ellerman,' Rathbone began after the formalities in the interview room were complete, 'as you are aware, in the course of our enquiries certain items have been removed from your flat for examination. I have a list of those items here and I believe you have a receipt for all of them.' He waited for a moment but Ellerman's only response was a slight tilt of the head that seemed to say, 'So what?'

'Among those items,' Rathbone continued, 'was this.' He lifted the sheet of paper that had been covering the carved box.

Ellerman gave a start and put both hands to his eyes. He was plainly moved. 'You had no right to touch that,' he said shakily. 'It was Julie's . . . it's private, a present from me that I bought for her in India. She called it her treasure box.'

'Doctor Ellerman,' said Sukey in response to a glance from Rathbone, 'we know that you loved Julie very much and we understand that you are still grieving for her, but we have a job to do and we believe that one of the items in this box may help us. It is even possible that it may help you.'

He raised his head. 'Help me?' He gave a short ironic laugh. 'Why would you want to help me?'

'Our only concern is to establish the truth,' said Rathbone. 'Two women have been murdered and we believe there may be a link between the two crimes. All the evidence we have so far points to you. You continue to maintain your innocence, so it's in your interest to answer our questions, however painful they may be.'

Ellerman lowered his hands and raised his head. 'I understand,' he said. 'What do you want to know?'

'Among some personal items in the box my constables found this diary.' Rathbone held it up and Ellerman reached out as if to snatch it away, but restrained himself. 'Do you recognize it?'

'Of course I do. It was Julie's. I saw her writing in it once or twice.'

'Have you read it?'

'Certainly not! It was private; I wouldn't have dreamed of it.'

'Then allow me to quote an entry which we think significant.' Rathbone read out the relevant passage. 'Does that mean anything to you?'

Ellerman nodded. 'Oh yes, she told me about Jay,' he said with a slightly condescending smile. 'She spoke very warmly of him . . . said he'd been very good to her after her parents died. She said he was a widower and she felt sorry for him because he was lonely. He actually asked her to marry him, but she thought he was probably looking for someone to look after him in his old age.'

'Did she mention his name?'

Ellerman shook his head. 'She refused to tell me who he was. I asked her why the secrecy and she said something about not wanting to cause embarrassment.'

'Embarrassment to whom?' asked Vicky.

He shook his head. 'She wouldn't say. I'm sorry, that's all I can tell you. I understand I'm being granted bail again. When will I be free to go?'

'As soon as the formalities are completed,' said Rathbone. Sukey noticed that his manner towards Ellerman had become slightly less aggressive. Back in the CID office he found a message asking him to call Sergeant Rook at a police station in Hackney. After making the call he said, 'They're pretty sure from the artist's impression that the dead woman is Aggie,' he said.

'Does that mean they've managed to contact her family?' asked Sukey.

'Not exactly. They heard from some neighbours with a daughter who used to be at school with Aggie and seemed pretty sure she's the woman in the picture. Anyway, this neighbour – a Mr Singh – went to the police station and said he'd called on Aggie's family to show them the picture. He spoke to the father who said that as far as he and the rest of the family were concerned their daughter had been dead from the time she left home. They didn't say in so many words that they thought of her as no better than a prostitute, but Mr Singh told Sergeant Rook that's the impression he got from the father's attitude.'

'Charming,' Vicky commented. 'So where does that leave us?'

'In the absence of an ID from a family member, I guess we'll have to rely on one of our other witnesses,' said Rathbone. 'As she was RC, Father Burke is probably the most appropriate. You'd better go and see him ASAP.'

Fortunately, Father Burke was at home when Sukey called. As soon as they explained the situation he agreed to meet her and Vicky at the morgue. When the attendant drew back the sheet to reveal the murdered girl's face, he nodded and said sadly, 'That is without doubt the young woman who used to attend my church. Will you allow me to spend a few moments alone with her?'

They withdrew a short distance. He appeared to be praying; after a few minutes he made the sign of the cross and then rejoined them. 'When will you be able to release her body for burial so that I can make arrangements for her funeral?' he asked.

'Probably quite soon,' said Sukey. 'We'll let you know . . . and perhaps you'd let us know the date of the funeral. I'd like to be there if possible.'

'Me too,' said Vicky.

'Of course,' he replied, evidently touched by their concern.

When they returned to headquarters. Mike and Tim were seated at a desk with Ellerman's laptop in front of them. On seeing them approach, Mike sat back and flexed his arms and shoulders. 'Any luck with that?' asked Sukey.

He shook his head. 'Nothing in the least bit iffy so far.'

'He comes across as very businesslike and methodical,' said Tim. He too sat back and linked his hands behind his head. 'How did the reverend react to your request?'

'He met us at the morgue,' Vicky told him. 'He said the dead woman is Aggie – that is, he's certain she's the one who worshipped in his church, which confirms what Minnie told us. Short of a family member coming to see the body, that's probably the nearest to an ID that we'll get.'

'At least she'll get a Christian burial,' said Sukey. 'I'm sure that would mean a lot to her.'

'We've heard from Mrs Shilling, by the way,' said Mike. 'She's pretty sure from the artist's impression that it's Aggie.'

Rathbone appeared with a mug of coffee in his hand. He listened to their reports and checked his watch. 'Just gone five o'clock,' he said. 'Ellerman's on his way home and there's nothing more we can do this evening so the SIO says we can push off. We can all do with an early night for a change.'

As Sukey was getting into her car a series of bleeps from her mobile indicated the arrival of a text. It was from Harry and read: 'When are you home? Urgent see you.' She keyed in: 'On way now' before starting the engine. As she drove home various possibilities ran through her head. Had he been doing some of his famous ferreting around and come up with a vital piece of information? Probably not, if he had he'd have said so, she thought as she waited at the traffic lights in Whiteladies Road. 'It's more likely you're out to try and pump something out of me,' she found herself saying aloud. 'Well, tough; you'll have to wait for tomorrow's statement.'

She had barely had time to park her car and switch off the engine before he arrived. She could tell by his manner that he had something to tell her. 'What's the urgency?' she demanded as she dumped her bag and slid off her jacket. 'Have you solved the case for us . . . or is it just that you couldn't wait to see me? No, it isn't that,' she added, pretending to take offence. 'You haven't even kissed me.'

'Sorry, love.' He gave her a quick embrace. 'I've just had a text from a mate of mine in London who has a contact with the police in Hackney. Ah, I see that rings a bell,' he added as she shot him a keen look.

She was at the sink, filling the kettle. 'Want a cuppa?'

'In a minute. This is exciting. That artist's impression you gave us of the Fiddler's Patch victim has been publicized nationally and Dave says someone in Hackney has identified her.'

'I'm listening. Go on.'

'Dave couldn't get a name, but his contact dropped a hint that led him to a certain street. He went there and hung around for a while. There were a few people in a huddle talking among themselves but as soon as he approached they shut up and wouldn't say a word.' Harry stood behind her, put his arms round her and nibbled her ear. 'If you'll tell me a bit more I promise to keep quiet until you say it's OK to release it.'

'Release what?' She moved away and reached for the teapot.

'You've been doing all the talking.'

'And you haven't shown any excitement so what I've just said obviously isn't a revelation. Oh come on, love,' he wheedled. 'I'll lie awake all night trying to fill in the gaps if you won't tell me anything.'

'All right.' She made a pot of tea and reached for some mugs. 'I can confirm that someone claims to know who she is and we have reason to believe them. We've had additional information and there'll be a statement to the press in the morning. And that's positively all you're going to get out of me.' She put two mugs of tea on the table and sat down.

'No hint of the source of the additional information?' Harry said hopefully.

'Not so much as a sniff of it.'

'I might have known. Anyway, it was an excuse to come and see you and – ' he checked the time – 'it's still quite early so let's go out somewhere for a meal. That Spanish place we went to a few weeks ago was very good. How about going there?'

'That's a great idea,' she said.

'We'll take a cab so we can both have a drink.'

Later, when the taxi dropped them at Sukey's front door, they stood for several moments quietly holding one another. After a while she said, 'Do you want to come in?'

He took her key and opened the door. 'I thought you'd never ask,' he said.

# TWENTY-SEVEN

'You're looking pleased with life,' Vicky remarked to Sukey as they reassembled in the CID office the following morning. 'Did you have a good evening?'

'Great,' Sukey replied. 'Harry took me out for a meal; it made a change after all the overtime.'

'It must have been a super menu to put that sparkle in your eyes,' said Vicky, inviting further details with a lift of one eyebrow which Sukey chose to ignore.

'Right troops, no time for gossiping.' Rathbone summoned the team into his office. 'DCI Leach wants us to find the mysterious Jay and our only clue to his identity is that Julie refused to tell Ellerman his name on the grounds that it would be "too embarrassing". Let's do a spot of brainstorming; what sort of situation between a young woman and an elderly widower is likely to be considered embarrassing?'

'Jay was a mutual acquaintance?' suggested Mike. 'One of his colleagues, perhaps.'

'They'd all be too young,' Tim objected. 'Do we know how and where Ellerman met Julie? Perhaps Jay introduced them.'

'Unlikely,' said Rathbone. 'If Jay thought so much of Julie and considered Ellerman to be a bad lot, he'd hardly have thrown them together.'

'I suppose not.'

There was a silence, interrupted by one of the civilian workers in the general office. 'There's a woman in reception, Sarge, who's asking to speak urgently with the officer in charge of the Fiddler's Patch murder. She says she has some information about the victim.'

'*Has* she?' said Rathbone. 'That sounds promising; fingers crossed everyone. I'll see her in here; Sukey, you stay and take her statement and the rest of you go back and carry on flogging your brains. If it's anything significant I'll let you know.'

Sukey judged the age of the woman who was ushered into Rathbone's office to be about fifty; she had fluffy grey hair and was wearing a lilac trouser suit. She was obviously ill at ease; she perched on the edge of the chair Rathbone indicated and clutched her handbag to her chest as if fearing it would be taken from her and searched.

'Thank you for coming to see us,' Rathbone began and she gave a slight nod. 'I am Detective Sergeant Rathbone and this is Detective Constable Reynolds. Now, I understand you are Mrs Elsie Maynard, that you are an employee of the Clean as a Whistle agency and that you believe you have some important information about the victim of the Fiddler's Patch murder.'

'That's right,' she said in a tremulous voice. 'I feel simply awful about not coming to tell you before, but I've been away you see and I've only just found out about poor Aggie . . . oh, I do hope I'm not too late . . . supposing he's done it again and the body hasn't been found yet? Such a nice gentleman, who'd have thought he'd do such a terrible thing?'

'Mrs Maynard,' said Rathbone, 'we do not believe Aggie was the victim of a serial killer, so please relax. Before we go any further, perhaps you'd like a cup of tea or coffee?'

The surprise in her smile made it clear that this was the last thing she expected. 'Oh . . . yes, a cup of coffee would be lovely.'

'Milk and sugar?'

'No sugar, thank you.'

He ordered coffee for the three of them. When they were settled and Mrs Maynard appeared less tense, he said, 'Just take your time and tell us in your own words exactly what you know.'

'Well,' she began, speaking slowly at first and then more quickly as her story proceeded. 'I saw her picture in a back number of the *Echo* when I got back from Italy yesterday evening and my first thought was "Poor Aggie" and my next was "Oh my God, that could have been me!" It was my regular day to clean for him you see, but I couldn't do it because my flight was changed at the last minute and so I asked Aggie . . .' Her voice trailed away; she fished in her handbag for a tissue and dabbed her eyes. 'I knew she didn't like working in the afternoon,' she went on, 'but I thought "maybe just this once she won't mind and anyway I did her a similar favour a week or two ago". It didn't even enter my head that he'd be there . . . he isn't usually . . . and now she's dead and it could have been me . . . and I'm so afraid you'll find he's murdered another poor woman and if I'd told you before I could have stopped him. I feel so guilty.' Her shoulders sagged and she scrubbed her eyes with the tissue.

Sensing that Rathbone's impatience was beginning to show, Sukey said, 'Mrs Maynard, there is absolutely no reason why you should feel guilty. We understand why you couldn't come to us earlier and DS Rathbone has already told you that we do not believe the person who murdered Aggie is likely to kill again.'

'You're sure of that?' she said doubtfully.

'As sure as we can be. Now, about this gentleman you usually clean for on Wednesday afternoons; he isn't normally in the flat while you're working, but you say he's nice so you must have met him at least once.'

'Oh yes, he was there the first time. Most clients like to be there the first time to show the cleaner exactly what she has to do, what things not to touch and where all the polishes and things are kept, that sort of thing. Some are there every time of course . . . it just depends.'

'But in this case the gentleman was normally absent while you were cleaning his flat?'

'That's right.'

'Do you know his name?'

She shook her head. 'I'm afraid I've forgotten . . . I haven't seen him since that first time and I clean for quite a few other people. Mrs Shilling will tell you.'

'Well, thank you very much for your help Mrs Maynard,' said Rathbone. 'DC Reynolds will prepare a record of your statement which we will ask you to sign before you leave.'

'Yes, of course.'

'We're getting somewhere at last,' said Rathbone as he returned to the main office. 'Mike, call Mrs Shilling and ask her who Mrs Maynard normally cleans for on Wednesday afternoons.'

After making the call Mike put down the phone and said, 'It's a Mr John A. Yardley of thirty Sycamore Park, Sarge.'

Rathbone gave a soft whistle and reached for his jacket. 'J A Y . . . Jay. Right, Mike. You, Tim and I will pay him a visit.'

*    *    *

'I've been expecting you,' said Yardley when Rathbone explained the reason for their call. 'I've known all along I'd never get away with it, but at the time . . . it was a knee-jerk reaction that got out of hand . . . fatally out of hand. I should never have been at home, of course; I normally meet friends for lunch on a Wednesday. It was very unfortunate.' He led the way into the sitting room. 'Do sit down.'

Studying him, Mike was astonished at his composure and dignity. He had as good as admitted to the murder of one woman and was almost certainly responsible for another, yet his manner was that of a courteous host.

'I never even heard her come in,' he went on. 'I'd just read the report in that morning's *Echo* about the arrest . . . there were no names of course but I knew it was him . . . and I couldn't contain a shout of triumph, probably something like "I did it Julie, I did it for you!" I think I even punched the air like some teenage football fan. It was so good to know that he was going to go down for something I'd done.'

'So what happened then?' prompted Rathbone as Yardley seemed to fall into a reverie. As Mike told the others later, he wore a trace of a smile that gave him a bizarre resemblance to the Mona Lisa.

He gave a slight start. 'Forgive me, I was just . . . anyway it was then that I heard a scream; I turned round and there was that woman . . . someone I'd never seen before . . . and she was obviously terrified and had guessed the truth. She was shaking and she wouldn't stop screaming; I grabbed her by the throat and squeezed it like this.' He raised his hands and mimed the action. 'I don't think I realized what I was doing, only that I had to keep her quiet. She stopped screaming and I let go of her and gave her a little shake and said something like "I'm sorry, I didn't mean to hurt you" but I suddenly realized that she was dead and I'd killed her.'

'So what did you do then?' asked Rathbone.

'I knew I had to dispose of her body, of course, but it was broad daylight so I just hid her in a cupboard and waited. I waited until some time in the small hours – it seemed an eternity – and I wrapped her in a blanket and smuggled her out through the rear exit, praying I wouldn't meet or be seen by anybody. I put

her into the boot of my car and . . . well, I don't need to say
any more, do I?'

'On the contrary, sir,' said Rathbone, 'we believe you have a
great deal more to say.'

'Yes, of course. I'll tell you the background to the whole story.
I've still got her handbag, by the way. I'll go and fetch it.' He
stood up and was about to walk from the room, but Mike barred
his way.

'No need for that, sir,' said Rathbone. 'My officers will carry
out a thorough search of your flat. We'll need to examine your
car, so kindly give me the key and tell me where it is.'

Yardley shrugged and sat down. 'It's in the garage that belongs
to this flat. I suppose you want the keys to the flat as well. They're
all on the shelf by the front door.'

Rathbone stood up. 'We'll continue this interview at headquarters,' he said. 'John Alfred Yardley, I'm arresting you on suspicion
of the murder of Aghami Hussein.' Yardley made no reply and
they took him downstairs and drove him to police headquarters.

During the interval before the case came to trial Sukey had a
hard time resisting Harry's pleas for information. At the hearing
at Bristol Magistrates Court Yardley refused legal aid and frankly
admitted killing Fenella Tremaine and Aggie Hussein, describing
them both as innocent victims of his determination to avenge
Julie Armitage's death. In the dock he expressed particular contrition for having killed Aggie, who had played no part in his
original plan but had merely had the misfortune to stumble on
the scene at what he described as "an inopportune moment".
However, he stated openly that had he been successful in laying
the blame at Ellerman's door he would have been more than
satisfied to see him sentenced to a substantial term in prison. 'If
we still had capital punishment I'd have been happy to see him
go to the gallows,' he finished defiantly. At this point, the magis-
trate adjourned the proceedings and remanded him in custody
for medical reports.

'He's obviously a nut case,' Harry remarked when he called on
Sukey with a Chinese takeaway a day or two later. 'He seemed
to regard poor Fenella as a kind of sacrificial lamb.'

'It would have made more sense to most people if he'd stuck his knife into Ellerman,' Sukey agreed, 'but as he considered him morally responsible for Julie's death – which of course he was – he was determined to make him pay what he considered a suitable penalty.'

'So his hatred of Ellerman had been festering all this time while he was trying to figure out a suitable way to punish him?'

'That's right. He admitted he suddenly got the idea from seeing the knife and took the opportunity of nicking it while the rest of the party were looking at pictures. His first thought after learning what happened to Julie had been to find a way to kill Ellerman, but then it occurred to him that if he could get him sent down for murder it would be a much greater punishment. That's what prompted that odd comment about it being a pity that Fenella was the one who had to die.' She sipped her wine in silence for a few moments, then frowned suddenly.

'Penny for them?' said Harry.

'I've just remembered . . . during one of our discussions I put forward a theory that putting the blame on Ellerman might have been the motive for the Tremaine murder. And guess who I thought the killer might have been? Jennifer Freeman!'

'You're joking!'

'We were just brainstorming, of course. I was on the right lines, but had the wrong suspect.'

'Going back to Yardley,' said Harry, 'I think he's got Italian blood. He's got that sort of look about him. Maybe he saw his mission, as he called it, as a sort of vendetta. What do you think they'll do with him? He's not likely to be a danger to anyone else.'

Sukey twirled her wine glass between her fingers. 'It depends on what the shrinks make of him,' she said after a moment's thought. 'As you say, he's done what he set out to do and as far as he's concerned it's end of story. He doesn't seem the least bit bothered about what happens to him next. He's not completely heartless; during one of the interviews before we charged him he said, "Tell Kate I'm sorry."'

'Who's Kate?'

'Kate Springfield; she lives in the same block as Ellerman and the SIO thought it would be a good idea if I went to see her. We still don't know for certain how he came to know Julie or why he became so concerned for her welfare. He flatly refused to tell us – in fact he got quite emotional every time we broached the subject. We thought she might have worked at Maxworth's and we asked them to check their records for a Julie Armitage, but no joy there. She might have been a temp, of course, but they had no idea what agency they used at the relevant time. Kate was another possible source of info; we thought he might have confided in her, but she knows nothing about his past except that he's a widower, used to live in Clevedon and had been "somebody important in a local business" before he retired. She's a single woman in her sixties by the look of her; he's been dating her quite a lot and I think she was cherishing a secret hope that he'd propose to her one day. She's really distressed; she kept telling me what a good, kind gentleman he is and how she found it hard to believe him capable of hurting anyone.'

'She sounds a simple soul,' Harry remarked.

'You can say that again. She said at one point, "Henry didn't trust him, so perhaps I should have been on my guard." Henry, by the way, is her cousin's cat and she said he "didn't take kindly to dear John". His owner seriously maintains he has near-human understanding.'

Harry chuckled. 'They sound a pair of really dotty old dears.'

'At least it's a harmless form of dottiness.' Sukey suddenly found tears welling from her eyes. 'Oh Harry, why is there so much sadness in the world?'

'There's happiness too,' he said meaningfully, taking her hand and squeezing it.

'That's true,' she admitted, returning the pressure, 'but in my job I see a lot of the dark side of life.'

At that moment her mobile rang and she picked it up. 'Hullo . . . oh Gus, lovely to hear from you! Got your results yet? A two one . . . well done! We must celebrate . . . what's that? Oh Gus, how exciting . . . yes, of course I am . . . I'm delighted . . . give Anita a big hug from me . . . yes, see you soon . . . bye!' She switched off the phone. 'Wonderful news! He's already been promised a job now he's got his degree, a good one . . . and guess what, he and Anita plan to get married next year. Can you beat that, Harry? I'll be a mother-in-law!'

'You'll be the nicest mother-in-law ever,' he assured her. 'Let's take them out for a celebration dinner.'

'That's a lovely idea, we'll do that. And there's another bit of good news as well. I almost forgot to tell you; our Sarge is now DI Rathbone. We only heard about it yesterday; it accounts for why he's been so edgy lately, waiting for the results of the final interview.'

'Well, good for him,' said Harry. 'I'm sure he deserves it. And I've just remembered something else; I've had a call from Major Howes and it seems that Brian Seaton is making a serious effort to mend his fences with Carla. He spotted them one evening recently in their glad rags as if they were off to some fancy do or other, and, according to the Major, he was holding Carla's arm and she was looking really happy – almost attractive. To use his own words, "Perhaps he's realized he's been a bit of a swine and is trying to make amends."'

'I'm really glad to hear that,' said Sukey. 'I'll never forget her saying pitifully, "If only he'd loved me just a little."'

'I thought that would please you. I wonder how the court will deal with her?'

'It depends on what charge they decide to bring. "Administering a substance with intent to cause temporary disability"? It should be a teaser for the legal eagles.'

Harry put down his empty glass and took hers away. He reached again for her hand and this time he drew her close. 'You're right, of course, there's always a dark side,' he whispered. 'Suppose I turned out to be a killer, for example? What would you do then?'

'Oh, but you are a killer,' she said softly. 'In the best possible way, of course.'